FROM
PULITZER PRIZE-WINNING HISTORIAN

GREG GRANDIN

A sweeping, revisionist work *of* American history
that spans five centuries *and* redefines our understanding
of North *and* South America forever

AMERICA, AMÉRICA

A NEW HISTORY OF THE NEW WORLD

GREG GRANDIN
PULITZER PRIZE-WINNING AUTHOR
OF *THE END OF THE MYTH*

"Dazzling . . . Destined to become
**OUR NEW REFERENCE FOR UNDERSTANDING
THE MAKING OF THE MODERN WORLD."**

—*Naomi Klein,*
New York Times bestselling author of *Doppelganger*

PenguinPress | prh.com/AmericaAmérica

GRANTA

12 Addison Avenue, London W11 4QR | email: editorial@granta.com
To subscribe visit subscribe.granta.com, or call +44 (0)1371 851873

ISSUE 171: SPRING 2025

EDITOR	Thomas Meaney
MD & DEPUTY EDITOR	Luke Neima
SENIOR EDITOR	Josie Mitchell
MANAGING EDITOR	Tom Bolger
ASSOCIATE DESIGN DIRECTOR	Daniela Silva
ASSOCIATE EDITOR	Brodie Crellin
EDITORIAL ASSISTANT	Aea Varfis-van Warmelo
PHOTOGRAPHY EDITOR	Max Ferguson
COMMERCIAL DIRECTOR	Noel Murphy
OPERATIONS & SUBSCRIPTIONS	Sam Lachter
MARKETING	Simon Heafield
PUBLICITY	Pru Rowlandson, publicity@granta.com
CONTRACTS	Margaux Vialleron
ADVERTISING	Renata Molina-Lopes, Renata.Molina-Lopes@granta.com
FINANCE	Suzanna Carr
SALES	Rosie Morgan
IT SUPPORT	Mark Williams
PRODUCTION & DESIGN DIRECTOR	Sarah Wasley
PROOFS	Katherine Fry, Jessica Kelly, Jess Porter, Will Rees, Francisco Vilhena
CONTRIBUTING EDITORS	Anne Carson, Rana Dasgupta, Michael Hofmann, A.M. Homes, Rahmane Idrissa, Karan Mahajan, George Prochnik, Leo Robson, Janique Vigier
PUBLISHER	Sigrid Rausing

This selection copyright © 2025 Granta Trust.

Granta (ISSN 173231 USPS 508) is published four times a year by Granta Trust, 12 Addison Avenue, London W11 4QR, United Kingdom.

Airfreight and mailing in the USA by agent named World Container Inc., 150–15, 183rd Street, Jamaica, NY 11413, USA.

Periodicals postage paid at Brooklyn, NY 11256.

Postmaster: Send address changes to *Granta*, ESco, Trinity House, Sculpins Lane, Wethersfield, Braintree, CM7 4AY, UK.

Subscription records are maintained at *Granta*, c/o ESco Business Services Ltd, Wethersfield, Essex, CM7 4AY.

Air Business Ltd is acting as our mailing agent.

The manufacturer's authorised representative in the EU for product safety is Authorised Rep Compliance Ltd, 71 Lower Baggot Street, Dublin D02 P593, Ireland (arccompliance.com)

Granta is printed and bound in Italy by L.E.G.O. S.p.A. This magazine is printed on paper that fulfils the criteria for 'Paper for permanent document' according to ISO 9706 and the American Library Standard ANSI/NIZO Z39.48-1992 and has been certified by the Forest Stewardship Council®(FSC®). *Granta* is indexed in the American Humanities Index.

ISBN 978-1-909-889-72-9

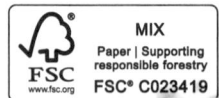

MIX
Paper | Supporting responsible forestry
FSC® C023419
FSC
www.fsc.org

CONTENTS

6   **Dead Friends**
Thomas Meaney

11   **Burning Mao**
Fernanda Eberstadt

27   **Posterity**
Joshua Cohen

41   **All Being Well**
Susie Boyt

59   **Mark Cawson Lives**
*Smiler, with an introduction
by Iain Sinclair*

91   **Nowhere**
*Yasmina Reza,
tr. Alison L. Strayer*

105   **When Rhinestones Star
the Night and You Find
Yourself Thinking Fondly
of Dave Hickey**
Anne Carson

107   **Remission**
Gary Indiana

122   **Watching, Content &
Colombia**
Audun Mortensen

129   **The Conservation of Mass:
On Resomation**
William Atkins

149   **Unruly Light**
*Ming Smith, with an
introduction by Tobi Haslett*

178   **Note to Self & Gentle
Rain**
*Robert Walser,
tr. Damion Searls*

181   **Killing Stella**
*Marlen Haushofer,
tr. Shaun Whiteside*

199   **Benoît**
*Michel Houellebecq,
tr. Luke Neima*

204   **Cell Phone**
*Krystyna Dąbrowska,
tr. Karen Kovacik*

207   **This Very Complicated
Cast of Mind**
*Renata Adler in conversation
with the Editor*

227   **V.S. Naipaul: The Grief
and the Glory**
Aatish Taseer

247   **Gian**
Tao Lin

270   **Notes on contributors**

A journalist in Sweden asked me – 'Why are those people your friends?' I'm like, why are you with your husband?

– Nan Goldin, in conversation with David Velasco, 2022

Introduction

There is a mysterious lack of mystery about friendship. Compared to love, it seems more stable and enduring. We find our friends earlier in life than our lovers, and they often stick around longer. Flattery and exaggeration may soften the ground for love, but friendship, what the Greeks called *philia*, has a reputation for being more clear-eyed, more transparent than *eros*. Perhaps for this reason there seems to be less to say about it.

But much of the distinction between love and friendship is dubious. For a long time in English, the word 'friend' blurred into 'lover', a fuzziness still preserved in words like 'boyfriend' and 'girlfriend', or in the German 'Freund/in'. The bleed-over is taken attractively for granted in Nan Goldin's photograph on our cover. Friendship and erotic love huddle together on a spectrum: they can both be 'romantic'; they can both involve distortions and the telling of truths. There is unrequited friendship just as there is friendship at first sight. It can be just as fragile as love, just as capricious. Why we make a friend resists analysis as much as why we fall in love. 'Because it was him, and because it was me,' says Montaigne.

There are two standard ways that dead friends are memorialized in the anglophone West. The first is the obituary, a matter-of-fact account of the life and deeds of the departed. The economy of the form is part of its power. The second is the eulogy, whose immediacy and observance of propriety tends toward cliché and sentimentality. This issue of *Granta* seeks to avoid these models in search of a different kind of reckoning.

One of the most celebrated literary portraits of friendship in recent years is Elena Ferrante's *Neapolitan Quartet*. The novels concern Lila and Lenù, two Italian women whose friendship is forged in childhood and becomes, at least for Lenù, the relationship that shapes her life. Ferrante's books captured an old-fashioned, even Old Testament-style bond, in which a friend can be counted on to hate one's enemies – when a boy-gangster in the neighborhood makes an unwanted advance on Lenù, and touches her arm, Lila takes a penknife to his throat. But the Quartet also testifies to the tenacious quality of friendship that many of us have experienced in our lives: friends made early in life, whom we cannot jettison any more than we can family, and who know a certain version of us so well that they alternatively stymie and comfort us.

Dead friends come to us unbidden – in unexpected moments, in dreams. They remain in conversation. In these pages, writers have transmitted the flickering aura of their departed friends. Michel Houellebecq told us he was relieved to write again about Benoît Duteurtre, because he was not satisfied with the rushed tribute he wrote at the time of his death. Tao Lin did not need a perfect memory to reconstruct his relationship with Giancarlo DiTrapano; he had saved all their messages, which he uses to unfurl the story of their friendship thread by thread.

Aatish Taseer's portrait of V.S. Naipaul and Fernanda Eberstadt's of Andy Warhol handle the same dilemma in different ways: both write of older mentors whose influence was as burdensome as it was formative. With time, they have been able to separate the gains of the friendship from the cost of its demands.

In 'Nowhere' by Yasmina Reza, translated by Alison L. Strayer, the author notes how absurd it is to feel nostalgia for a world that no longer exists. Though Reza refuses to indulge in sentimentality, her mind circles back to 'covered-up and silenced things'. In reporting that took him to Ireland, William Atkins introduces readers to a new, watery way of doing away with the dead.

Susie Boyt, in our fiction in this issue, returns to the cast of her novel *Loved and Missed*, only this time the relationship under examination is between friends, rather than relatives. As we watch the final act of a long-standing friendship, Boyt encourages us to redraw the line that sometimes separates friendship from family. Marlen Haushofer's novella *Killing Stella* was originally published in 1958, but unlike her most well-known book, *The Wall*, it has never been available in English. Haushofer recounts the story of Stella, a 'stupid young person' who runs 'headlong into a murderous, metal machine'. Guilt-ridden and resentful, the narrator sinks into a carousel of feeling and tries to piece together the events that led to Stella's death. In Joshua Cohen's short story, a man's entire posterity – or entire hope for posterity – suddenly vanishes.

Hannah Arendt was something like a high technician of friendship, who embalmed her friendships in her books. She believed friendship was inherently political because it modeled an ideal world. Renata Adler, one of Arendt's youngest friends, spoke with *Granta* about how their relationship was formed. Like Houellebecq, Adler was unsatisfied with an appreciation she wrote after her friend's death, but upon revisiting it, she found aspects of herself and Arendt that she could not grasp at the time.

A friend of this magazine died while the issue was in production. I got to know Gary Indiana toward the end of his life, when it seemed most of his closest friends were already gone – a long trail of the dead stretching from the doorstep of his East Village walk-up all the way back to Derry, New Hampshire. He ventriloquized these dead friends all the time. Gary had a rare stamina for long telephone calls, in which he insisted on unpicking the world's inanities and evils together, not alone. I was one among many lucky recipients of his talent for friendship. He died the day before he was meant to come to the *Granta* party in New York for the China issue:

Dear Tom,

Imma commin'. Probably with Xian. There is another party the same night for NYRB, I think. They're funny. I like Edwin. Also Nick. It will be fun to go to both, I've been housebound for the con of the void.

Janique told me she'd seen a galley or layout of my piece, would it be possible for you to send that to me? I'm so pleased that you're running it. I never publish anything. I could, of course, but it's been nicer not to for a while.

Aside from the novel I have been working on a little film with some friends in Paris and Arles, via phone and email, based on a Balzac novel. Funnily, Balzac was a devotee of Mesmer. This was not unusual for people in France before, during, and after the Revolution, but Balzac's involvement with it had escaped my notice until I read this late novel, where mesmerism really comes into the story in a conspicuous way. We're playing this up in our movie in absolutely serious fashion. Mesmer would bind a group of patients to a tree he had 'magnetized,' the rope couldn't have any knots in it because they would interfere with the circulation of invisible fluids. If a patient proved recalcitrant, Mesmer himself would sometimes appear, in a lilac taffeta robe, and 'drill fluid into the patient from his hands, his imperial eye, and his mesmerized wand.' He could cure anything, apparently.

Best regards,

Gary

The opening of the novel Gary Indiana was working on appears in this issue. In a turn of events that would have drawn his grim laughter, the collection of his books and papers – sent to California for safekeeping after his death – was consumed in the Los Angeles fire on the day it arrived.

I thank Sigrid Rausing for her steadfast support. Her friendship with Johanna Ekström, expressed in their book *And the Walls Became the World All Around*, was one of the seeds that got this issue started. ∎

TM

BOB COLACELLO
Andy at the Factory, 860 Broadway, New York, c. 1976
Courtesy of the artist and Vito Schnabel Gallery

BURNING MAO

Fernanda Eberstadt

The summer of 1977, when I was sixteen years old, I started work at Andy Warhol's Factory.

I was a teen stalker, a fantasist who mostly preferred sitting on a stoop opposite someone's house, noting the street-scene in my diary, to actually meeting the person inside, and Andy had long been one of my simmering obsessions.

My parents – New York society people with an interest in downtown art – had first met Andy in the late fifties, when my father was working as a fashion photographer and Andy was still an illustrator dressing windows for Bonwit Teller. My father liked to say that back then he'd thought Andy Warhol an embarrassing little creep whose determination to be famous was clearly doomed. But my mother had a taste for oddball dreamers and she and Andy became friends; she appeared in one of his 1964 *Screen Tests*. I'd been raised on her stories of the Factory – the silver-tinfoil-walled spaceship where Andy, pedaling on his exercise bike, swigged codeine-infused cough syrup and watched his superstars squabble and self-destruct. Watched and subtly egged them on. At a certain point, my mother got spooked by how many of his beautiful, lost young creatures ended up dead.

In 1968, Andy was shot by Valerie Solanas and he too, briefly, died. It was a time when America's chickens, in Malcolm X's phrase, seemed to be coming home to roost – Andy's shooting was edged off the front pages by Robert F. Kennedy's two days later – and when Andy came back from the dead, with his insides shattered and sewn together again, he was seemingly cured of his taste for watching other people detonate.

O n 7 December 1976, I finally succeeded in pestering my parents into introducing me to Andy Warhol.

By then, they had devolved into merely social, semi-professional friends who exchanged poinsettia plants at Christmas, and the Andy I had wanted to know – the ghostly cyclist who could mesmerize you for eight hours with a flickery image of a skyscraper – had been supplanted by the art-businessman flanked by pinstripe-suited managers. And I too was in a different phase. By the time I actually made it to the Factory, I was less interested in Andy than in dancing at Studio 54 with his managers.

O ur first meeting was at La Grenouille, a fancy French restaurant in Midtown. My parents had invited Andy to dinner, and later that night, I wrote my first impression of him in my diary. Andy was *'standing there in his dinner jacket and blue jeans, tape recorder tucked under his arm, looking shy and uncertain but friendly'*. He had brought as his date Bianca Jagger, gorgeous in a purple fox stole and a gold lamé toque. They ordered oysters and a spinach soufflé, which she sent back because, as she explained to the waiter, it was *affreux*. *'Halfway through dinner Mummy asked me to switch places with her so I could talk to Andy. Andy said something about my mother being "mean" not to let me sit next to him before. So we talked the rest of the evening. I was a little shy and ended up feeling oddly depressed and dispirited, sort of drained. He said I looked like a movie star, had I ever thought of being one. That seemed like the sort of thing he says to about five hundred people a week ... He asked me to bring down my whole class to the studio – that too I found depressing. I asked "Why don't you come to Brearley* [the private girls' school where I was in eleventh grade]*?" He said no, he could never* *do that, something about being too shy. I said, "Well, a lot of them are really awful." He said, "Well, bring the awful ones too." He's very easy to talk to, I kept saying things I wished I hadn't.'*

My mother had told Andy I was a writer and he asked if there was anyone I wanted to write about for his magazine *Interview*.

He said they needed something for the January issue. ' *"We want someone young and really new – what have you seen on Broadway, who can you think of" on and on, I was completely stuck. Ludicrously I suggested Mr [Edward] Gorey. Andy said, "Oh come on. He's creepy – he's really old. I saw him walking along Park Avenue the other day. He's too peculiar for me." That made me laugh. "Too peculiar for you? He's just a bit moldy. I was obsessed with him for about two years." Mr Gorey's star was pretty dim that night.'*

I suggested other writers, photographers, film-makers whose work I admired. All too old, too peculiar. Finally, I proposed the choreographer Andy de Groat, who had just collaborated on Philip Glass and Robert Wilson's *Einstein on the Beach*.

Andy agreed, '*though he thought* Einstein on the Beach *was "stinky". He wanted some more people. I told him I'd provide some later. Andy said to call A de G tomorrow, and then him. "The piece has to be in really soon."'*

Andy's description of the evening, published in his *Diaries*, accords with mine, but he added a nice coda. '*The Eberstadt daughter didn't say anything during dinner but then she finally blurted out that she used to go to Union Square and stare up at the Factory, so that was thrilling to hear from this beautiful girl. I told her she should come down and do interviews for* Interview *and she said, "Good! I need the money." Isn't that a great line? I mean, here Freddy's father died and left him a whole stock brokerage company.'*

As a kid, I used to feel this need to be outside in the dark, looking up at lighted windows, imagining the life inside. I still do. But nowadays the lighted window is my own, my husband and children are inside, but something broken and uncured keeps me outside, sniffing the night wind and rain, unable to join the circle by the fire.

The Andy I was drawn to was dogged by this same self-imposed and unassuageable loneliness, though his version of the family fire was the VIP lounge at Studio 54 with Truman Capote, Halston and Liza Minnelli. Yet no matter how famous he became, he was still the 'embarrassing little creep' who, when he first arrived in New York, had harassed Truman Capote with daily fan letters, phone calls, and camped out on his doorstep; he was still the balding twenty-something sitting every day at the counter of Chock full o'Nuts, eating the same cream-cheese sandwich on date-nut bread; someone who founded his art on boredom, repetition, because only unvarying sameness could soothe his raging anxiety.

I told Andy the first time we met that this was something we had in common – that although, as he put it in his *Diaries*, I was a 'beautiful girl', a banker's granddaughter, I was also a freak like him, a person who in some way would rather stand outside staring up at the Factory windows than be invited in.

Even today, it's this same dividedness in Andy that gives me a pang of fellow feeling, the same compulsion to hide away that overrules your hunger to belong, a compulsion that then leaves you feeling too lonely, too weird, too left out of everyone else's fun. And why does the loneliness feel truer, more essential than any love or acclaim?

By mid-December, I was heading down to Union Square every day after school to transcribe my tape-recorded interview with Andy de Groat. I would install myself at the front desk of Andy Warhol Enterprises, play back a couple of sentences, and type them up two-fingered, dragging out the process tortoise-slow. My pretext was that I didn't have a working typewriter at home, but in truth the Factory had become my happy place.

My favorite moment was at the end of the day when Andy put on his apron, picked up a broom, and swept the floor clean – I liked the monastic discipline, the humility of the act. If I got lucky, I would then share a ride uptown with either him or his business manager

Fred Hughes, the enigmatic Texan dandy who was the one I actually had a crush on.

O ne night, Andy and I were sitting in the back of a yellow cab hurtling through the sooty entrails of the Pan Am Building and out onto Park Avenue.

We were discussing our evening plans – in my case, studying for a Russian history test with my friend Martine; in Andy's case, a dinner party given by Fereydoun Hoveyda, the Iranian Ambassador to the UN who had been the conduit for Andy's portraits of the Shah and his family. (This was two years before the Revolution, which the ambassador survived, although his brother, the Prime Minister, was executed by firing squad.)

On these taxi rides, I became familiar with Andy's conversational technique, how he negotiated his mix of shyness, curiosity, malice. He was a persistent questioner, and what he wanted to hear was the most shameful thing about whomever it was we both knew, and because I wanted to please him, I inevitably divulged some incriminating tidbit and his reaction was always, 'Oh come on. *Really???*'

I was used to this kind of inquisition from my mother, though she never feigned disbelief, and as with her, I ended up cursing my inability to keep my mouth shut. Andy knew all about mother–child oversharing; his mother lived with him for years and coauthored his first art books, and my guess was that he inherited his malice from her, it was his mother tongue, although it coexisted with a certain vestigial innocence: a part of him that was stuck at an age between child and cat, that wanted to timidly lick the boy he loved all over.

6 January 1977.
I was home sick in bed; I was often sick in bed growing up.

Catherine Guinness, Andy's assistant, phoned to discuss a photograph to go with the de Groat piece. They had decided that Robert Mapplethorpe should take the picture.

I asked after Andy.

'Andy's busy sweeping up cigarette butts.' She put him on the phone. I heard the mechanical-man voice with its campy singsong intonations, teasing, a little flirty, and my heart leapt.
AW: Gee, it's really too bad you're sick. How did you get it? Who have you been carrying on with?
Me: No one – it's really disappointing.
AW: Well, are you typing and typing away?
Me: I'm in bed all day. My mother has to read aloud to me.
AW: Did you get nice presents for Christmas? Did you get what you wanted?
Me: Well, not really. Will you get me what I want for Christmas?
AW: Oh I meant to get you a Christmas present but I never got around to it.
Me: Yes, I was so jealous when you gave Mummy something and not me.
AW: Oh were you? Well, I'll get you something. When are you coming to the Factory next? I'll give you a present when I see you at the Factory.

I was a resourceful kid; all winter and spring, I produced a steady enough stream of interviews to keep me coming down to Union Square with pieces to transcribe. One day Chris Hemphill, the office assistant, had good news for me: their receptionist was going on maternity leave in June.

As soon as school let out, I started my summer job at Andy Warhol Enterprises. The mid to late 1970s marked a low point both in Andy's reputation and his creative output, and in those days the Factory's chief business seemed to be managing the Warhol brand: racking up corporate sponsorships; drumming up advertisements for *Interview*; above all, getting portraits commissioned. I too was inducted into the hustle – how many of my parents' rich friends could I persuade to commission a silkscreen portrait? If I succeeded, I would get 25 percent of the price, which I noted as being $25,000. ('*Good! I need the money.*')

Despite the corporate veneer, the atmosphere at the Factory was one of slapstick merriment. That I answered the phone in an inaudible mumble and couldn't switch from one call to another without cutting off both parties made me the dream receptionist. Andy, Fred, and Catherine all took turns imitating my telephone voice; callers wanted to know if I was still asleep in bed.

In a TV interview from the same period, a reporter accused Andy of being 'commercial'.

'I'm a commercial person,' Andy conceded testily.

'Why?'

He considered. 'Well, got a lotta mouths to feed. Gotta bring home the bacon.' His tone was curt, he was sick of this criticism, of never being taken as seriously as peers such as Robert Rauschenberg or Jasper Johns.

But his answer also reflected his image of himself as 'Pop' in the sense of someone who was running a mom-and-pop store with no mom to help out, a single father who needed to keep his feckless kids in line.

If he weren't there with his apron and broom, we would drown in cigarette butts.

Every morning, I was supposed to be in by nine, in time to answer the phone when Andy called from home to check that all the slackers on his payroll were in the office.

Vincent? Fred? Ronnie? Chris? Everyone was present, though some were looking a little ragged: Ronnie Cutrone had got locked out of his apartment the night before and had to shack up with an ex-girlfriend; Fred Hughes had a black eye. 'I got into a fight with someone who said Andy was queer,' he told me, and I believed him; the next inquirers were told respectively, 'Nenna [my nickname] hit me', 'Andy hit me', and 'It's supposed to be punk – that's a fad that's so new not even Nenna knows about it'. In fact, Fred's tendency to fall down stairs turned out to be an early sign of the multiple sclerosis that would kill him at fifty-seven.

Andy came in later, just in time to hide before the first guests arrived. Even on his own turf he was awkward, and gave the impression, I noted in my diary, '*of hanging around people, rather than the other way around*'.

At noon I used to go to Brownie's, the health-food store around the corner, to pick up a stack of avocado and tuna sandwiches for lunch. There were always visiting rock stars, Hollywood directors, European princesses. A lotta mouths to feed. In the afternoons, Victor Hugo, Halston's Venezuelan boyfriend, usually showed up with models he'd scouted in gay bars and baths. Andy and his assistants disappeared into the back of the Factory – an area that was tacitly out of bounds to me. This was where Andy made his 'Landscapes' – Polaroids of naked men posing and having sex that were then turned into prints and silkscreens.

There was an effort to keep me sheltered from the nude photo shoots, although the finished canvases were sometimes propped against my desk for Victor's inspection, with much joking about 'King Kong unclothed'. I looked elsewhere while they estimated cock size. How would I know and why would I care whether this particular specimen was XXL or XXXL?

After work, Andy and his crew, me included, went on to fashion shows, tennis matches, movie premieres, dinner parties, winding up at Studio 54 or Xenon. But even when I got home at 3 or 4 a.m., I still sat down and recorded the previous day in my diary.

All summer I was soaring on a wave of adrenaline, drugs, alcohol and teen hormones. But there were times when I crashed, needed to reassure myself that '*this is just the trashy segment of a very real life*'. At such moments, I found myself increasingly drawn to Andy, whose presence – in contrast to my mother's experience of him ten years earlier – felt mild, steadying.

Towards the middle of July, something changed. There are holes in my diary – events so disturbing I could only allude to their aftermath. There was the weekend when I was supposedly staying with a school friend in Southampton, but I persuaded this really sleazy fashion designer to hire a speedboat and zip me out to Andy's

BURNING MAO

compound on Montauk – an escapade that was relayed back to my
parents by a journalist.

When my parents and Andy next met – on board a chartered
bus to a soccer match of the New York Cosmos, a team founded by
Atlantic Records mogul Ahmet Ertegun and his brother Nesuhi – my
father yelled at Andy. Andy accidentally called him 'Mr Eberstadt',
and my parents realized then that some border had been crossed of
who was friends with whom.

Was Andy really Pop, the boss who had a lotta mouths to feed, or
was he a child still frightened of other people's fathers?

I too had a scare. My father threatened to yank me from the
Factory and only agreed to let me keep working there on condition
that I was home every evening by 8 p.m. Though I wasn't cured of
my thrill-seeking, the curfew gave me a welcome breather.

And weirdly it was this blow-up, in which Andy had been
humiliated and made to suffer for my misbehavior, that altered
our relationship, deepening it into something more intimate, more
fusional.

Our morning phone calls were now long-drawn; telephone-
friendship was freer, unencumbered by the embarrassment of bodies.
We slipped into a comfortable routine: as soon as I got into the office,
after watering the plants, I dialed up astrologer Jeane Dixon to hear
everybody's horoscope, and when Andy phoned, I relayed his fortune
for the day. Hello Leo, I intoned in Dixon's rich cheery voice, and
Andy feigned either excitement or alarm. Was an old rival really
going to make trouble for him? That was so rotten! Who could that
be? Was today really the right day for important financial decisions?
Did that mean he should be asking for more money for the Toyota
endorsement?

Andy told me what he'd been up to that morning: he was in his
kitchen making marmalade. This particular batch was too runny, it
hadn't really jelled. He complained about his boyfriend Jed, whose
mother and sister he found tacky. He hated the way Jed behaved when
his family was around.

He asked about the boys I'd been seeing. Was Michael behaving himself? What about Fred? A sharp plaintive note entered his voice, the bite of jealousy, of feeling left out.

We floated in this disembodied, homey place, thick with orange rind. The intimacy depended on the illusion that I would always be there, although we both knew I was leaving in August.

My last week at the Factory, William Copley, an artist and collector who lived in a townhouse with a circular bar, a pinball machine, lots of Warhols, and twenty-odd stuffed sheep by the French furniture designers Les Lalanne, gave a dinner party. Andy got me invited, and I negotiated a no-curfew night with my father.

It was a complicated evening, a kind of Midsummer Night's Dream in which most of the guests seemed to be unhappily chasing after someone who didn't love them.

Halfway through the party, a cocaine dealer arrived, and Bob Colacello – editor of *Interview* – and Fred Hughes and I locked ourselves into the bathroom, and Andy, who didn't do drugs, was left outside.

'*The next day, August 2nd, as soon as I got in, Vincent said, "Andy called and wants to speak to you," but when Vincent called him back, Andy wouldn't speak to me,' I wrote in my diary. 'Later Bob called to warn me that Andy had called <u>him</u> and screamed at him about last night. He told Bob he was a terrible person, the scum of the earth to have taken me to the bathroom – that the way we'd behaved was utterly unforgivable. When Andy called the Factory next, he wouldn't even say hello to me but got put on to Catherine. I knew he was telling her about it, but when I tried to pump her afterwards she wouldn't say ... When Andy got in, he began yelling at Fred about the new issue of* Interview *and only after ages admitted that it was about last night he was mad. When no one was around and Andy was hanging around my desk, not looking at me, I finally said, "Andy, I hear you're really mad at me." His face was positively*

contorted with anger and embarrassment – he was blushing and twitching.
"Yeah, I am mad – <u>very</u> mad. After the way your father bawled me out, it
was terrible for you to behave the way you did. I'm trying to protect you
and you went and did that. I'm really disappointed in you."

When I talked to Bob later, he said that what Andy had really got mad
about was not the coke which he is scared of and blows out of all proportion,
but that he said that <u>he</u> had asked me to that party and I was <u>his</u> date but
I hadn't spoken to him at all.

Fred Hughes and I were planning to go out to lunch but it didn't
seem tactful so we just ordered sardine sandwiches from Jason's and took
them to the park in Union Square to eat. After that, we looked at some
antique stores and Fred showed me an enormous birchwood Adirondack
sofa he was getting for Andy's birthday, and I bought Mummy some green
Bakelite Art Deco jewelry to wear with a dress of hers . . . Andy really liked
it but when I gave it to Mummy she thought I must have done something
really awful.'

It's odd. The year I worked at the Factory felt like the happiest and most exciting period of my life, a whirl of discos, parties, famous people. Yet afterwards, when I looked back, it seemed a dangerously empty, soul-destroying time, and today what pierces my heart is the morning Andy stood by my desk, blushing, face contorted, too angry and hurt to speak.

Rereading my teen diaries, I have the impression of someone driving a car repeatedly over a cliff, seeing how often they can walk away alive. There weren't many adults who were looking out for me, but Andy felt like one of them. 'I'm trying to protect you,' he said. It was true; he was. And he trusted me enough to tell me that I'd hurt his feelings . . .

My last day at the Factory, we invited my mother to a farewell lunch, and in the afternoon I got paid my summer's wages. I'd been given the choice between being paid in cash or in art, and I'd chosen art.

Ronnie had laid out stacks of silkscreens across the wooden floor. It was like picking a puppy from a litter, a carpet from an Ottoman caravanseray. I pored through sheaves of flaming macaw-colored Elizabeth Taylors and Mick Jaggers and Chairman Maos, and opted for dictatorship over entertainment.

When I'd chosen two Mao silkscreens – one blue-black and ochre-brown, the other turquoise and Astroturf-green – Andy scribbled over them in Magic Marker. He added two pink-and-purple prints of cows, and scrawled on the front of all four, 'To Nenna, with love Andy.'

Fred was watching. 'Andy never dedicates them on the front.' He sounded put out, as if I were getting away with more than I should.

I gave Andy a big kiss. 'Oh gee,' he said, startled. 'You just gave me a French kiss. Did Fred teach you how to do that?'

'I'm going to miss you,' I said.

He looked surprised. 'Aren't you coming back to work for us in the fall?'

I said of course I was but I didn't, I never really came back. In September, I brought Andy, Fred, Bob and Catherine to lunch in my school cafeteria, and after that we still met up occasionally, but it wasn't the same. We were no longer floating in the marmalade fug of the morning phone call, we no longer knew each other's horoscope or what parties we'd each been to the night before.

The next year, 1978, I went to England to study for the entrance exams that would get me into Oxford. It was a conflicted move: I was desperate to escape my parents' world, the glittery, over-sophisticated, fame-studded New York in which I'd grown up; I felt as if my survival depended on it. But I also wanted to take my Manhattan glamor with me.

My final year at Oxford, I brought one of the two Mao silkscreens to hang on the wall of my undergraduate room. But some Oedipal impulse intervened, an urge to murder my elders: going off to find a picture hook, I left the Mao propped against an electric heater and it caught fire.

I never got the picture restored; in my arrogance, I felt as if its scorch marks were as integral a part of the Mao's history as its 'To Nenna with love'.

In 1987, I was back in New York when I heard that Andy had died after a routine gallbladder operation. I was flooded by a raw grief that even today I can't begin to process. I hadn't seen him for a couple of years: we had each entered different phases of our lives. Andy had been taken up by younger artists like Basquiat and Keith Haring and had gone back to painting, and I was going through a puritanical reaction against my wild teens, but I'd nonetheless counted on a future where we would reconverge.

At his memorial in St Patrick's Cathedral, the art historian John Richardson gave a eulogy about the intensely lived spirituality that suffused Andy's art, and it seemed like a turning point in how his work would be viewed, a recognition of the religious faith mixed in with the cynicism.

It's now almost half a century since my summer at the Factory. All these decades, I've only allowed myself to think about Andy through a kind of dissociation, focusing on him not as someone I actually knew, the boss who was sometimes mean and petty, sometimes cozy, vulnerable, loving, but as a historical figure, a prophet of contemporary America and its fame-and-death-and-money machines.

The burnt Mao hangs on my wall: its midnight-blue face is haloed in black smoke and shards of its crinkled flesh have got stuck to the Perspex frame. The damage from that long-ago electrical fire has turned the Mao into what the French after the First World War called a *mutilé de guerre*, it's a cultic sacrifice, like a Madonna that bleeds tears.

When I look at the Mao's charred flesh, I think of Andy's own stigmata, the molten lacerations of his acne-devoured face, the purple-and-white sutures from the shooting that kept his guts from spilling out, and I can feel the daily mortification, the pain of inhabiting his body.

I'm picturing Andy at the end of the day with his apron and broom; he's a tightwad who is teaching his employees a lesson about hard work, but there is an expression on his face of sweetness, humility, resignation, and suddenly I want to kiss him. *Oh gee*, he says, *you just gave me a French kiss.* ∎

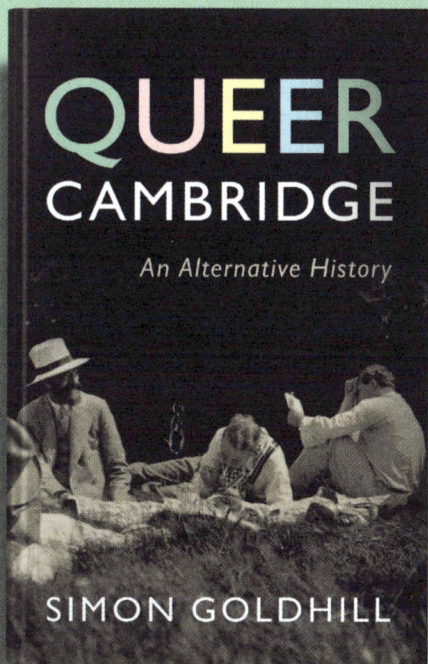

POSTERITY

Joshua Cohen

I am proud to call myself my father's son
    but I am even prouder to call myself my father's reader
    The books he wrote
    The ~~classic~~ novels he composed
    The ~~vanguard~~ literature that Dad persisted against all odds in
creating was an incitement
        a direct indictment
        an impassioned critique
        an impassioned protest of a culture whose highest honors are
essentially betrayals

'Would you mind putting that away,' the flight attendant said, 'we're getting the cabin ready for departure,' and Acker left off his shaky typing and shut his computer and stowed it in the pocket of his business-class pod and as the plane got in line for takeoff, as the plane sped and lifted and rose up through the sky, it was as if all his thoughts were left behind on the ground except: I've fucked up badly.

The festival dedicated to his late father was scheduled to open tomorrow evening on the Mediterranean island of Midorca and the evening after that Acker was set to present his remarks at the Biblioteca Pública de Midorca. It would be the festival's main speech, the organizers had told him, it would be the keynote address, the organizers were seeking his permission to record it, and yet most of what he'd managed to write of it so far was this beginning: 'I'm proud to call myself my father's son, but even prouder . . .'

From there, he had a few stunted anecdotes that he could use to wing his way through the lecture's middle, as he'd been winging his way through the middle of his life, but as for an ending, he had none, he had no hope of one: 'I'd like to take this opportunity to thank –' is not an ending.

His intention had been to finish a draft in transit, to use all this dead delayed time otherwise wasted waiting between flights and on flights to pressure his jumbled troubled filial notions into a more final respectable form – sensitive, intelligent, did he mention respectable – but drinking vodka sodas high above clouds that looked like tiny brains or like the tiny pills currently seeping into his brain, he was suddenly too woozy and drunk to get anything done and instead of trying to type any more under such slurry conditions he spent most of the flight out of Newark sitting plugged into some trash on his swivel-mounted screen, wallowing in the watching of a popular superhero franchise, watching the original and then the sequel and then the rest of the installments, but somehow, unsuspectingly, watching them out of order.

'– a refill?'

'What?'

'– ice?'

'What?'

'Would you like another drink,' the flight attendant had to yell, 'and would you like it with ice?'

If this were a scene in one of his father's (classic, vanguard) books, it would've been written this way: the main character, drunk and pilled, self-loathing, self-disgusted, gross and gassy and distinctly un-sober, would be watching 'a popular superhero franchise', but since this isn't fiction but reality, we can say that Acker, failing to complete his remarks, was wrecked on Ketel One and Ambien and watching all the Batmans. He'd fucked up badly. He'd known about this festival honoring his late father for about a year now and he'd known about his late father's hundredth birthday for – about a hundred years now? And yet despite having had all that warning to prepare, he was flying to the occasion equipped with just a few weak memories of youth, none of the emotional ones really emotional and none of the intellectual ones really intellectual, along with a trite diatribe against identity politics and cultural illiteracy in what he thought was his father's style, which wasn't really in his father's style. A sad-because-too-revealing account of this one summer day together when his father showed him how to polish shoes (and then gave him a half-dozen pairs to polish and left him to it). A sad-because-too-revealing attempt to turn that polishing account into a metaphor (for what?). Short sketches of his father as a bad driver and swimmer, a lugubrious if dubious description of his adolescent drift from his father that tended to flatter himself in accounts of his flirtations with one of his father's young girlfriends in Sicily and of his sexual experiences with another of his father's young girlfriends on Crete, along with an embittered sour section – one that should be the ending, but could not be the ending – about what it was like to grow up on Midorca and then leave, when his mother left and took him with her back to the States, leaving his father behind to write the books that helped make him and the island famous.

About a decade ago, his father had returned to Midorca after picking up one major literary prize or another and, as the press coverage went, the moment he'd entered the house and set the award atop the only empty shelf in the crowded alcove reserved for trophies, diplomas, and other such encomia, he'd suffered a stroke and died. He was buried in a grave high up on the cemetery cliff above the sea and eulogized by old rich hippies and celebrity friends who flew in, name-brand painters and singer-songwriters along with investment bankers and property developers, while he, the dead man's son, had stayed behind in honking New York to care for his ailing mother. She could not be left alone. If he'd left her alone that winter in cruel and

brutally cold New York to fly to his father's funeral in Midorca, the
heavy traffic of nurses and doctors would have told her where he was,
and she would've keened and raged and ripped the tubes and wires
straight out of her havocked body and dropped dead on the spot, the
way his father had, as opposed to what happened, which was that her
consciousness continued to flicker and fade until she passed away
peacefully just a few days later.

His father died on a Monday, his mother died on a Friday,
something like that, and the more extensive weekend-edition
obituaries of Geoffrey Acker – 'the author of acclaimed volumes
that skewered capitalist pieties' (*The Times*), 'who chronicled the
Americanization of Europe and the banalization of America' (the
Guardian) – went on to note in an update that his first wife had
outlived him only briefly.

Acker had never gotten along with his father – the man who
everyone meant when they said 'Acker', even the man he himself
meant when he said 'Acker'. He was the first son of his father's first
wife. He was the only son actually, the only child actually, of the first
wife of two. There were also three biographers, five translators, and
about a dozen dazed shambolic scholars from Europe, all gathered
together in Zurich, specifically in Zurich Airport, specifically in a
small, neglected terminal from which the smaller budget flights
departed on airlines that shouldn't exist, airlines that didn't exist,
special charters with nonsensical names and non-sequitur logos
that kept changing. Something called EUsky with a winged cow.
Something called Flingling with a bubble font in fire colors. The
gate for MidAir (represented by a palm tree whose fronds were also
whirring rotors, its lettering proto-Phoenician) was at the end of the
farthest hall, a dingy, gray-carpeted, bathroom-less and café-less
mustering point that slowly, gradually, over the torporous course
of the day, became populated by experts, academics, men (mostly
men) just shy of emeritus age, who seemed to all know one another
personally or at least by reputation and greeted one another with

stern handshakes (the Germans) and hugs and kisses (the French and Francophiles) and traded witty quotations in flavorfully accented English of favorite lines of the work of the man whose posterity had brought them together ('over the torporous course of the day'). Some had been waiting for hours already and were relieved to finally have others around to complain to, the jet-lagged others who were just showing up on flights from Mexico City, Hong Kong, and Seoul. There was one flight a day from Zurich to Midorca and apparently much of the festival would be on it. The director of the Acker documentary, who was due to be interviewed onstage after what would be the world premiere screening of the Acker documentary. The author of the passive-aggressive memoir about informally studying with and even serving as an informal secretary to 'Geoffrey', who kept referring to Acker's father as 'Geoffrey', in print and in person, every chance he got. Acker was the last to arrive – last and late – even after the late-because-of-a-tardy-pilot flight from Los Angeles, and the late-because-of-a-volcano flights from Scandinavia. They'd been waiting for him, they were impatient for him, he could feel it. As he rolled his fancy metal-armored luggage down the hall toward the gate, he felt their eyes roll over him like wheels, and in his stomach, in his throat, he felt a trepid rising nausea. Here we go, he thought. Time to be the son and heir, the head of the estate, the gatekeeper of the flame, the flamekeeper of the gate, the standard-bearer of the Jesus Christ enough already. YES – you have the permission to quote such-and-such my father wrote about so-and-so. YES – you have the permission to reprint said text, to reproduce this photograph, that clip. But NO – you may not use any of those diary entries where the old graphomonster was overtly misogynistic (*if only* XXXX *were as sweet as her sweet tits*) or racist (*it's as if* XXXX *thinks he's owed a living for having been born a poor and boorish African*). Oh Dad! Oh Geoff! It was time to be his face – there was a certain resemblance of uncertain chin, invariably remarked upon – time to be the interface for a group of people with their own relationships and stakes: people who had some claim to his father and then exaggerated the rest, people who'd exaggerated some claim and then imagined the rest. The scholars whose tenures were made out of interpretations of his father's early novels or late novels or the increasingly detached and elitist political non-fiction the man wrote to mark the years in between; the leather-swaddled former Marxist who cared only about Acker as a former Marxist; the plump and wistful Jew who cared only about Acker as a Jew; the crunchy, dreadlocked Jamaican-Estonian who wrote that article on the 'mirror inversion expatriate aesthetics' of Acker and Nabokov; and the bald, gay, very fit cyclist from Amsterdam who'd brought his folding bike along with copies of the jargonated monograph he'd authored entitled 'Hetero-conservative influences in the pseudo-radical novel: the cis/systems fictions of Geoffrey Acker', which mined fatuous meanings out of fabulous misprints and derived wishful phallic inferences from every mode of transport – taxi, bus, train, horse – Acker's heroes ever rode.

As the flight's pilots and crew arrived harried gateside and commenced with their checks, Acker was introducing himself to people he'd forgotten he'd already met and being introduced to others with whom he'd hazily corresponded, trying to keep everyone straight and placated from among the swarm of frumpled necrologists he was going to be sequestered with for the next lauding week beachside and poolside at the over-starred resort where they were being put up, asking where was the guy who'd edited that collection of his father's letters (Acker owed him an email) and where was the guy who was supposed to profile him and write about the festival for some magazine (Acker wasn't quite sure which magazine and was eager to confirm the *New Yorker*)? '– but did anyone tell you about the pub at the resort?' an academic from somewhere in Britain that wasn't Oxford or Cambridge was saying. 'A pub, bar and grill, called Acker's – unclear if that was always the case or they've just renamed it after your dad for our event.'

Acker was considering joking about whether that meant he could drink and eat for free when an Aussie academic asked, 'Have you been back since your father's death?'

But before Acker could answer, some other professors around him were chiming in about how 'the island's changed a lot, like most things for the worse' and 'it's become all touristy and commercialized now that it's a stop for the cruise ships' and 'there's really nothing left from the era of your parents, when that whole countercultural wave took the island by storm, I assume you've read the book by –'

'I haven't,' Acker said, and though he was still answering that earlier question, saying that he hadn't visited Midorca since his father's passing, his father's Portuguese translator thought Acker had meant that he hadn't read the book he was recommending to him (which Acker hadn't, anyway), the book he was offering to send to him (to which Acker nodded in a way that might've signified thanks, anyway).

A man who'd identified himself as 'your father's voice in Polish', said, 'I think they did a wonderful job, actually, converting your father's house into that museum.'

'Casa Acker,' the Brit said. 'They did an excellent job.'

'And they've been keeping up the grave,' the Aussie said. 'I was there for the dedication of the monument.'

'You know,' said an Ackerite from Paris, 'I did a fair amount of research and consulting for the museum when it opened, when I was working on my dissertation.'

'If by research and consultation you mean a fair amount of shagging the staff and vacationing Danes, then sure, I'm sure you did,' said an Ackerite from Frankfurt.

The acolytes stood clustered around the living son, breathing in the terminal's stale, recirculated air and blowing it out again as one-upmanship and banter, while readying to queue for boarding, putting away into their backpacks their much-thumbed editions of his father's books and cocking their pretentious straw hats and clutching the handles of their battered suitcases, as if their suitcases were canes or walkers – ambulatory assistive devices that just happened also to be luggage, plastered over with stickers advocating world peace and declaring affiliations with distinguished institutions of higher learning.

Already – so soon, too soon – Acker had the desire to flee, to run away, but it wouldn't be that easy. The business class on this flight wasn't true business class, at least not like it had been from Newark to Zurich, where he'd had that private capsule all to himself, replete with spinny screen and a seat that stretched and yawned out into a bed. Here, the business class that he'd requested from the organizers – that he'd demanded from the organizers, once his daughter had insisted he not relent and keep demanding – was just a seat up front, in the first row alongside the window where everyone boarding passed him and greeted him again and exchanged some words or a wave with him again and resented his extra legroom.

Along with the festival participants passing him, he also noted some regular tourists or people he took for regular tourists, retirees mostly, whose curiously pre-tanned faces had also been lifted and tightened in such a way that only emphasized their bafflement when they encountered these sloppy bookish creatures gibbering to one another and blocking the aisles: Aren't we headed out on a golf and tennis and spa-massage holiday? Who are all these losers, trying to cram their book-stuffed schoolbags into the overhead bins?

Acker was seated by the window in the first row that was ostensibly business class with one empty seat next to him on the aisle and he kept watching that seat and watching the boarding passengers as they passed down the aisle and thinking to himself: please let me be seated here alone or please if it's not my luck to be here alone then let me share this row with one of those older, surely husbandless ladies with the cleavage. He didn't know who he was praying to and enjoyed for a moment pretending that he was praying to his father.

One of the biographers – not the author of the so-called academic biography and not the author of the so-called popular biography but the author of the so-called *revisionist* biography – sat down next to Acker in the empty seat, a woman who'd lambasted Acker's father and criticized his 'turn inward and rightward', harangued him for his treatment of women 'as shabby in fiction as in life', pilloried him for his position or lack of position on the American civil rights movement, and just generally went after the man with the energy and conviction of someone who'd truly loved him and felt jilted, though it was unclear to Acker whether they'd ever actually slept together. She's old now, Acker thought, she's my age. 'I always put in the request to sit either in an emergency-exit row or up front,' the woman said, 'because of my knee.' Acker forced a smile and looked down at her knee. It looked normal below the stretchy jeans. Maybe a little puffy. Maybe her knee was a little swollen or she was wearing a brace. Acker didn't want to ask her about her knee and neither did he want to talk about the biography she wrote that was being republished for his father's centennial in a new edition, nor about any of the other subjects that the woman wanted to talk about, from the unfortunate circumstance that the biography was being republished by a worse publisher than had originally put it out ('but these days the alternative to a bad publisher is no publisher at all'), to the sabotaging editor who wouldn't let her incorporate any new changes or corrections ('this time the errors aren't on me') and the delinquent publicity and marketing departments that had pretty much resigned themselves to the fact that the literature of Geoffrey Acker was unlikely to entice the interest of the younger generation ('who spend all their time online, where you haven't even digitized your father's archives . . .').

They were already airborne at this point – so insistent was the biographer's patter that Acker had barely registered takeoff. He'd wanted to see Zurich from above but by the time the biographer had given him pause to look out the window, the city was already behind them. There was rain dribbling down the window and then they were up above the rain, where the air was bumpy. Acker said something about how talking on planes made him nauseous. The biographer couldn't sit with her knee flexed for hours and Acker couldn't talk on planes, or actually, he was explaining to her, while in any type of motion.

The biographer, abashed, tugged at her long white braid and apologized, and as Acker was assuring her there was really no need, a memory opened like a flower in his mind of this woman doing that very same apologetic braid-tugging years ago at his mother's in New

York: there had been some sort of Q&A his mother had consented to, either to advance her own agenda against her ex-husband's reputation or merely because she herself wanted the attention, but one of the biographer's Qs had rankled his mother who, instead of providing an A, had threatened to toss her out onto the street, and the biographer, in an attempt to wait out his mother's rage, had said 'sorry I'm so sorry', and in the very same nervous anxious way had stroked and pinched and tugged at her long braid, which was black back then, not white, tugging at it like tugging at the rope that rings the bell at the church by the Midorca cemetery . . . and then what? Acker couldn't remember the rest of that day . . . had Mom calmed down enough to let her stay?

The next time Acker turned from the window, the biographer was asleep, she was snoring, and then – despite the plane being cramping small and the flight being short and occasionally turbulent – he was also succumbing. It was the drinks, it was the pills, it was the cumulative social obligations along with the sudden realization that he'd been awake all night – his head was lolling just as the land beneath gave way to sea and his dreams turned watery too: his mother, years ago, giving him some lawyerly document to take when he went to meet his father for one of their island summers together, a document it was important that he get his father to sign and bring back, he couldn't forget, but then he'd forgotten . . . his daughter just yesterday, which didn't feel like just yesterday, dropping him off in manic, frigid Newark and telling him once again how guilty she felt that she couldn't accompany him, although the truth was that she hadn't been invited officially and he'd never invited her unofficially himself, and then her saying to him, 'I know you didn't ask me, but if you did ask me, I'd say you can't go out and talk about Grandpa without admitting what an asshole he was,' although the truth was that she'd met Acker's father only once, 'an asshole to Grandma, an asshole to you, just an abusive controlling narcissistic asshole you only care about,' and here his daughter's voice was changing into his mother's, 'because of the money he brings in, the royalties and licensing fees and prestige that you can't live without,' and here his mother's voice was changing into his father's, 'because you yourself have never been able to do anything . . . nothing of your own . . . nothing original . . . you've just sailed your way through life like a favored parasite who –'

He was jolted awake. The plane was jolted. In a way that Acker's dead father would never have written it, the plane was shaking. In a way that only the dead author of the universe would have written it – and gotten away with writing it, because who would have criticized – it bucked and trembled and shook. In what would later be called, by one of the festival organizers who was already on the ground in Midorca, 'a tantrum of coincidence', and, by the magazine journalist who'd been assigned to profile the festival who'd canceled at the last moment due to a virus, 'an affront to the subtlety of Acker's corpus', it dipped and juddered and dove. The tray in front of Acker was loose and flapping and the oxygen mask that had dropped from above was flapping like a wing against his mouth as if begging him to swallow it and the biographer was twisted around in her seat and with heavy breaths as if she were snoring while awake, she was appealing to him, she was panicking, showing him blood on her jeans, blood on her blouse, blood on her head. She'd bashed her forehead on something – on the bulkhead just in front, which was smeared with blood. Acker had a pain in his gut, where he'd been thrown against his seatbelt buckle. He went to loosen the buckle, loosen the seatbelt, but it was fastened too tight, his weight was against it, and the pain remained. The plane was diving, convulsing and diving, and the overhead bins sprung open like laughter and backpacks and totes were falling out and books were falling from the bags and other bags from the back of the plane were sliding and tumbling down the aisle, along under the seats toward the front of the plane, as the plane rocked and tipped and kept tipping and rocking forward at a sharper angle and choking on its own speed, until to sit in it was to sit fully aslant with wet plastic cups and cans and bottles and loose ice and popcorn and mixed nuts and shoes and the books these passengers had both read and pretended to read and even written themselves rolling down to Acker's row and collecting at his feet. The biographer gripped her bad knee and with her other leg stomped on whatever detritus rolled in her direction along the floor of the plane, which due to the ever-more-severely pitched angle was becoming almost a wall of the plane. Thick black smoke obscured their row's window and the window across the way. Below them, or behind them, or wherever it was their feet could be said to be, a telephone rang, shook like the plane shook, rang. Acker couldn't hear it ring but it was vibrating and lighting up amid the pile of books and the loafers and sneakers of wildly different sizes and for a moment he didn't recognize that the phone was his. The biographer was howling – she was trying to tell Acker something in shrieks, while trying also to untangle her braid from her oxygen mask and hold Acker's hand and Acker swatted the mask away and raised the armrest and grabbed the woman's hand and held it tightly and felt the blood sucking warm and slick between them. This is it, he thought, this is the end – stuck with a bunch of helpless experts strapped into the seats of a flying lecture hall that, tipping to a pivot, now flips over and over and over itself and spirals down and down through the clouds and splinters apart in midair, the victim of a flock of large black birds that until their very last moment, when they were shredded by the engines, had been no symbol. ■

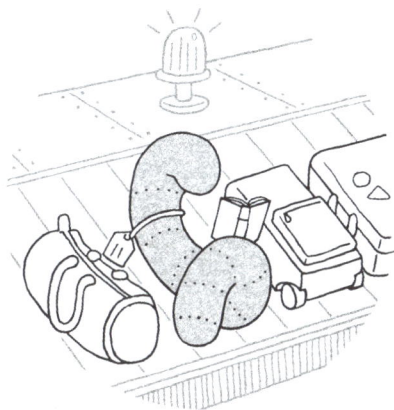

SABINE HESS
From *You Felt The Roots Grow*

ALL BEING WELL

Susie Boyt

This fine creature falling into your lap when you were sixty-two and looked it *and* felt it was no hardship. Jean just needed to get the hang of things, that was all. Lily was an orphan in every regard – apart from the embarrassing fact there were two parents extant. To say they were not up to the job was to mock the notion of employment. Eleanor, the mother, a walking catastrophe – her self-murdering zeal matched only by a talent for staying alive. The wolf lived permanently at her door without quite reaching the upper chambers. The father – a complete nothing – to the extent one didn't know his name.

There was something about Lily going out into the world, a girl in a hoody with a basket in the forest, hem of her dress caught up in her fingertips, heart pried open so you could almost hear the pumping of her heroic (O positive!) blood type, urging her to receive life without judgement or grudges or speculation . . . Perhaps that was what was unbearable, the sense she would get mashed and pulped like all the other bright heroines, if Jean took her eye off her.

She hadn't had such worries with her own child. Louisa wasn't vulnerable she was solid, thoughtless, flushed-cheeked, curly of hair. Like a small red car in an Enid Blyton she was self-reliant, forward-moving. She was lucky and had a tendency to land on her feet, whereas Lily stepped through rooms on tiptoe, peering behind her for ghosts. Powered by whirrings of bright moral energy, a ripe determination to emerge unscathed – those were strong things – but was it enough?

The facts were sharp if not entirely clear. As luck would or wouldn't have it, Lily had been brought up since late babyhood by Ruth, her grandmother. Seven weeks before her last breath Ruth asked Jean if she would take Lily on. They were not family but best friends of long-standing, colleagues at the coalface of the blackboard wiper, sober doler-outers of the detention baguette. Ruth's voice struck an elaborately casual note, as one might ask, before a journey, if a neighbour could shake a hose at the sweet williams or put out and roll back the Wednesday bins. She spoke as though there was a possibility of a no, which there was not.

'Sure,' Jean said, matching Ruth in tone.

'*Sure?*' the word was queried, found wanting, condemned.

'It would be a great honour,' Jean bowed.

'Thank you.'

She promised Ruth, at the end, she would not let anything bad happen. 'Not on my watch,' Jean said. 'No! Never! No way!' Who in their right mind dished out such pronouncements? Frank Sinatra? Lily would thrive and Eleanor would stay alive. Jean rubber-stamped it. Had they actually shaken hands? But Jean's night self, which was less staunch than her day self, wanted some backup, some heavies, some sentinels. So here she was going to sleep singing 'For Those in Peril on the Sea'. And sometimes 'Those in Peril *or at Sea*' to broaden its application.

*

'I don't want her to feel unentitled to mind things,' Ruth was saying. She was propped up in the hospital bed, clipboard at the foot, clipboard at the head, as though the bed itself were conducting a thorough survey. Two winded pillows barely reached four inches thick. 'Days not weeks,' the doctor said, a certain shyness round the well-worn death sentence. Minding things *was* an entitlement, Jean pondered it. It was a step up from suffering; it was the belief your suffering was unjust. That you weren't afraid to show you thought something of yourself. Very important. (Of course, some people made a blood sport out of minding everything – so dreary.)

'That it wouldn't destroy anyone if she thought now and then she had been dealt a cruel hand,' Ruth spoke slowly but her diction was immaculate.

'You have never been cruel.'

'I know, but a start in life ought to be more solid.'

'Yours wasn't.'

'Still. She may need at some point to allow herself to wail and flop a bit.'

'These things can't be forced.'

'I don't know. They can be accommodated.'

Oh. So I'm to accommodate the unspeakable things because you did not? Jean moved the words round her mouth with stealth. Instead, 'She will need buffers. Mechanisms to hand that will help. But of course she may be that rare soul with the kind of hardware to weather tough things. In which case that tendency, that *infrastructure*, should be respected.'

'Christ, Jean! Buffers? Infrastructure? You hate resilience. You think it's a racket. That it's what's expected from those who aren't treated well. They'll put it on your headstone!

'OK. God! You're impossible!'

They both laughed.

'Sorry,' Ruth said.

'No, I'm sorry,' Jean said. 'I suppose I want to tie things neatly in a bow.'

'Well you can pack that in for a start.'

'Understood.'

'Isn't it great we can still drive each other mad?'

'I agree. I think it's very authentic of us.'

Then – 'How will she grieve me?' Ruth asked.

What a question!

'I wish I could slip away, so she wouldn't notice. How could I wound her like this?'

'It doesn't work like that.'

'I've let her down.'

'I don't see it that way.'

'I do.'

Later when Ruth woke, Jean steadied herself. She had a speech prepared and practised in the visitor's chair. Trial and error, a good deal of editing, a passable dress rehearsal with moving lips. 'I've a good plan,' she said. 'Would you like me to say what I think we would –'

'Please.'

'Well, we will miss and mourn you together. We'll celebrate you as we do our teeth and drink our morning tea. You'll top and tail our days.'

'But how will you actually –?'

It was evening now – a crescent moon, very still, in the corner of the window like a stamp. Ruth said it looked Parisian. One of the side lights in the ward was on the blink. It cast a queer throbbing intensity over the dangerous talk. A man in a blue boiler suit was up a ladder, fiddling away, quite merry.

Jean reeled off her list like a little poem. It was as though she was scaling a tall glass building, but she tried for a restful atmosphere. 'We'll speak of you every day. We'll continue some of your favourite routines and make the food you made and read the books you loved. We'll walk through London parks, marvelling at all the different greens. We will cook now and then from Elizabeth David although, as you know, I'm not big on her superior tone. We'll get out letters and photographs of you on Sunday afternoons, if there's nothing decent on TV. We'll come and visit you to say hello or when we have news, good or bad, and we'll sit on the bench and fill you in on what's going on at school and in the world. What's on special at the supermarket! And we'll bring coffee and viennoiserie sometimes to where you rest and just sit and chat there, showering you with croissant crumbs. We might sing, if you can stomach it, I know you're not a fan of my country and western side. We may suggest we have read more than we have to impress you, so you can discount twenty-five per cent of our claims. If I say I've learned Russian to read Chekhov in the original you can take it with a pinch of salt. We'll laugh and we'll have a cry, I might bring the travel backgammon in case boredom sets in. We will have cream cheese and cucumber sandwiches and slot plain crisps inside for the crunch factor. That do you?'

'Oh oh oh!' Ruth murmured. There was pleasure there. Strong pleasure, weakly expressed. Jean stood and leaned over the bedside. She held out her hand and stroked Ruth's hair. She thought suddenly of babies' hair, the way when their hair first came in it didn't always look real.

'Oh yes, and I forgot, we'll plant snowdrop bulbs beside you; I'll order a load of them when I get home. They should be up nicely by mid-Jan. And we can put in something more scented and frothy for the spring, Lily can choose it, but I'll steer her away from yellow, if I may. Soft blues and lilacs would be more my –

'And I will answer any questions that she has about her life, and your life. I'll do it carefully, laying things out little by little. And I'll wait to be asked, like we said.'

Jean exhaled and cast her eyes about the ward. It was one of the more difficult exams she had taken.

Ruth was beginning to look uneasy. Had she under-delivered? Had she over-? There was something crass in giving all the details. It was always better to preserve your mystery. Were there omissions that grated? Had she hoped for more sorrow in the delivery? Did she require mention of black garments – on a *child*? Jean put her hand gently to her mouth to convey she didn't blame it. She wasn't going down that road.

The sadness was spreading thickly between them now. Words couldn't do anything, not really.

After school, Lily arrived at the hospital. She often took refuge in the lavatories on the ward, disappearing for ten minutes or so, the days in need of breaking up and brokering. Her face damp and glistening on her return gave Jean the idea that she splashed herself for courage, taking time to think and feel the things necessary to her emotional privacy. But one couldn't know. It might have been the remnants of tears, or steps taken to hide or dilute them. She came back refreshed-looking in any case. She was professional in that way, not in the sense of being controlled or businesslike, but in knowing what she needed. She was respected by the hospital staff who looked her up and down with great approval. They addressed their comments to her in the main – family had a higher status to friends in a hospital setting – but she was only fifteen. There was a lozenge-shaped pink patch of dry skin under Lily's chin, and she rubbed away at it without seeming to notice. It expressed a form of physical sympathy with Ruth's state, Jean thought. A dab of Vaseline ought to do the trick. Perhaps when they got home she ought to – no, it would be better coming in the morning.

The doctor made his evening rounds, the tall, grand English one. His august look held both glamour and humility. 'More like three or four days, now, I'm afraid.' Then: 'Less than a week, certainly.' He lingered for some sort of civilised response. Jean rose to her feet, but she could not speak.

'OK then. Fair enough,' Lily murmured, nodding, meeting the doctor with a cool thin smile. That was incredible. The way she took it upon herself to lead them all into this new phase. Such maturity and authority. And if Lily could accept it, it meant they all could/must follow suit. So now it was just about how to colour in those precious hours. Just!

L ittle tableaux from the past bobbed about them all the time, marking the scene for future memory. When Lily was small, five or six, something difficult happened, Jean half remembered, to do with her mother, it always was, who had shown up in bad order, or more likely not shown up at all. There was some kind of ensuing episode or confrontation, and Ruth took it hard, which was unusual, and had to go to bed for a time. Jean was put in charge of taking Lily on an outing, but on being asked what she'd like, Lily thought she was being quizzed about a present, and had spoken, if it wasn't too expensive, of a new nail varnish she fancied. The shade was called Sunflower Mist; the stockist the chemist next to the laundrette. With ceremony, not quite marching but almost, they went and bought it, took it to a bright cafe.

They ordered hot chocolates, not too sweet as Lily liked it, and she did them both with concentration, as good as a nail bar, pushing back Jean's cuticles with an orange stick she brought from home, massaging the nail beds with the edges of the napkin, applying the colour with the tiny brush in three even strokes. The yellow had a greenish tinge, more Van Gogh's chair than his sunflowers, the shade of Jean's-Ex-Alan's fingertips before he gave up smoking, Jean remarked. Still, Lily was thrilled. The atmosphere between them deepened. It was a powerful connection to have matching nails. Jean asked her if she felt OK, what with her mother coming round in a bad way or not coming when she had said she would or whatever it was that had gone awry – 'It's got to be tough to take' – and Lily said, quite sensibly, 'It's cheered me down, Jean.'

Jean fell for her then. She reached for something outlandish such as, 'From now on instead of Jean will you call me . . . Gigi?' but it might have pissed Ruth off, the wanting and organising of a special name. It smacked of that dread phrase 'Our little secret'. It was enough their nails were twinned. Still – tempting.

Gigi though, Jean rolled her eyes now, looking at Lily on the other side of the bay. What on earth had she been thinking? Gigi, my arse.

Jean watched Lily approach the nurses' station, take the nurse in charge to one side asking if it wasn't time for a syringe driver. The nurse said no, not yet. There wasn't any discernible breakthrough pain, apparently. How on earth did Lily know about syringe drivers? Jean was amazed.

'I don't think we should wait until there's breakthrough pain,' Lily said. 'That would be bad, if we left it that late. No. Can we revisit tomorrow when the doctor does his rounds?'

Revisit! What a mild and elegant way of saying I don't agree.

The day before, while Ruth slept fitfully, Jean and Lily had a conversation about 'life-savers'. 'When someone doesn't see things my way,' Jean said, 'I used to tell them to get lost but now I just say,' she sweetened her voice to benign automaton setting, '"Do you have any *flexibility*?" And although it's less satisfying I seem to get better results.'

'Like wiggle room,' Lily said, her face creasing. 'Or is it wriggle room? I'm never sure.'

'It's wiggle,' Jean said. 'Easy to remember because a wiggle is a small flexible movement whereas a wriggle . . . a wriggle room would be a room in which to twist and writhe!'

'Sounds good!'

'Another one is, "What would you do if you were me?", which is meant to get the other person to walk in your shoes. Swap allegiances,' Jean said. 'Change their perspective, at least. So they *say*.'

'I heard Ruth say it on the telephone once. I don't know if it worked. It was when my – when Eleanor was in the prison that time.'

'Oh yes,' Jean said. She heard her breathing coarsen. 'I remember how unusually warm it was, that autumn, sometimes even hot, until halfway through November . . .'

'Did you know I was born here?'

'Yes I did know.'

'SO cool!' Lily said. 'I might pop down to the baby place. Revisit the scenes of my earliest youth!'

'Yep!' Jean said. 'Amazing!' She closed her eyes. She'd heard of scenes she couldn't stop herself animating – an infant trailing wires in a see-through box, skin crawling with sores and rashes, trembling unfocused limbs, despair. A babyscape ought to be soft and sweet but here there were only sharp-edged things. It was faintly pornographic in its crisis and craving. Failure and insufficiencies as far as the eye could see. It provoked in Jean a moral vertigo. She closed her eyes more tightly. *It's all right,* she reassured. *You're beginning the grief I expect, that's all. It's starting.*

'What?' Lily said. 'What? Why have you gone all weird?'

'I was . . . I was just thinking how the time flies, how it has flown, from that day to this. Incredible. All in the blink of an eye in the same building. One minute you're down on the second floor and . . .'

'OK?' Lily said, grinning warily. 'What have you done with Jean?'

'What do you –'

'Aren't you the person I once heard say to the whole school in assembly, "Teenagers, they grow up so slow"?'

'Well,' Jean said. 'I suppose I may have done. All right. All right. Got a laugh though, didn't I?'

The next day Ruth lay like a mound of ashes. Her mouth was a separate species though, the lips a good firm red, apart from some white marks that flecked the borders. She was not going to go quietly, that was certain. Odd when she'd never been exactly chatty before. Perhaps that was why it was necessary – shop now while stocks last. Unless the need for privacy was dying too . . . privacy had always been her dominion. Jean admired her for that. Her high, dry style – the things she bit down on habitually.

'You won't outdo me will you Jean?'

'Well I'm going to outlive you, unless you've got a gun.'

'No, I mean you won't be so much better than me that you make me look awful.'

'Of course I won't. Wait – what?'

'Can you mess up a bit, not do everything perfectly?'

'These things happen naturally in households staffed by human people.'

'It's just your standards are higher than mine and you're calmer and you've got money. And you're cuddly and cosier too. You have a pink sofa and sweet things in pretty boxes in a cupboard.'

'Everyone's more cuddly than a cancer patient.'

'Oh.'

Then after a minute: 'I mean, you're being crazy. People idolise the dead! You're not thinking straight.'

'I don't know.'

'I'm not sure I can sign up to this. I know you want me to do my best for Lily. You said to knock myself out in every way. Think of the lists of instructions we drew up together. Twelve pages, single-spaced, both sides of the paper. Times New Roman! I am going to give it everything I've got – that's the plan. Also, let us not forget, you don't have any choice! There isn't anybody else.'

Ruth's skin had altered subtly in tone and texture this last half-hour. Her arms had gone the colour of cement.

'You're just, you're just feeling sorry for yourself!'

'I *am* on my deathbed Jean.'

'You don't want me to fuck it up to make you look better. Not really. That's not your style. Come on.' Jean's voice descended into its *Tippex is the Devil* timbre.

'I'm so jealous. All the things I'm going to miss.'

'Well – yes. I know.'

'How can I compete?'

'Well – but you've already given Lily the earth.'

'It makes me think all sorts of terrible things about you.'

'That's all right. It's normal. I can take it.'

'It's not very nice though.'

'You're going to need to die soon if you keep this up,' Jean said.

Ruth almost giggled but her face was watery against the parchment skin.

'You know I think what I'm going to take from this little *talk* is that when I do err as I inevitably will, I'll imagine you punching the air with the angels.'

'I'm not much of an air puncher, though, am I? Could you imagine me clapping with them and their golden harps all in a row?'

'Yes, I will, that's much better. And I shall bow and feel the warmth of your approval beating down on my skin. That sound all right?'

Ruth nodded painfully. There were vivid waves of pride and waves of shame. It had always been her currency, Jean thought. She pictured a passport with dual nationality.

'There's a girl in year seven at school,' Jean began, 'told me every night her big sister says to her, last thing, after they've done their teeth, "Night Sophie. Hope you die in your sleep."'

'Oh?'

'Isn't that . . . severe?'

'Maybe she means I hope you die in your sleep when you're an old lady, peacefully and not in pain or in a car accident or at the hands of some axe murderer. I hope you have a good death. It's sweet.'

'You think? She's twelve years old.'

'Well yes, I think so. Why not?'

'Whatever you're on can I have some?'

Ruth pointed at two brown bottles on her nightstand. 'Fill your boots.'

'They just leave them lying about? I thought it was all under lock and key.'

'Not really,' Ruth said. 'I'm not sure. The nurse does usually . . . there's different stuff for different things. They bring round little paper cups.'

'I see!' Jean picked up the bottles and tried to read them but the writing was impossible.

'Maybe I will try one,' Jean said. 'I need *something*. What's that one there?'

'A strong one, I think. Tramadol, or is it the other –? There's the pale blue ones. Lovely colour. What's that play where the man says "That's a lovely shade of blue on your woolly"?'

'Not sure. Is it Pinter maybe or more like Joe Orton? Whoever it was makes *shade* sound filthy!'

'I know! And Gabapentin is the yellow ones with the numbers. Quite strong. I like that one. We could take it together, bit like holy communion?'

'Ha! What time you due your next? We mustn't be silly about it.'

'I just wait until the nurse comes usually. It's my favourite one today, Irene. She's got four sisters in Jamaica but she is the cleverest and the most beautiful.'

'Even so, she's unlikely to hand out freebies to visitors. Or is there happy hour on Fridays?'

'Is it Friday? That was quick. Thank God it's Friday Jean!'

'Maybe,' Jean said. Then, 'No I mustn't, it's irresponsible. What am I thinking?'

'We *are* in a hospital.'

'Yes, but we're not in the business of creating more patients. The nurses don't need extra dramas.'

'But I never ring my bell or anything. Wouldn't *dream* of it. Even if I was –'

'I know. I know you wouldn't . . . I, on the other hand . . .'

'Yes, yes you would. Night and day.'

The song 'Night and Day' hovered in the air between them, but neither had the heart to take the bait.

Jean unscrewed the nearest brown bottle and lifted a yellow pill to her mouth. She imagined Ruth's daughter Eleanor swinging onto the ward, putting on a bright brave blank face for her mother, although they all knew there was no saving things, not now. All the damage imprinted on Ruth's flesh. Broken tissue scarred and inflamed. And that very odd thing indeed of no one ever judging her. Did they try hard not to, did it just come naturally?

At home in the private solace of her sofa, Jean judged Eleanor mercilessly. She permitted herself little fetishised stints. They hit her system with force, like whipped cream folded into melted chocolate.

She admired the judgements that she fashioned, the severity of their tone and tilt; above all their certainty. The wry internal musings of the critic. The sharp observations in the vocative case. What you put your mother through! The breathtaking cruelty of your leisure activities. Wrecking lives with no awareness or compunction. To dedicate your life to torturing others – what venomous career counselling did you attend? *And* forcing everyone to feel sorry for you in the process. Pitiful girl.

Eleanor ruled through fear, left her mother and daughter routinely stunned and quaking. Afraid to answer the telephone. Afraid to take breaths. The amount of daily courage she exacted from them was an obscenity. Lily wearing yellow to prove she wasn't crushed, dotting her i's with hearts to convey optimism. What a strain to perform *I'm all right* with your every move, hopes pared back beyond what was decent, unable or unwilling to take the measure of the pain.

Eleanor brought Ruth to her knees, kept her there, liked her there. And for what? To what aim? Jean flexed her strict beliefs before her like the founder of a cult. That Ruth also depended on opiates now was a parody of homecoming. Of leave-taking. What ugly parallels. Scoring in the morning, scoring in the evening. Jean shook her head with great bitterness. Still Ruth preferred parody to satire, she had said so more than once. Parody was playful. Less mean-spirited.

Jean's skin grew hot. It reddened with injustice. She held the pill from the nightstand against her lips in the spirit of *can't beat 'em join 'em*. She saw three witches, in her imagination, ancient, cobwebbed and with red-rimmed eyes, but it was just Ruth, Eleanor and Jean when you looked closely – all lolling on the hospital bed singing songs and nodding out. Broomsticks ahoy! Night and Day. Death and Life. They would all go down or all go up together.

The reality was, there was not a single spell left to be cast. A terrible Brecht poem called 'I am Dirt' sprang at Jean from God knows where. 'Unfortunately, I had to do lots of things / That were harmful, purely to stay alive.' The speaker took so many drugs she called herself a 'bedsheet with no bones'. Sheets never have or have had bones, Jean was doubtful – but still the phrase had great power. It was how Eleanor was.

The way Jean's thoughts were going it was as though *she* was dying. She was too close to things. That was it. All of life was contagious. Of course your head would get muddled with the other person's at the end. It was just the practical side of 'for better or for worse'. That was friendship so much more than marriage. No one had a husband from seven to ninety but with women's love it wasn't even especially unusual. It would just merit an 'Oh' of recognition from another. No one would faint or anything.

Lily arrived and sat with Ruth while Jean palmed the pill and made a raid on the vending machine. A four-finger KitKat detached from its coil and fell with a clunk to the grey trough at the base. Suddenly Jean lifted her hand and banged the glass front with her fist as though it had cheated her. Something was cheating her. Everything was. She didn't stop beating until the whole machine rattled and began to emit a disastrous echoey wail. She nipped back to the ward in disgrace then, sitting on the blue vinyl chair at the edge of things, giving Ruth and Lily some privacy. She could see they were plotting something.

I'll get my mum here, leave it to me, no problem.

God. Please not that.

Lily came over to kiss them both goodbye. She was going to a friend's for a sleepover. It was a good idea and Jean encouraged it. They must pace themselves. She could hold the fort. 'I'll ring you at Beth's if I –'

'Sure.'

Jean gazed at Ruth in her parlous state. Perhaps Eleanor would come but in what condition? People being absent was more acutely felt by a certain type of individual than people being there. The tendrils of un-love went deeper. A disposition for grief. The impact had been searing, unforgettable, beyond endurance. There was nothing equal to it.

She blinked and took in the facts of the room. Easy does it. Well done. It was routine for her to congratulate herself. Her high opinion was important. She named all the white things she could see on the ward: pillow, sheet, clipboard paper, teacup and saucer, Ruth's ghost-face beginning to shut down. Ruth was peaceful in her slumbers. Concentrate, Jean told herself.

She sat herself up, stiff in the visitor's chair, the yellow pill still in her fingers. Sensible and calm now, she weighed things carefully. The truth was she could do with a lift, a break from all the pressure. Lily was off for the night, leaving Jean free to retire from the human race briefly. Saturday tomorrow – no school – excellent. It wasn't an insane idea. The pill might help her sleep, which would be good. Sleep had become a complete stranger to her nights. She was feeling the strain now, all the time, no denying. Work hospital, work hospital, marking at the bedside, watching over Lily, helping Ruth get to the one thing she didn't want. Fuck! This hinterland was stretching out for weeks and weeks. Aspects of her personality were becoming inoperable. She needed *something*. She popped the pill in her mouth – why not? And the way Ruth opened her eyes and shimmered with delight!

'Oh no Jean stop! I'm so stupid. Christ! That's Dulcolax.'

Jean yanked it out with the tip of her little finger, scarlet nail nicking the fleshiest part of her gum. The pill was intact and still dry. 'Ah, that I *don't* need,' she said.

'Sorry about that.'

'Never mind. No harm done. I wasn't thinking.'

'No you weren't, I am a bit shocked.'

'Good!'

'You ever taken drugs much Jean?'
'Well,' she said. 'I have and I haven't. I had a very bad time with Dexedrine when I was young. Put me off for life. It was dreadful. I went mad for six weeks, but when you go mad you assume it's forever. It was a shocking time.'

'Why d'you take it?'

'This,' she said, grabbing a handful of belly.

'Did you go very thin?'

'It's hard to know when you're insane. They had to take me away in a van. It wasn't pretty.'

'Christ.'

'Same thing happened to Muriel Spark! That was some consolation anyway. She wanted to get all slinky one Christmas, save money on her food bills – Dexedrine seemed the perfect answer. But one unexpected side effect – she got completely obsessed with T.S. Eliot! His most Christian play *The Confidential Clerk* – she thought it held special messages for her, beaming directly from T.S. himself. Then she started to believe he was communicating with her through the *Times* crossword.'

'*The Confidential Clerk*? The crossword? Jean you're making this up.'

'No. It's all there in black and white. All her hallucinations starred Eliot. Isn't that just so *chic*? Then she convinced herself he'd taken a job as a window cleaner with some of her friends to get even closer. Rumour has it news reached him of her predicament and he wrote to her to say he wasn't trying to reach her at all.'

'Christ! Sending a message to say he wasn't sending messages. Only a man!'

'I know.'

'Mine are mostly weddings and christenings.'

'Well a hallucination ought to feature rites of passage I think. That sounds good and proper. I think it's healthy.' At her 'healthy', Jean winced. *What the fuck is wrong with you?*

Snoozing happened to both of them then, Ruth's head on the pillow, Jean's nestled against the chair. It was very warm in the bay – Jean couldn't help think free heating. And later, in the night, when the ward was lightless apart from a pale column of blue and almost dead apart from a pair of drowsy nurses, Jean woke and started whispering.

'Hey! You knew all along about that pill! God I'm slow. You were teasing me. You beast!'

Ruth stirred and rigged up a dim smile. Her eyes lit a little. Were there the dregs of mischief there?

'Oh, I could kill you! You villain!'

'Better get a move on then.' Her voice was dry and sore and inhospitable.

'Don't . . .'

And after a few minutes, 'Jean?'

'Yep?'

'I do love you.' Their fingers wove together hungry on the damp top sheet.

'You're not so bad yourself.'

It was their last speaking. ■

MARK CAWSON LIVES

Smiler

Introduction by Iain Sinclair

In his calling-card self-portrait, Smiler isn't smiling. With good reason; he has been assaulted, traditional British street violence under the protective rubric of festering resentment, ugly politics. National Front collision, 1980. Full face, front on, abraded. Presented as evidence. His friends and associates, fellow travellers in the art-squat-music, just-do-it community, testify to his charm, his affability. 'Charismatic and beautiful,' wrote Tim Banks.

Smiler was on the scene with his weaponised camera, but he came from another planet: Nairobi. He has an older identity, shaken off by his submerged London life. His passport says: Mark Cawson.

Cawson's mother arrived here in 1939 on Kindertransport and was adopted by an English family. Her parents had been killed in Riga death camps. Cawson's father worked with both Maasai and settlers, until he was washed off a bridge, drowned. The wild colonial boy is dumped, well before he has acquired his alias, at a Nigerian boarding school. 'When Smiler's stepfather went to visit him, he could not understand a word Smiler said,' notes Neal Brown in *Smiler*, a telegrammatic book published by Sorika in conjunction with the photographer's only mainstream exhibition, at the ICA. And then, on achieving his majority, a stroke of fortune, the young man, exiled in a shifting and shiftless community, inherits £2,000. He buys camera equipment. He lends Keith Allen £500.

Smiler is a spectre from a subcultural milieu. His outline feels as opaque and enigmatic as David Bowie – anaesthetised in cocaine reverie, finding himself two miles out of a nowhere town in Nicolas Roeg's film of the Walter Tevis novel, *The Man Who Fell to Earth*. 'Human, but not properly, a man.' A shivering spook with special interest in future-world camera technologies, privileged ways of seeing. Smiler, like Bowie, has come to ground: a forced landing in an airless environment in which he sustains himself by making fallible records on photographic paper. Records that threaten to melt the page if we don't imprint them on our consciousness. The image journal is time travel.

Smiler's catalogue of the lunar faces of his cohorts in the countercultural squatting nexus is pure romance. Wrist-snap documentation becomes essential poetry. Images as natural as sneezing. And as plosive. Solitary dancers cakewalking in a night-world are scorched in atomic aftershock. They are like casualties collected from hard-news crime scenes by Weegee and his dustbin-lid flash. These are the junk-jolted undead, reanimated by Smiler's predatory and pitiless gaze. By being noticed. Surveyed before surveillance was universal. Before all-seeing conceptual snoop systems became the art of the state, where everything is captured in present time but nothing matters. The patina of excitement in Smiler's portraits of dead friends, of drug parties like wakes, comes from our sentimental attachment to a past that never was, but which is vividly here when resurrected and reforgotten. Cawson's prints are bleak Xeroxes referencing generations of resistance and addiction; from the punk orphans of Thatcher to disaffected Class Warriors; from the bohemian colonists of Notting Hill to sit-in polytechnic radicals; to second- and third-generation Situationists chasing a viable thesis. And all those dressed up and drifting particles looking for shortcuts to a good time.

Smiler hibernates. He has no interest in the long game, the blind faith of the courageous (or demented) outsider, hoping to be elevated from cult status to post-mortem name-check inflation. The bits of a past he is prepared to confess emerge when he lets rip, drink taken, on a late-night Tube ride. A strung-out barefoot walk in the early hours across a carpet of broken glass. The essence of squat occupancy is that it's finite, performative: nicknames but no surnames. 'Spotty Pete, Lulworth House'. No identity papers are required in King's Cross, Camden Town or Latimer Road. In Smiler's confrontational images, the dead outnumber the living. The salvaged account presented for future historians is Homeric. Eros and Thanatos. Named casualties. And opportunistic fucks. Survivalist routines with heroin punctuation in borrowed or invaded terrain. Demigods ascend or descend, playing their part in the comedy of squatocracy.

The pre-famous and the doomed children of television character actors cohabit, sharing their goods and affections. Smiler is in the room. He responds. Makes portraits. The visitant from another planet is finessing an autobiography of fragments. What he sees is who he is. A 'no future' aesthetic enhances the potential of the trigger instant: this print is awkward but it is all you are going to get. The 'decisive moment' of Cartier-Bresson, when chaos behaves itself, with all aspects in unique alignment, solicits admiration. Smiler, on the other hand, anticipates a coming world where compulsory pocket devices will do the heavy lifting. And every image cast against boredom carries consequence. He labours to keep his captures raw. The subjects are not consumers for anything freighted from a warehouse. They do their own shopping.

It can't be claimed that Smiler achieved a Hogarthian critique of the society in which he lodged. Putative artists here, dismissed by a smashed Barry Flanagan in their Hornsey assessment, are beating their shaven heads against concrete columns. Brutalist blocks designed as indestructible monuments to social blight are laughingly called 'House'. Smiler validates that privileged interval between 'considerate' construction and pitiless demolition. From a high window he notices a fire nobody can be bothered to put out on the wrong side of the tracks. Firemen watch. Location scouts evaluate the potential for screen time, documentary or cop show?

The broken teeth of that other London, CGI towers and investment silos, nibbling at a misted horizon. If the photographic seizure works, and appeases reality, you are transported, directly, to this other set.

Cawson has left a record that cannot now be challenged. His considerable and largely unseen archive accurately represents its own history. The prints look disposable, casually framed, throwaway. They flirt with happenstance. Action before theory. If we take them seriously, as indeed we should, they challenge the necrophile calculation of Warhol's Polaroids, the silk-screened multiples for investors. Smiler's photographs are *like* the heroin-chic versions that dressed style magazines of the period. But they have the integrity of accident, managed carelessness. They could survive without the witness of the artist responsible. The figures Smiler opts to depict quiver on the cusp of refusal: their eyes register affront, suspicion, weary tolerance. To be exhibited is to acknowledge mortality. This moment will become all moments. Brown recollects walking across a park – 'twilight, plants and animals' – towards 'a recovery gathering'. Smiler has entrusted some of his archive to his friend. Then he decides that he wants one particular print back. But Brown says that he never had it. Smiler 'was giving archives to me and others in quiet anticipation of his death'. The images we are permitted to access here, by way of Cawson's son Louis, have a defining quality: resistance. The survival of these negatives, beyond the evidence of those lost lives, is miraculous. Preconceptions around the vulnerability of the strictly limited selection of images chosen for an exhibition are challenged when we inspect the untapped potential of a rescued contact sheet. Now a fuller, rounder version of Cawson's autobiography emerges: he lives again.

There are alternative choices beyond the nakedness of that self-portrait after the assault. There are excursions to the seaside, remembered pleasures. Associates relax over tea and ciggies in greasy spoons. They smile! Young Black men gather on the streets of Notting Hill. And there is a prophetic long shot, pulling back from the intimacy of the portraits, the nudes, the haircuts. It offers a Ballardian vision of the Westway as a discontinued future. The elevated highway is flanked by a twenty-storey tower block, fresh from the 1970s. Its long shadow falls across the estates, the curve of railway, and the coming spread of incontinent development with its terrible consequences.

The prints from which Smiler's integrity must be tested belong to a limited number of specific London locations at a specific period. In a very smart move, the photographer asked for the emphasis on the commissioned text for *Smiler* to be placed on Brown rather than himself; thereby assuring his mythic status as a Harry Lime ghost in his own novel. He landed Brown with the task of listing the lost, libelling those who deserve it, while giving up addresses of relevant squats, fast-food pits, clubs and addiction parties.

Property and possession: the continuing shame of London. Back in the sixties, strategies were imported from Provos in Amsterdam. Warehouses were found in anarchist alleys. The sleeping-bagged floors of Whitechapel were like performance tributes to Jack London's photographs from *The People of the Abyss*. There were meetings in Stoke Newington and Shoreditch, addressed by European activists, and attended by locals, bruised in physical battles to maintain occupied terraces in Redbridge. Loose associations of like-minded drifters invaded council-owned properties left empty, while they waited to become under-resourced tower blocks. There is a long and complex history, beyond the scope of Smiler's portfolio. He worked at one remove, highlighting the quotidian. A predicated overdose with high heels and empty file boxes in King's Cross. A figure, head in a bag, reversed balaclava, bonelessly slumped like a political prisoner forced to stand against a wall. And described as 'Psychosis, All Saints Road'. Temporary occupants, warming the stones for grand development projects still in the pipeline, are under notice. The surrounding microclimate, also registered by Smiler, features the terminal dread of waiting for service at a McDonald's franchise in Kensington. Along with a suited and muted celebration of Jehovah's Witnesses at a wedding in Monmouth Road. Hard to tell if 'Spotty Pete' of Camden, with his flowered shirt and parrot tattoo, is lockjaw-yawning or deceased. A naked, smoking Jane holds – as instructed? – a print of a young Sophia Loren over her face. Seamus, on the sixteenth floor of a squat in Shepherd's Bush, is embedded in the scattered ephemera of possession: a hulking safe-sized Dansette, floor-mattress with tartan rug, ties and belts dangling from a waterpipe. Whitewashed prison bricks and barred window. The harsh reportage offset by painterly light dignifying the sitter: fine eyebrows, moustache, dimpled chin. And provisional acceptance of fate's cruel hand.

End notes in *Smiler*: eleven friends dead. AIDS cull. Overdose. Self-harm. 'Property prices go up. Squatting criminalised . . . Joy upon joy of intensity of love. Drinking lots of water . . . Smiler doing new work.'

The revealed alignments of small interconnected groups in unwanted properties under permanent threat. Possession of self-medicating pick-me-ups persecuted. Dispossession a fact. Smiler's portrait after the NF beating, two or three stages beyond what is comfortable to see and know, recalls Étienne Carjat's famous photograph of the runaway outlaw Arthur Rimbaud, who also had his subterranean London period. 'Right now, I'm damned. My country appals me. The best course of action: drink myself comatose and sleep it off on the beach.'

Aidan Andrew Dun starts to write, after 'seven or eight years of study and research', *Vale Royal*, a poem of place. He tells us that he looks up from his copy of Rimbaud, over the unresolved and ultra-urban particulars of King's Cross: railway, canal, burial ground. It is 1973. He nests in a squatted building. Uncollected by Smiler, Dun was one of those who disinterred local mythology and made it universal: the ground plan for Blake's Jerusalem. Rimbaud, a trans-dimensional neighbour from Royal College Street, risked the only possible escape. He gave up poetry, went into colonial trade, and became his own portraitist, with a remotely triggered selfie on a coffee plantation in Harar in 1883. ∎

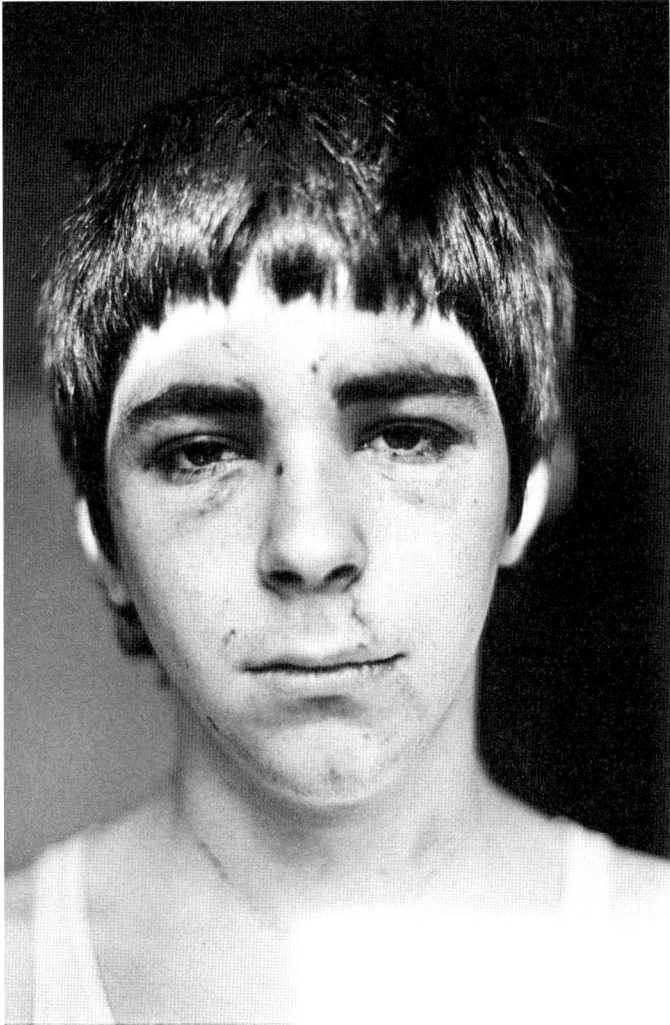

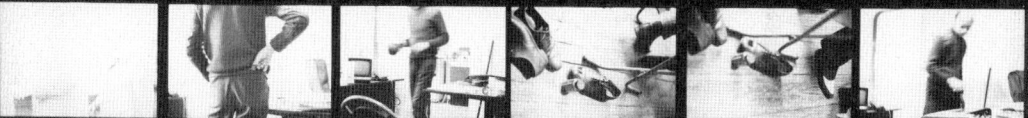

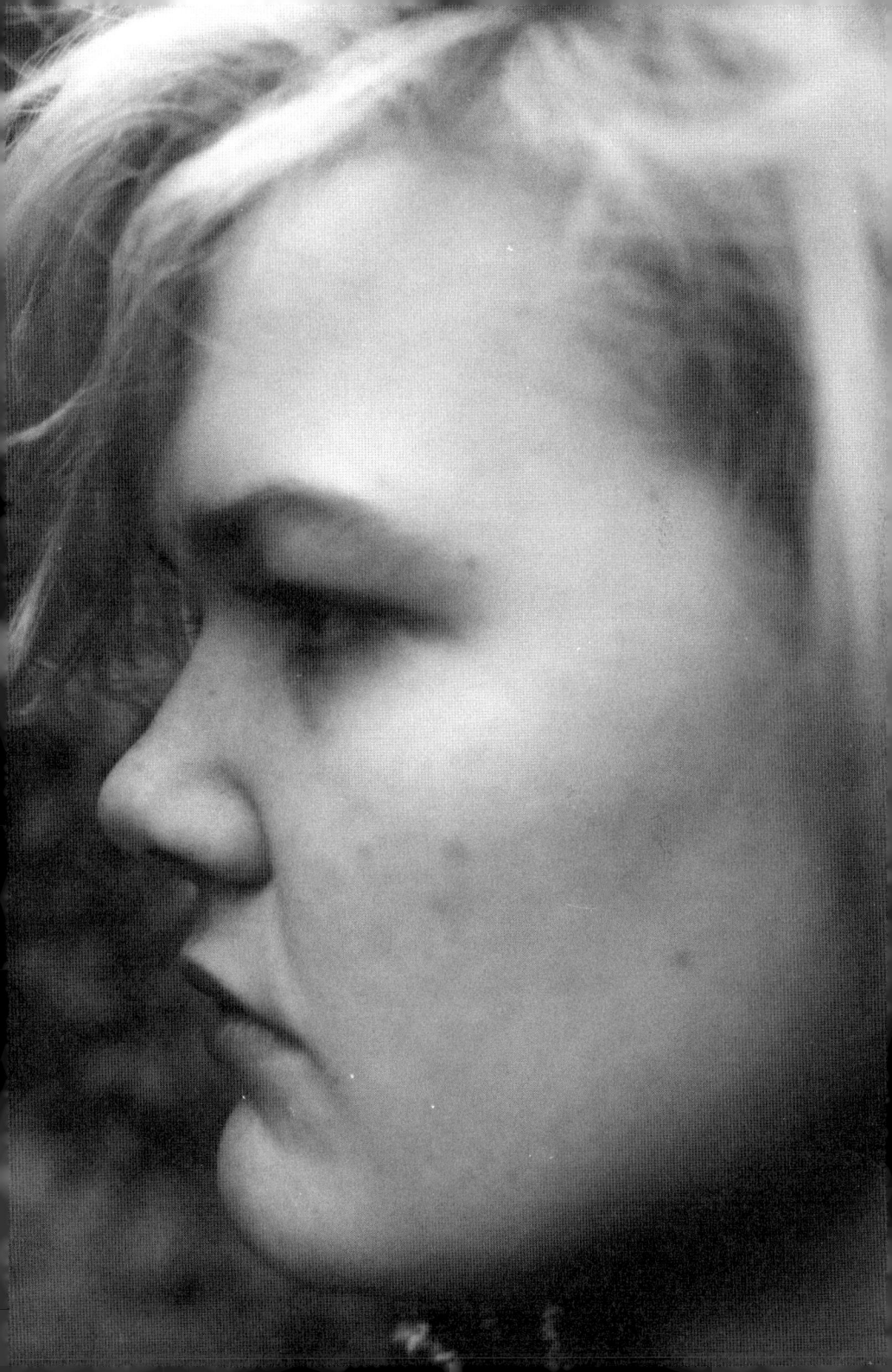

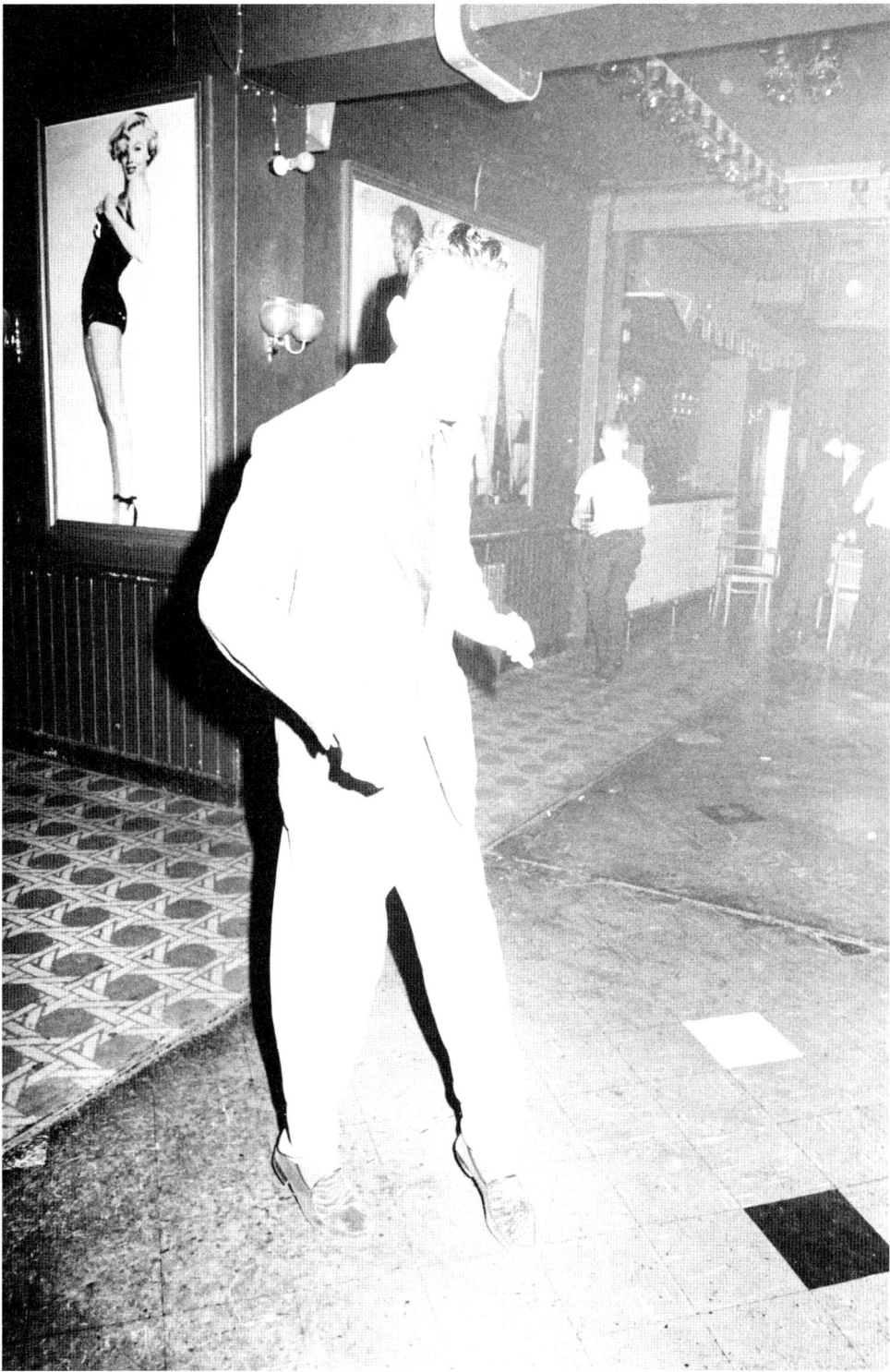

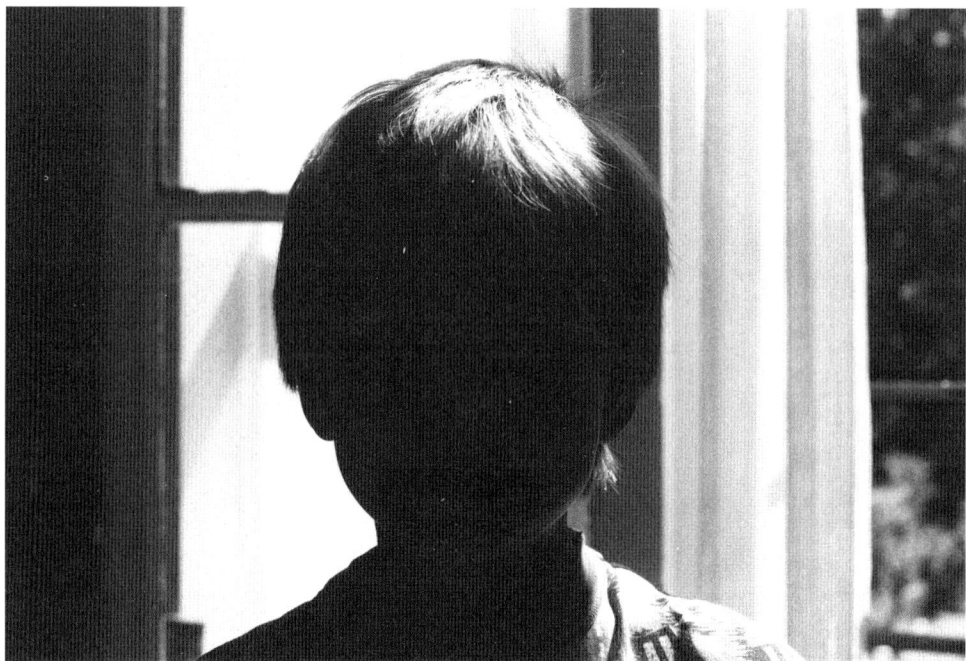

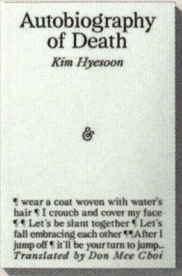

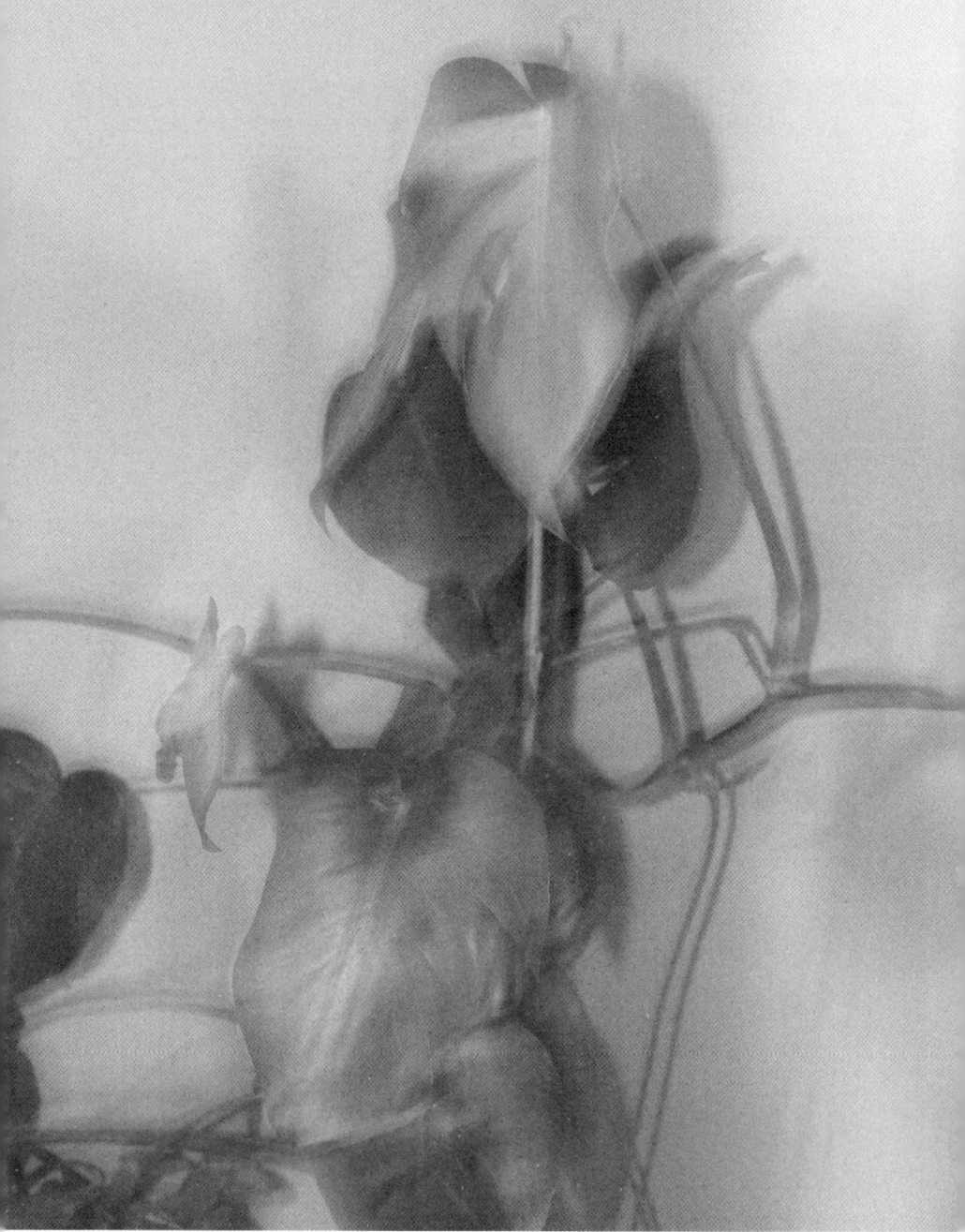

KALPESH LATHIGRA
Bird of Paradise / Strelitzia

NOWHERE

Yasmina Reza

TRANSLATED FROM THE FRENCH BY ALISON L. STRAYER

I do not know the language of my father,
my mother, or my ancestors, not any of
their languages. I recognise no soil or tree,
no soil was ever mine in the way people
mean when they say 'that's where I'm from'.
There is no land where I would ever feel a
sudden longing for childhood, no place for
me to write who I am. I do not know what
sap I fed upon, the word 'native' does not
exist for me, nor the word 'exile', though
even so, it's a word I think I know, but that is
false. I don't know any music for beginnings,
no songs or lullabies; when my children
were small I rocked them to sleep in a
language I'd invented. Where my father
came from my father himself could not say
– Tashkent, or Samarkand, which he had
never seen, Moscow, where he was born, or
Germany, where he learned his first
language, later forgotten. He came from
nowhere he could speak of, or whose trace

he had retained anywhere but in his body, his eyes and the abruptness of certain ways he had of doing things. I saw my mother's city, I heard my mother's language, there's a country called Hungary that was hers, of which she told me nothing and which is nothing to me. I can't dress a table the way my mother did – my mother never dressed a table. I don't know how to do the things that mothers do, learned from their own mothers in their tradition. I have no tradition, I have no religion, I don't know how to light candles or arrange any kind of celebration. I don't know how to tell the story of our people, I didn't know I had a people. I like the names of French regions, Creuse, Vendée, Haute-Marne, Franche-Comté and other names too, realms of land with names that are more distant than countries, and which exclude me. I have no house, from time to time I dream of having one, not a holiday home but a house to bury myself in. I do not want well-being but austerity, I dream of refuge, I want hills and woods to walk in. That is what France is and has always been – place names, the names of *communes*, those unattainable havens, burial grounds to generations. I have no roots, no soil has ever lodged itself in me. I have no origins. When I read in the newspapers Iranian, Russian, Jewish, Hungarian, these are only words I've said. There are no images, no lights, smells, nothing. There aren't even any photos. I found photos that Marta Andras took of Veronka Ligetti and me at her place in nineteen-ninety. I am moved by these photos, in which we never stop laughing, we are laughing from exhaustion – Marta never pressed the shutter, she only complained about our lack of spontaneity. Marta died one year later, I don't know what became of Veronka Ligetti. But what moves me most about these photos is Marta's flat, a stateless flat with stateless china, paintings, elephants, Buddhas, teapots, lamps – even the flowers are stateless – and the pale wispy print of the settee which cried 'from now on, I want things clean and new and upbeat'. She was my agent and my friend until she died, I talk about her in *Hammerklavier*. The first time we met she said, I'm in no hurry, think it over, take your time, I don't want to rush you. She gave me an orchid, which sat waiting for me on her desk. I left in the night with the flower, my head spinning with excitement. The next day at first light, on the phone, Well? she sighed with her Hungarian accent, more Hungarian than my mother's, which I never hear, What's going on? What have you decided? Why do you take so long? Yes, yes, Marta, I replied, forgive me, I realise it's been long, absurdly long, yes, let's be quick because I don't know where we're going, or whether it's far or near or high or low. Questioned by me about her childhood, my mother says at

least ten times during the conversation,
which bores her, we must turn the page.
Turning the page comes up again and again
without my ever getting to see the page. She
says, we cannot dwell on what we used to
be; she says, it's absurd to feel nostalgia for
a world that no longer exists. In a hallway of
my childhood there was a picture, a painting
of her playing the violin. My mother was a
violinist, I never heard her play. Still, I wrote
'violinist' in the blank where you wrote your
parents' occupations, at school. The violin
was abandoned in a cupboard at the back of
a high shelf, I only saw it with my own eyes
as an adolescent. Not long ago, she decided
to sell it, just to get it out of the house, it
wasn't worth anything. In the end, she gave
it to a young Portuguese guy without saying
anything to us. I do not regret. There's
nothing that I miss. When it comes to places
I have been, there isn't even one I miss, no
real specific place, I think as I'm writing
this. I miss only times and spaces I don't
know. I can feel the most violent nostalgia
for places I've never been. To my
amazement, I discovered this passage in
I-Another, the journal of Imre Kertész: 'I've
never analysed the significant fact that my
favourite reading as a child was *The Ugly
Duckling*. I read it many times and wept
over it diligently every time. I thought of it
often, on the street, in bed before I fell
asleep, etc., as a type of consolation that
takes revenge on everyone for everything.

Perhaps it does a much better job of illuminating my life's secret guiding principle than the grand readings of my youth that I took to be the fundamental turns of my fate and determinants of my perhaps straying path.' How many times, over random readings, have I told myself, 'I'd have loved to have written that', or, 'I could have written that'? But when a person says, I could have written that, it's the idea they're referring to, the phrasing almost never. The excerpt from Kertész strikes me *word for word* as something that could have been written by me. I don't think I've ever come across such a close resemblance, which is all the more uncanny when you consider that it's a private reflection, a confession. Perhaps the only difference lies in this last point. Of my own devices, I'd have never written it down. Without Kertész, the connection with *The Ugly Duckling* would have remained buried in my memory with other covered-up and silenced things. The way in which Kertész relates it, word for word in the way I might have done myself, had I dared transform it into *matter*, compels me to disclosure. I cannot stand idly by and allow another person to exhume a part of my existence. There is a hard piece of earth, trod upon for years, in which, if I have the strength and daring, I may one day have to dig. For a time in my childhood that was short and which I don't remember, my father filmed us with an 8 mm camera. In those few films discovered in adulthood I see myself leaping, spinning, moving in the most chaotic way – flailing alone in front of the lens in every film in which I appear. I thrash about on a beach or in some other place, and no sooner have I stopped moving, or run out of breath, than I start right up again. Watching this crazy child, I can hear my father cry: move, move! To confirm the magical function of the camera, the subject had to move. Me, I moved to make him happy. Other children were more natural, more defiant or indifferent. Me, I moved absurdly. I knocked myself out to make him happy. All I have in the way of animated relics of the past are the images of that electrified little puppet; it may have been better not to have seen anything at all than to see all that anxious breathlessness. I have no memory of the places we were in the photos. I'm even quite amazed to see I'd been on a beach. We didn't go to the seaside, or I just don't remember it. You could not say that these are images of joy. In the eyes described as sparkling, and in spite of the wide-open mouth showing all its teeth – for my father must not have just said move, move, but also laugh, laugh – I see not only the desire to please, and to do it well, I also see *uncertainty*. I'd like to know where we were. I've not a single memory. I often don't know where I am in the photos in our albums. The scenery doesn't ring a bell, nor

do the people. I came across this story told
by Klaus Mann about Stefan Zweig. 'The
last time I met him, he was coming towards
me on Fifth Avenue. He didn't notice me,
he was, as they say, deep in thought . . . As
he believed no one was watching him, he
allowed himself a fixed unhappy gaze. No
sign of the cheerful faces for which he was
known. Moreover, he had not shaved that
morning and his face looked strange and
shaggy. I looked at him, the stubble and the
dark lifeless eyes, and thought, "well, what's
going on with him?" I walked towards him.
"Where are you going, why the hurry?" He
stopped short, like a sleepwalker hearing
someone speak his name. A second later
he'd pulled himself together and was
smiling, chatting, joking, as courteous and
lively as ever.' I've always written like a man
of other people, the man who knows he's
being looked at. I've *lightened up* gloomy
subjects and made them likeable. Is it
possible to write like a man who doesn't
know he's being looked at? Yet in Klaus
Mann's account, I see two sides of the truth,
because the desire to behave in a courteous,
lively manner reveals a person's essence just
as much, if not more than, a passing state of
gloom. Where are you going? Why are you
in such a hurry? Where are you going in
such a hurry with your lifeless eyes? Going
down that avenue, hurrying for what? 'Yes,
Marta, forgive me,' I replied sixteen years
ago, 'yes, let's hurry yes because I don't

know where we're going, or whether it is close or far, or high or low.' I've been hurrying without you for a long time, Marta. Wherever you are, you'll know by now whether that place was far and high. Since you stopped wanting to live, I've been hurrying without you, and if no one is looking at me, you can see the way I really am. On my balcony is a plant that climbs a little whose name I do not know. From time to time, a stem with leaves at the tip shoots out and bends towards the outer wall; it retreats around the corner to hide. It has all the room it needs to stretch out elsewhere, but it doesn't seek the sun. It goes off to hide, to be alone. I go after it and put it back in the sun. I've already mentioned Barthes's poignant phrase, 'to know that these things I am going to write will never cause me to be loved by the one I love . . .' A thing that one produces is like a piece of clothing, an element associated with oneself, an external attribute, inalienable but external, so that recognition, esteem and expressions of appreciation are of very slight importance. It is an illusion to believe that admiration can turn into emotion. Amongst my grandfather's effects in New York, we found a photo of the Ugly Duckling. I'm fourteen, photographed full length on a lawn in Switzerland (I know because of the wooden railing in the background). I wear a white short-sleeved blouse, white shorts, a wide white belt with a gold buckle and black loafers, my hair hidden beneath a printed fichu, an outfit not at all suited to my age, and completely out of sync with the times. Still, there's an attempt at elegance, though that may not be the right word, so graceless are the face and body. An attempt at elegance, lacking in conviction. I see it in the curled-up wrists, the slightly misaligned feet, the look of unhappiness. That body, that face and get-up are still inside me. They are scattered through the characters, dissembled on the pages, unbeknownst to all, unbeknownst to me as well – no one knows where they come from, the things we command words to do. Nothing to take from childhood. Writers return to childhood, sooner or later. I don't return anywhere, there'd be nowhere to return to. Long walls walked along, long waits, the fallow lands of new suburbs, devoid of history. Buildings replacing houses, clusters of buildings that people called apartment blocks. Hallways, corners of the flat, a bedroom tidied ad infinitum. Certain landscapes. Certain events. If I applied myself, I'd find more, but it's of no interest whatsoever. Josiane, on tour in the city of Lyon, writes: 'In the neighbouring park where my father's soul drifts about, the park where he came almost every day of his life to run, the first of all the joggers, and then to pedal when he could no longer run, I retraced the steps I took at every stage of my life. Once I saw my mother furtively

pick acacia blooms and eat the petals. She
who was so measured and so wise, a
worshipper of reason, eating flowers whilst
hiding from park wardens, before the eyes
of her dumbfounded (young) children.' My
gardens are safe. I can walk past and even
through them worry-free. There are no
wandering souls. I am left in peace. A happy
childhood is a useless burden for the future.
Childhood period. No matter which
childhood. Josiane retraced the steps she
used to take between her father's surgery
and the family flat: 'I did the walk, which as
a child seemed to me a true journey,
between the Surgery and the Flat. A five-
minute walk. Sun in the street. My father so
proud of having made it possible for us to
live in that bourgeois district, near a
beautiful park.' She put capital letters on
Surgery and Flat. So she retraces her steps
and without her saying so, or without it
becoming apparent (or maybe it is apparent
in that wonderful detail), her heart grows
heavy, I can feel it. In 1987, from a distance,
with a single camera and no lighting, Didier
filmed a performance of *Conversations After
a Burial* at the Théâtre Paris-Villette. I no
longer know why we did it. To begin with,
things that seem natural to others are not
natural for me. I've never felt it necessary to
archive (awful word) a show. A few months
later, I watched the tape, but only the
beginning, the first few minutes, until the
characters walk, enter, exit. We couldn't see

much, couldn't see the faces in detail, but could hear the sound. I don't mean the words, I mean the sound of the actors' steps on the stage – a certain kind of footstep-sound on that wooden floor, to which I'd never paid attention but which, for some unknown reason, contained the soul of the play. With its uneven tones, it signalled distance and oblivion. That sound of steps which I will never hear again in real life provoked in me a savage, unquantifiable melancholy, related to both past and future. I could not keep watching the tape, and never viewed it again. Is this not the same melancholy people suffer when they run into their childhood again? On the side of the street the school was on, for a long time there was only a long wall that concealed a piece of undeveloped land. Most of the time I walked on the opposite sidewalk, which was even bumpier, but sometimes I crossed the street and walked by the wall. It was a street in progress that went up to our building. I asked my sister what had become of our room after I left at around age fifteen. I say, I have no memory of your room when you lived in it alone. She replies, it hasn't changed, it's just the same. I think about our room, eternally tidied, nothing left about, no toy or piece of clothing, not a single object of no immediate use. I say: same wallpaper? (columns of daisy bouquets) – Yes. – Desk? –Yes. – Did you put things on the wall? – No. – Did you like our room? –

No. But I liked the chestnut tree out the
window. I say that I don't remember the
chestnut tree. She's astonished, yes you do,
the nice horse chestnut! I suddenly think of
Desolation and the character of Lionel, who
every day in every season contemplates the
chestnut tree outside his window, and I'm
struck by an absurd idea, which I
immediately reject: the invented chestnut
tree at the corner of rues Laugier and
Faraday could only be a transplantation of
our chestnut tree from childhood, of which
I have no memory, but I reject the idea. The
chestnut tree of childhood has been erased
and there have been many other chestnut
trees since. It was not for me, nor mine, that
tidy room in which I kept myself for years,
now occupied by someone else looking out
at the same square of outside world, at the
tree if it still exists, the life of the railway,
the freight trains and the little hill behind
– a half-empty room facing north, a
passageway with two doors on the diagonal
that one abandons without regret to escape
into the future. Once in a while, I think back
on the short trip we took with my mother to
Budapest. A return to her native city in her
native land, a serenely detached journey, as
if there were no such thing as a native city
or a native land, as if those words to which I
ascribe such weighty and even ancient
meaning (one really wonders why) were
nothing but literary phantasmagoria.
Someone told me recently that he loved

such-and-such a place because it was his
country. People who can say 'my country'
often mean a village, a neck of the woods.
That's what a country always is, anyway, an
inaugural setting, a piece of earth – it
cannot be too big. What's the difference
between people who have a neck of the
woods and those who don't? What's the
good of having a place, a soil, roots, because
when all is said and done –? There have
never been graves, no places of the dead. I
had a little sister who died, I don't know
where she is. My maternal grandparents are
ashes somewhere in New York, my mother
doesn't know exactly where. As for my
father and his parents, I was the one who
brought them *into town* before my father's
death so I wouldn't have to inter him in the
suburban hinterland next to the ring road,
where he'd just buried his brother and
would have buried his father and mother,
repatriated from who-knows-where, in a
plot that wasn't even Jewish. One day, in the
street, knowing he was sick, knowing he was
done for, not to put too fine a point, I asked,
'When you die do you want a religious
burial?' He stopped walking to properly
take offence: 'Of course, what a question!' I
said, 'Grandma isn't buried in a Jewish plot,'
he said, 'Well that is a mistake.' So now I
know where he is, and I know where his
father, mother, brother are, they're in that
Jewish section in the Montparnasse
cemetery where by some miracle we got

three spots, but the land is absolutely new, without any roots. Bodies are put there at random, with no connection to anything. I feel a sort of coming up in the world to have them there in the heart of Paris, next to famous people of French culture, like the nouveaux riches of death. ■

Anne Carson

When Rhinestones Star the Night and You Find Yourself Thinking Fondly of Dave Hickey

Oh tell me, is it not nearly day?
(you said and I said) Look, the
blessings should surprise you, not
the pain. Pain is normal. After all,
we die! Our fathers die. Or refuse
to, their sweaters still hanging in
the kitchen, making us 'leftover
Dave' in the living room,
wondering why it's called that.

NAN GOLDIN
Daily dose, Berlin, 2015

REMISSION

Gary Indiana

W e had all followed the news stories about Evan Greene, followed them, I ought to say, with the scurvy interest that 'people like us' take in stories that could, either in part or entirely, involve people we know, or even people we are, or once were.

At least one of our crowd had actually met Evan Greene at an earlier moment in his, Evan Greene's, life, his political life if I may call it that, before Evan Greene succumbed to the dark beckoning of lethal excess.

NADIA STEIGER, 44, TENANT OF HESPERUS COTTAGE, VAN MEERGEN ESTATE
When was I first aware of him? He probably introduced himself at some point. I didn't realize he was living at Number Six at first. Clam Shell Cottage it's called. I knew the woman who lived there before. I'd been away for a few months, and when I came back, there he was.

I wasn't aware of him the way you mean until that first incident three years ago.

Who was living there before him?
Jackie Something. Jackie Banning. She was a club promoter, a PR person. She lived by herself.

Did she know Evan Greene?
I have no idea. Why would she?

She might have recommended him to the landlord.
I wouldn't know. We weren't friends. I knew her the way you know people you see all the time without thinking about them. I like having neighbors, but they're usually horrible when you get to know them. Jackie was all right. She gave parties. I went to a couple. But I can't remember anybody I met there. I don't know what happened to her.

What were your impressions of Evan Greene before the incident three years ago?
If you look at Number Six from here, you only see that side of it through the trees really. I didn't run into him every day. I mostly saw him getting in or out of his car.

Just a general impression.
I honestly never gave him a thought. Before, I mean. They say he did modeling when he was young. I could believe that. He has very waspy features. But when I try to picture his face he really looks like nothing. He got very thin. I did notice that. Almost skeletal. His skin started to resemble parchment. We didn't speak often. Hello goodbye in the parking lot, and a few times at the pool. Or I'd run into him at the supermarket. This isn't a close-knit community. We're not up each other's noses. I see most people here at the supermarket, if ever.

Can you recall any of those conversations?
He was always on about local politics. I have no interest in local politics. In one ear out the other. Dogs, also. He talked about dogs quite a lot.

He had a group that rescued golden retrievers.
Why would you *only* rescue the most expensive type of dog? He didn't even have a dog himself.

What else did he talk about?
Nothing memorable. Talked your ear off but nothing you'd remember afterwards. Other people had more contact with him. I didn't like him, frankly. Something about him wasn't right. He had scary eyes. Empty, icy blue eyes. They say he used to scream at city council meetings. Even when you had an ordinary conversation with him, he had the look of someone screaming, even though he wasn't.

Pepper Gillespie was friendly with him. In Coulibri Cottage, over the way. And Dr Balvet, Dr Balvet's place is the one behind his. He knew him socially, I think. I'm sure Solberg in the front cottage saw things, he spies on everybody. Stargazing, he calls it.

PEPPER GILLESPIE, 31, TENANT OF COULIBRI COTTAGE
The way it was reported made more sense than what actually happened. I never heard of this slamming thing until the article came out in *The Times*, but I imagine Evan Greene was as fucked up as they were. It excited him to keep it going. He wouldn't have been rational. Addicts never know what they're doing, in my experience.

Did you notice these young men coming and going all the time?
It wasn't all the time. That's been exaggerated in the press. They weren't all young, either. The first one that died was almost sixty. None of them were children. It's a tough thing to decipher. It's hard to imagine getting off on that. Each to his own and everything but . . .

Anyway, sure, I noticed them. I saw things. I have a pretty clear view of Number Six between the trees. I don't sleep much. It would've been hard not to notice the traffic in and out of Evan Greene's place. But for a long time it just seemed like, an old, gay white guy with lots of young Black friends. After the first one died, Roderick Williams, I think we started to look at Evan Greene differently.

You were friends with him?
Not at all. If somebody told you that, I bet I can guess who it was.

What were your encounters with him like?
He came on to me once, a few years ago. You know he posed as a photographer for a while. I think he had some delusions of being a Robert Mapplethorpe or Nan Goldin type or what have you. He dropped the pretense after a while, apparently. The news stories never mentioned it. Anyway, once, this was by the pool, he said he wanted to photograph me for an art show. He found my tattoos fascinating, he said.

Did he photograph you?
No, I told him I don't like being photographed. I guess he thought, because of the tattoos . . . I was standing there in my swim shorts and his eyes kept zooming in on my crotch, not furtively at all, he made his interest obvious. It was a bit creepy. He didn't like being turned down. He took a negative attitude toward me for a while after that. Later, when he really started to change, visibly change, he suddenly became insanely friendly and talkative.

You thought he was insane?
I thought he was taking a lot of speed, or coke, to be that intense. Anyway, now we know, the guy's a monster. Became one. I don't think he was that way before the drugs. It was a real Jekyll and Hyde thing. I feel slightly sorry for him, because it sounds like he's going to get what amounts to a life sentence at his age. They've piled on all these charges like 'operating a drug house', which is going overboard in my opinion. It doesn't seem fair.

What do you think would be fair?
I'd rather see him sent to rehab than prison. It's just an opinion. None of this would've happened if he hadn't gotten into meth. Meth turns people into robots. The way he's been painted, he's likely to get murdered in jail.

He shouldn't have preyed on those people, if you want to frame it like that, no doubt. They weren't the brightest bulbs in the box. On the other hand, they kept going back after they knew what they were getting into, so . . . It's hard to know what to think about it.

AKSEL SOLBERG, 59, AND ROSA SOLBERG, 56, TENANTS OF MARLIN COTTAGE

If the press uncovers anything to grab on to, any stray detail, to make an ugly story sell, they will. It was lucky nothing about the estate figured in the reporting, aside from him living in a 'fantasyland' or 'storybook' cottage. Otherwise, we'd get tour buses coming through here. It was bad enough that that boy's family and their political friends turned up every weekend before the arrest. They seemed to think everyone on the estate was somehow implicated in the whole thing. But once Greene was in custody it all went quiet as far as where he lived and all that. Otherwise, some of the old stories about this place would come to light again, no doubt. Not just the suicides, either. The press stuck to its political morality tale and left the neighbors out of it.

This is a totally different –
I know that. I know that. But the reporting has been horrendous. You can see it's been blown up to fit a particular narrative. Two different ones, in fact. What happened was disgusting. But things like this happen somewhere in this city every night. The race factor got played up, along with the myth about Evan Greene being a billionaire with powerful political connections. What billionaire drives a shitty car like that beat-up Prius he drove?

These cottages are rent-stabilized. You wouldn't think so, for such prime property. Nobody on the estate has anything like a billion dollars. Evan Greene sold a small data-processing service in Scottsdale ten years ago for two point three million dollars and he's lived off that nest egg ever since. I looked into it. Tesseray bought the whole property for less than that. It's no billion dollars.

It's nice here of course. Exceptional for what we're paying. The cottages are sweet. Very comfortable, even if they do look a bit Disney. 'Disney Whimsy', someone said, with grace notes of perversity. On clear nights I watch the stars above the clouds, through that telescope. The night sky puts things in perspective. We're nothing but lint on a tiny ball of dirt and water. I mean from a cosmic angle. We all get tossed around on the currents of the universe. That's the Evan Greene story, more or less.

Were you living here the first time the police showed up?
The police have been here more often than you think. But I know which time you mean, obviously. We were. We've lived here almost as long as Dr Balvet or Theresa Lennox, who has the place near the side gate. She's not one of the original tenants, but she's been here the longest. She's a hoarder, apparently. A real fruitcake.

There were several minor incidents leading up to the first really serious one, in the weeks before.
One night a young man wearing a pair of white underpants came running out of Evan Greene's house up to the side gate and away into the night. He was clutching his clothes. I suppose he pulled them on when he got to the stairs. Definitely in a panic. I happened to be out here stargazing. Another time one of Greene's charming guests sat masturbating on that bench over there at two in the morning. Rosa was awake for some reason and happened to look out. She came into my room and told me about it. I threw on a robe and chased him off. I had words with Evan Greene about that. He fed me some convoluted tale about volunteering at a mental clinic years earlier, and this guy being a former client who somehow found out his address. I didn't believe a word of it but I just let it go.

Men sometimes showed up at the main gate or came in through the street entrance. And they often came out stumbling and looking seriously wrecked. I just assumed they were rent boys. They were rent boys, as it turned out.

Did you or, if you know, any of the other tenants call the police when –
These people coming to see Evan Greene at all hours were often
familiar to me. If I saw someone going there once, chances were I'd
see the same person again over the course of a week or a month.
After that it would be someone else. They were generally pretty well-
dressed. I wouldn't call the police just because someone I recognized
looked wasted or turned up at weird hours, unless they seemed
threatening. Theresa Lennox would, I imagine. Nadia Steiger might.
They're both a little nuts, in my opinion.

They didn't, though.
That was more out of laziness than consideration, I'm sure. The
thing is, people would shout his name from the front gate, where he
couldn't possibly hear them. Someone who did hear them would have
to go down and explain that after sunset, when the gate gets locked,
you're supposed to have the code, or phone whoever you're visiting
to let you in. I had to do that a few times. I let them in, just to avoid
trouble.

You might have kept them out for the same reason.
Looking at it now, that's probably true. Of course they didn't need a
code for the side gate. There's just a flight of narrow steps that runs
up from the boulevard and then an ordinary wrought-iron mesh
door, if they knew where it was. It's a bit hard to find. There's a lot
of overhanging vegetation. There's no light there. That gate's almost
never locked. It's overgrown with ivy.

Actually, the police came more than once about Evan Greene
before all this. Something to do with drugs. But that was all handled
quietly. They never arrested him.

Did the owner ever try to evict him, do you know?
What, Mr Tesseray? Not at all. Him and Evan Greene have certain
interests in common, I would think. It's probably why he rented to
Greene in the first place. They were friends.

What interests?
Well, not rescuing dogs, let's say.

THERESA LENNOX, 76, TENANT OF STARFISH COTTAGE
I'm not set up for company at the moment. We can sit out here.
 I just have to send a text message.
 Okay.
 I look after the plantings and landscaping. Not all of it, but some.
The walkways and the shrubs, the hedges, the trees, the fieldstone
benches, and so forth, were laid out in the late 1940s, but a lot of it's
changed over the years. I came here in '86, after Tesseray bought the
estate from the original owner's trustees.

Who was the original owner?
I can't think of his name offhand. He built these cottages . . . houses
really . . . shifted a lot of the hillside, flattening parts of it out. None
of it's exactly flat, but flat enough where the houses are to put up
structures, with all this foliage and garden areas between them. You
make the foundations level when the land's crooked.
 He thought of himself as a sea captain. I read that somewhere.
There're nautical motifs, little seafaring touches in all the cottages.
McAvery. The name just came to me. People called him Captain
McAvery. In reality he'd never been on a ship, I'm told. He made all
his money in noodles. Spaghetti imports, farina wheat from Spain or
Italy, something like that. Captain McAvery the spaghetti king.

So, Elio Tesseray hired you –
No, not until long after I moved in. It happened more recently, that
Tesseray needed help with the grounds. He knew I worked with plants
and gardens. It's only an occasional job. He hires a crew for heavier
work. For instance, replacing the soil. The soil here is too alkaline for
sycamores, and he wanted sycamores. They're valuable trees. The
ones over there were brought in from Idaho.

The drought has affected things. We can't use the water we normally would. The fires don't help either. Soot from the big fires gets carried here. Soot is oily, it reduces photosynthesis. By the time it gets here it's particulate matter you don't really see. It does a lot of damage. Leaves develop chlorosis and turn yellow. It isn't that severe now, because of these torrential rainstorms. Which are pretty weird in themselves. But the fires are just going to continue to come in the dry season, and get bigger. The landscape is taking its revenge. Anyway . . .

Anyway –
Yes, anyway. What can I tell you? The tenants had a meeting after Roderick Williams died. Then another meeting after Jason Crosby died. Fat lot of good it did.

You went to these meetings?
At Solberg's place. I didn't stay long at either one. All they wanted to do was drink Solberg's wine from Solberg's vineyard and talk about Evan Greene for ten minutes and then chit-chat about Solberg's butterfly collection and Solberg's vitrines full of exotic spiders and beetles. Solberg also has a big collection of guns over there, I happen to know, though he wasn't showing them around. I kept saying we should do something, but nobody wanted to stay on the subject. It was as if they just wanted to express their horror at the whole thing, to show how normal they are, and have done with it. The truth is, I didn't want to do anything about it either. But I felt that someone should.

Yes, but who –?
Someone Evan Greene would be afraid of.
    I don't know who that would be.

Tesseray?
Tesseray lives in another world. He spends all his time at body-building competitions as far as I can tell. When he needs something done, he

sends this kid Bobo. When he pays me, the kid brings the check over. Or we subtract it from the rent. Nobody ever really sees Tesseray. The police wrote them off as drug casualties. Still, you'd think having illegal drugs and paraphernalia in the house would have had some repercussions. The papers say he had important friends, that that's why it all got buried at first. You have to wonder if it was that, or simply that the victims were Black. It wasn't until their families went to the press that things came to a head.

DR RICHARD BALVET, 67, TENANT OF PEQUOD COTTAGE
People aren't telling you all they know. That I can assure you. They want to distance themselves as much as possible. It's understandable. It wasn't their doing, so they resist any suggestion . . . Of course, that's how I got pulled into this as the first doctor at hand, and even though it had nothing to do with me either, I'm not going to disown having any relationship to Evan Greene. I wouldn't say he was a close friend, but we certainly spent time in each other's company, in my place or his place, or on the grounds, we talked, I thought I knew him pretty well. He lived right there, everyone on the estate knew him to some degree. He was even something of a public figure. I mean in local politics, if you went to any public meeting of any interest, he would be there.

Did he speak a lot at any meetings you went to?
I think there was a zoning meeting and a city council meeting that was open to the public. He always had a lot to say. Much of it didn't go down well. He harangued people who were speaking. I always had an odd feeling that . . . that he was 'acting'. That he wanted to be seen as someone 'passionate' about his ideas, which were . . . convoluted, would be a way of describing it. I'm sure he believed in whatever he was voicing his opinions about, but there was also this slightly artificial edge to it. Wanting to be seen, wanting to be regarded in a certain way.

Evan Greene brought you both times to his place before calling the police?
He thought the men could be revived. The first time I went in more or
less unawares, the second time I phoned the police or anyway tried to,
as soon as he described the situation to me. I couldn't get a signal. In
both cases it was way too late for CPR or anything like that.

Can you talk about the first incident and what happened that night?
Well, there too, a lot of the news stories distorted things. Some of
the neighbors have probably added to that. Contrary to what's been
written, Roderick Williams was living with Evan Greene. He was known
to everybody on this estate. He was living here when he died. Whether
he was a house guest or a roommate is irrelevant. Everyone knew him.

Jason Crosby too: he'd been staying with Evan Greene for at least
two weeks before he overdosed. He left, I believe, for five or six days,
and then came back late one afternoon, and died the same night.

But look, I'm pressed for time today. I have a meeting with my
lawyer, unpleasantly enough. If you're seriously interested in what
happened I could possibly see you next week. We can discuss it over
coffee. Preferably somewhere off the estate. Now that you're known
here, the village gossips will be taking note of all your comings and
goings . . .

WESLEY CARTER, 34, RESEARCH ASSISTANT
I went to the estate several times. Some of the tenants wanted to
expand on their initial statements. But after a certain point, the subject
of Evan Greene melted away somewhat. They talked around the
subject. Their own lives and so forth dominated these conversations.

*Did that happen naturally, or were they deliberately avoiding talking
about Evan Greene in too much detail?*
With some it was hard to tell. I think they became worried about
saying something 'on the record' that might contradict what they had
already sworn to in affidavits, or, who knows, might implicate them in

some way. The Evan Greene business was very touchy. This in spite of knowing I was only drilling into it as the basis for a possible film script. On the other hand, this was right at the end of the pandemic. People had been stuck in their houses for months and desperate to resume some kind of social life. Even spilling out their personal shit to an investigator made a welcome change. As opposed to going mad from isolation. They didn't care to talk about Evan Greene, but they loved talking about themselves.

And Balvet? Did you speak with him again?
I did. A few times. Never on the estate. He was intent on keeping his neighbors out of his business. I'm not sure they were that interested in Balvet. But he wanted to keep them uninterested. We met at a coffee shop in Silver Lake, not far from the estate, another time we took a long walk together in Hollywood Forever Cemetery. Another person with obsessive problems, though his seemed a lot more real than others. Theresa Lennox, for example, was a complete paranoiac, steeped in conspiracy theories.

Pepper Gillespie?
Well, look, it's all in the notes and interviews I compiled. I'd rather you read through them and draw your own inferences from what's in there, rather than listen to my third-hand paraphrasing of all that material. There are transcripts of the recordings I made, notes I took after every visit. I think you've got plenty there to work with, if you really think a viable script can come out of it. It would have to be an indie film, so-called, because a studio wouldn't go near this stuff.

There's always someone happy to do drugs with anybody who has an apartment. That seemed to be what Evan Greene had done, harvested interested persons out of polyester tents in freeway underpasses, or scooped them off Santa Monica Boulevard, promising to get them high, maybe promising other things, and whisked them back to his curious nautical cottage. Two of these fun-seeking friends, unfortunately, died on his premises. A third one ran half naked to a gas station, where police were called, and this individual said he'd been injected with drugs while unconscious. There is a legal way of describing Evan Greene's life pod, which no news outlet failed to do, as a 'drug house', with penalties on that basis alone involving jail time . . .

When the story broke we all immediately thought of Daniel – whom some considered a friend, while others, like myself, tended to keep him at arm's length, albeit in a friendly way. Daniel could be an oblivious, scarily effusive meth head when he was using. He once picked me up by the waist and swung me around someone's living room like a hapless rag doll, in an excess of what he apparently considered affectionate high spirits, and I simply found obnoxious and frightening. Others liked him better, or at any rate put up with him with greater indulgence. I never knew what to do with my face when I caught Daniel's attention. He brought his own face uncomfortably close to yours when he spoke to you, as if he intended to chew your nose off and suck out your eyeballs. He refused to let any gathering end, and if hard drugs could be brought into it to keep things going far into the next day, or the next week, so much the better from Daniel's point of view. People who do meth often feel a need to do it with others; it's a sociable drug, although it often leads to homicide. Daniel has been known, in the absence of anyone closer, to find transient drug pals in the jhuggi colonies that crop up all over any fallow stretch of land in Los Angeles.

Apparently, Evan Greene's reputation as a methedrine candyman had spread among the city's street-dwelling riffraff, particularly among men of color down on their luck, mainly young men of color, but some others too, older men of color, younger men of less color, it could go like that. Evan Greene was often too high to be picky about who he dragged home with him. It's after three in the morning, you want to do speed with somebody else to get that nice orgiastic feeling going. Not that you'd be able to do anything especially orgiastic. As the Porter in *Macbeth* observes of drink, 'it provokes the desire, but takes away the performance'. A drug friend could really be anybody. Not someone special (and then, as the song goes, *I'm only me, not someone better, not someone good, I'd be a soldier, that's if I only could* ...). Los Angeles is a physically big city, but a rather small conurbation when it comes to artists and writers, and people driven to extremes, if they didn't start out in extremis in the first place. (I'm not counting actors, who take up so much space.) Word travels fast.

Evan Greene was sexually attracted to Black men. That much is established. But a few 'in-depth' stories in the press suggested that he also had contempt for the very people he was attracted to, that he sometimes, casually, used jarring racial slurs in conversation among Caucasian listeners. So the later explosion of outrage against him doesn't seem unjustified, even if it looks cooked up from a cynical misreading of what actually occurred between Greene and his house guests. (Was it cynical? A question for later.) Apparently Greene could only gratify himself with men rendered fully passive after he shot them up with a combination of methedrine and other drugs, sedatives for the most part, men who lay on his polished living-room floor naked except for 'tighty whitey' underpants and white athletic socks. How he happened to locate men already clad in this under-attire when he brought them home has never been reported, and possibly Evan Greene was never questioned about it. Perhaps Evan Greene provided the socks and underpants. Whether Greene achieved any sort of sexual release in this situation also isn't known, in fact it isn't known whether Greene even made physical contact with these prone individuals, except while injecting their arms or other body parts. For all we know, he may have fondled their privates, fellated them, licked their testicles, rubbed his body against theirs, rimmed their anuses, or done other things to them, but nothing of this nature has been reported. We do know that he videotaped many of his sessions, encounters, whatever these episodes might be termed, but of course his videotape collection was confiscated by the police, so we really don't know what he did or didn't do with these men. ■

Sadie Coles   HQ

Alvaro Barrington
Back Home / I Am… I Said

62 Kingly Street W1
05 March — 26 April 2025

62 Kingly Street W1
info@sadiecoles.com

1 Davies Street W1
+44 (0)20 7493 8611

8 Bury Street SW1Y
www.sadiecoles.com

Audun Mortensen

Watching

I make a certain effort
to give my sister in Korea
the impression
that I am interested,
since, after all, I reached out to her.
Anything less might be seen
as vengeful,
as if I'd sought her out
just to turn away.

I watch her Korean life,
I watch diligently,
several videos a day,
of this Korean life,
with two children,
with face masks and bucket hats,
colorful shoelaces,
and Korean comfort food.

I recognize kimchi,
and other dishes
I don't know by name
but might have tasted
in Seoul, Berlin, Stockholm,
San Francisco, Oslo, Seoul,
in that order, I think.
Once, I even commented,
praising her food
with a hungry-faced emoji.

Another time, the children played
with frogs in the living room,
white, polished, freshly mopped surfaces.
She shared many videos of the frogs,
as if they were family pets.

I've seen the children
watching TV from the floor,
eating their Korean comfort food,
then dozing off, half-sleeping,
in front of their screen,
mirroring me.

I don't always understand
her videos or who they're meant for.
But I assume she notices
that I've watched,
so I don't have to respond any more
to show her that I witness
this Korean life
on my phone.

Dutifully, I watch
her videos of Korean meals,
Korean frogs,
Korean children,
and Korean landscapes,
which I once in a comment,
mostly out of courtesy,
called 'beautiful'.

Content

My sister in Korea sent me photos
from the funeral of our father.
A few days ago I tried to look
for the photos in my inbox,
but I didn't remember her name,
at least not the Korean characters for it.
I searched for English words
that could have occurred in our emails,
to retrieve the funeral photos.

Apparently, I didn't want to download them.
That would have meant creating a folder,
naming the folder,
moving the image files from Downloads
into the newly created folder,
and pasting that subfolder
into a fitting main folder
I didn't have at that moment.

Now, I have a document with the speech
I gave at my adoptive father's funeral,
a document I didn't want to delete just yet.
Now the document lurks on the hard drive,
haunting me, kind of.

Perhaps I should create a folder
for content related to these two men:
photos from my Korean father's funeral,
the speech from my Norwegian father's funeral.

I remember an urn and a framed portrait,
the urn placed in a sort of cabinet,
and I didn't see any people,
only those gleaming objects
in a clean, freshly mopped white room.

I don't remember what she wrote,
or what the subject line said,
or if she only savagely sent the photos
without a subject line or message.
I haven't mentioned to her
that my adoptive father died shortly after,
that I gave a speech at his funeral,
and that I'd like to know
what they said or thought
about our Korean father
in that white room.

Maybe I could translate
my speech into English
to share my thoughts
on the Norwegian
who passed away
shortly after the Korean
to tease out her takes
on our father.

Colombia

A colleague mentioned
that she knew an adoptee
from Colombia,
who had recently become
a leader in an adoptee organization
and suddenly became very Colombian,
which she found strange and suspicious.

She seemed to assume I agreed
and that I shared her point of view.
What could I have said
to give her that impression.

Suddenly, I felt inclined to take
the Colombian's side.
Why did she find it suspicious
that the Colombian adoptee
had become curious
about Colombianness,
whatever that might mean.

You're not supposed to change
ethnicity or disrupt your identity,
my colleague seemed to suggest,
at least not more than once.

We looked at each other,
seemingly carefully contemplating
this moment that had occurred
in our quiet office space.
My colleague seemed offended,
I seemed secretly offended,
we played it cool.

All photography by CHRISTOPHER NUNN for *Granta*
The Resomator, 2025

THE CONSERVATION OF MASS: ON RESOMATION

William Atkins

1

If it has ever fallen to you to scatter someone's ashes, especially those of someone you loved, you might share my sense of the process as tantamount to fly tipping, the stuff resembling nothing so much as cat litter: coarse and grey, inarguably a waste product. It is surprising how much you get. I had imagined sprinkling a few handfuls to the wind and being done with it, but on the occasion I am thinking of it took four of us about an hour, using a Persil scoop, to deposit half. The remaining kilo-or-so still sits shut in a dresser at my mother's, a niggling source of unfulfilment. What I wanted, at the time, was for the remains to vanish altogether: *puff*. But anyone with a GCSE in physics knows what Antoine Lavoisier confirmed in 1789: that matter is indestructible.

It is at those points where the skin is thinnest and most quickly oxidised – the forehead, the ankles, the hips – where fire will first expose the underlying bone. The head burns from the crown to the nape, for instance, from the thinnest flesh to the thickest. The skin tightens and splits to expose fat, tendons, ligaments, organs and bones. With the protective dermis gone, fat renders and becomes a secondary accelerant. Bone turns yellow, then black, then white, finally grey. Ninety minutes have passed. The gas is switched off, the cremator cools, a technician gets to work with a rake.

You'd rather the alternative? Once blood has ceased to transport oxygen through the circulatory system, cells die and discharge digestive enzymes, breaking down the body's soft tissues. The stomach, groin and limbs bloat, then, after a week or so – deflate. The skin discolours, sloughs. First to decompose is the head flesh, the eyes, ears and nose. Upper limbs before lower. The stomach, spleen and intestines go relatively quickly; the kidneys, heart and liver are more enduring. One by one the joints disarticulate. After eighteen months, little remains in most cases but a set of greasy bones in a cake of hard-set fluid. The body has begun its migration out into the world.

Over the course of human history most human corpses, 100 billion or more, have been either cremated or buried. Even the least conventional of us, or the least religious, might be forgiven for feeling discomfited about having to consider a third option after all this time, all these generations. We might wonder what it means for the dying and for the dead, and not only them.

Elizabeth Oakes's Resomarium, in the town of Navan, about twenty-seven miles north-west of Dublin, is leased from an adjoining firm of funeral directors, James Fox, which in turn is attached, as such businesses often are in Ireland, to a pub, Fox's Bar and Lounge. There is a mural of a fox and hounds but no obvious signage to indicate the premises of Oakes's company, Pure Reflections, where I spent a morning in early December. In addition to Oakes's desk there were in her office an empty wicker casket on a bier and, on the windowsill, three droplet-shaped ceramic urns. Otherwise the room was almost bare. From the next room, however, I felt a force, something akin to gravity. It was strange to think that the machine was just behind that locked door, in this ancient town on the confluence of the rivers Boyne and Blackwater. But then doesn't the Large Hadron Collider lie beneath fields of French cows?

The first thing I saw when Oakes took me through was a coffin. The second was the Resomator S750, a sculpted monolith of stainless steel, at once industrial and clinical, and thus inherently terrifying. It was the size of a horse box, with a massive-hinged circular door like a submarine hatch. (A submarine hatch is precisely what it was.) It resembled something from a prison kitchen or a milking shed. The prone body, Oakes explained, would be hoisted from the coffin and slid into the unit head-first before the hatch was swung shut. With a fingertip you tap in the body's characteristics – weight, height, sex, embalmed, un-embalmed – and the computer calculates the right volumes of water and chemical. The vessel fills with water until the body is covered. The requisite dose of potassium hydroxide, usually about 5 per cent, is added, and a heat-exchanger – a metal coil snaking under the corpse-tray – heats the mixture until, after an hour or so, the machine's working temperature of 150°C has been achieved. The 'Resomation phase' initiates.

The chemical term for the process is alkaline hydrolysis. 'Hydrolysis' describes the destruction of chemical bonds by the insertion of a water molecule. In alkaline hydrolysis, an alkali operates as a catalyst, increasing the rate of reaction. The effect, in combination with heat and agitation, is to reduce biological material to a sterile solution. This includes proteins, carbohydrates and lipids, as well as deoxyribonucleic acid, or DNA. For an hour or two (more, if the body is big, or drenched in embalmers' formaldehyde), the fluid is recirculated via a network of spigots. Outside, all that is audible is a muffled sloshing, like a high-end dishwasher, and the occasional pneumatic *phut* of solenoid valves opening or closing. After an hour or two the agitation ceases, the bath stills, the unit is cooled with a cold spray, the fluid or hydrolosate – 1,500 litres resembling weak black tea – drains away to be neutralised in a separate tank. And with a *thunk-hush* and an exhalation of steam, the submarine door unlatches. All that remains, across the bottom of the unit, are the bones and teeth. Once dried and ground up (about twenty seconds in Oakes's cremulator, the same machine used in cremation), these resemble not ashes – the gritty tephra I scattered in those Hampshire woods – but something much cleaner and more homogenous, a white powder fine as talc.

When Oakes says she has always been entrepreneurial she is not just talking about a disposition for risk-taking or innovation. For her the condition presents as a hunger. When she was eight she bought two rabbits, a male and a female, with a £20 note she'd found in a bin. Soon she had thirty-six, which she sold to local pet shops at £15 each. At St Joseph's Mercy Convent School, she developed an understanding with the nun who ran the tuck shop: Oakes would take orders from her fellow pupils and deliver their Mars bars and Taytos, keeping the change as commission. By the time she left, Ireland had joined the Eurozone and she was clearing €150 per week. She knew she wasn't academically minded, but she was resourceful and practical, and she knew something else – in her life she wanted to make money.

She and her sister lived on a farm outside Navan, where their mother ran a saddlery. At seventy-three years old Clare Oakes can still mend your perished reins or snapped stirrup straps as well as anyone in County Meath. The smell of worked leather is one of the smells of Oakes's childhood. One of them. During her last two years of school it was her job to care at night for her two elderly great-aunts, washing them and helping them in and out of bed and onto the commode: 'then I'd get up the next morning and head off to school'. When the time came, Oakes helped lay the sisters out to be waked. The dead are not such strangers to the Irish as they are to, say, the English; it is still a common practice for the body to be lain out for viewing. When Oakes's father died six years ago, a thousand people, men, women and children, attended his wake, filing through the front room past the open coffin. The family's hands were raw from being shaken.

When she left school and moved to County Mayo, on the other side of the country, those years of stitching leather turned out to be helpful, as did caring for and laying out Great-Aunt Noreen and

Great-Aunt Olive. The apprenticeship she'd signed up for was among hundreds listed on a vocational-training agency's CD-ROM: one year as an apprentice, it said, then 40k per annum straight out the gate. 'I remember going into my mam and being like: "Mam! I'm going to be an embalmer!" And she was like: "Oh God."'

Finding that she had a flair for caring for the dead to match Clare's flair for saddlery, Oakes moved to Los Angeles to take a three-year degree in Mortuary Science. The qualification was unavailable in Europe and virtually unheard-of in Ireland's funeral sector. Pathology, mortuary law, counselling and 'restorative arts' ('reconstructing ears, eye sockets, nose, eyebrows . . .'). But when she came back to Navan with her degree and a business plan for an American-style, community-centred cemetery she wanted to call Slumbering Oaks, she was met by turned backs and slammed doors. The Irish funeral industry operates more or less as it did a century ago: as a network of family monopolies, with no licensing requirements and minimal regulation. '"Cartel" and "mafia" – those'd be good words.' Unlike the United States, where funeral directors must have a degree, written qualifications are not required or expected and do not necessarily work to your advantage, especially if you are a twenty-one-year-old woman, fresh from California, with powerful notions about how the sector might evolve. 'It's such a male-dominated industry – and older males, as well. They just didn't want to know about me.'

The mountain, as she puts it, was too high. Oakes abandoned her cemetery idea and instead opened a business in another of the restorative arts: permanent make-up, a form of cosmetic tattooing she learned while she was in LA: 'I remember people saying to me, "What woman in Ireland is going to let you tattoo her *face*?"' It's a mark of her instinct for what the Irish public wants that the business was soon thriving. But she hadn't forsaken the world of 'deathcare'. In 2017, eight years after she got back from America, she attended a funeral-industry seminar run by her old mentor from Mayo. The speakers included Damon de la Cruz, an American embalming specialist she knew from LA, who happened to mention, in passing, the growing popularity in his country of alkaline hydrolysis as a means of what is known in the trade as final disposition. It was not the first time she'd heard of the process, but she decided there and then, as Cruz was talking, that she would be the first in Ireland, and therefore Europe, to make it available to the public.

The nuns at St Joseph's Mercy would tell you that a person's body is a temple in which the Holy Spirit dwells. To destroy the body, even the dead body, is a sin. It is the *body* that is baptised, the *body* that is confirmed, the *body* that receives the Eucharist – and what is the Eucharist but the body and blood of Christ? In 1886, as cremation was emerging in Europe as an alternative means of final disposition, Pope Leo XIII issued a decree forbidding the 'detestable, impious custom'. Two years earlier, in the winter of 1884, an eighty-three-year-old Welsh archdruid named Dr William Price carried the body of his five-month-old son Iesu Grist (Jesus Christ) to a hillside, placed the tiny personage in a cask of paraffin oil, and lit it, an act that, in avoiding the contamination of the earth, he believed to be consistent with ancient druidic practice. Price was arrested, the fire was doused, and the half-burned scrap retrieved; but once a coroner had ruled that Iesu Grist had died of natural causes, his father was released and the remains returned to him. Two months later, Price tried again, with half a tonne of coal and what remained of his son's body. This time he was successful. Again he was exonerated, with a judge ruling, for the first time, that 'a person who burns instead of burying a body does not commit a criminal act, unless he does it in such a manner as to amount to a public nuisance'.

A legal precedent was set. The Cremation Society of Great Britain, which opened the first British crematorium the following year, championed the practice as a hygienic, efficient and civic-minded alternative to burial. (Its motto: 'Save the land for the living.') But in his epic cultural history of mortal remains, *The Work of the Dead*, Thomas W. Laqueur observes that, in fact, 'there were no new discoveries that would support the view that burning the dead was better for public health than burying them, and beautiful, clean cemeteries had recently triumphed over overcrowded old churchyards'. The poisonous miasmas associated with those churchyards had long since been dispelled. Nor could the embrace of cremation be attributed to any major shift in attitudes to death or religion. Instead, Laqueur says, cremation had become a way of *mobilising* the dead – in the interests of, among other projects, 'anticlericalism and laicization, spiritualism, heterodox and liberal religions, socialism and materialism'. The Church's long-standing opposition was as much a matter of rejecting a practice associated with anti-catholicism, specifically Freemasonry, as it was a liturgical prohibition. In 1963, with cremation ubiquitous in the West and the Masonic threat gone, Paul VI removed the papal ban, declaring that 'the burning of the body, after all, has no effect on the soul, nor does it inhibit Almighty God from re-establishing the body again'. Nevertheless, 'all necessary measures must be taken to preserve the practice of reverently burying the faithful departed'.

In Ireland, whose first crematorium did not open until 1982, cremations account for about 26 per cent of funerals, compared to 78 per cent in England. It was one thing, therefore, to try to bring a new final-disposition technology to England; quite another to introduce it to a country, a still Catholic country, where even cremation remains a minority choice after 150 years. Was our Lord hydrolised? He was not. But if the Irish public was ready for tattooed eyebrows, Oakes reasoned, why not alkaline hydrolysis?

The brochure she has had printed emphasises the environmental advantages of the procedure, that it represents a 'more positive choice about how we leave this world for future generations'. My father's cremation, assuming it was typical, released into the atmosphere at least 27 kilograms of CO_2 and about the same amount of pollutant nitrous oxides as a car would disgorge during a 2,300-mile journey. Say, Paris to Aleppo. Burial would have been better, but the cemeteries are almost full, we are inescapably chemical – and when we go, we do not go naked. Copper naphthenate, chromated copper arsenate,

arsenic, barium, zinc, copper alloys: all are used in the manufacture
of coffins. Formaldehyde is a carcinogen; chemotherapy drugs and
antibiotics maintain their effects as they seep from the corpse into
the soil. In alkaline hydrolysis, conversely, there is no coffin, only
a woollen shroud, and even the nastiest of chemicals are annulled.
What Oakes is offering is a kind of vanishment, a final act of kindness
to the earth.

2

'The skull is designed to protect the brain. Even in flame
cremation they have sometimes to move the body to get the
flames aimed at the head, to get the residual brain tissue. In alkaline
hydrolysis, what happens is the head will break off quite quickly from
the rest of the torso, and the brain's in the skull, which is like a little
boat. Although there's recirculation, the brain's sitting in the skull and
the skull's floating on the top; the chemical's not getting to it.'

The speaker is Sandy Sullivan, the Scottish biochemist whose
company, Resomation Ltd, has pioneered alkaline hydrolysis in the
UK. He is describing one of the main technical challenges he has
faced in bringing his machine, the Resomator, to market. A week after
I met Oakes, I spent a day with him, first at the Resomation factory in
Pudsey, outside Leeds, and later at a mothballed Resomation facility
on the outskirts of Durham – but most instructively, as it happens, in
his car during the two-hour drive in between.

'Resomation', the name he gave to the company he founded
in 2007, is his own word. *Soma* is from the Greek for 'body',
while the suffix is borrowed from 'cremation'. Sullivan was also
thinking of the founding declaration of the Cremation Society of
Great Britain, written in 1874, which stated its desire to substitute
for burial 'some mode which shall rapidly *resolve* the body into its
component elements, by a process which cannot offend the living,
and shall render the remains perfectly innocuous'. The prefix 're-' is
important. Resomation Ltd's logo shows two beads of water above

three concentric ripples. Pure Reflections' logo is a droplet morphing into a two-leafed seedling. The symbolism of water, and the water cycle, are crucial to what both companies are marketing. The liquid biproduct of 'water cremation', as Sullivan prefers to call the process, is not 'poured down the drain', to quote one perturbed American archbishop: it is simply *re*stored to nature – to the glittering stream, the roaring ocean, the April shower.

The machine itself, the Resomator, is manufactured by a 150-year-old firm called the Leeds and Bradford Boiler Company, an organisation whose managing director, Howard Pickard, has engineering so deep in his bones that he can make a statement like 'Life is very simple: just physics, chemistry, maths, that's all it is', and leave you wondering if he's right. When Sullivan's original majority shareholder, Co-op Funeralcare, Britain's largest funeral provider, pulled out in 2016, he persuaded Pickard to buy its shares, making Resomation Ltd a division of the Leeds and Bradford Boiler Company, and Pickard its MD. The company's trading name, LBBC, has the happy function, for anyone involved in dealing with the bereaved, of disguising its origins in industrial engineering. Its signature technology, based on a design of Pickard's great-grandfather, is a pressure-containing door. Among its modern-day customers are Rolls-Royce, which uses LBBC's autoclaves for precision-casting turbine blades, and BAE Systems, whose submarines the company supplies with hatch doors.

In person, as Oakes learned when she flew to England in 2016 to negotiate the terms of a contract, Sullivan has an air of warm insouciance that might be mistaken for resignation. It took me a while to realise it's actually self-belief, albeit of a quieter form than Oakes's. He speaks about her with avuncular affection, recalling their first meeting: 'She goes "I want one, and I want to be the first, and I want a good deal, and I want that one, in the factory, and I want it *now*!"' Oakes, who left Pudsey with an exclusive twenty-year contract to practise Resomation in Ireland, remembers it this way: 'I had nothing to lose and they had nothing to lose.'

The use of alkaline hydrolysis as a way of disposing of the dead is usually attributed to an English chemist named Amos Herbert Hobson, who in 1888 registered a patent for a 'process for separating gelatine from bones'. This entailed stewing livestock carcasses in a solution of boiling water and potassium hydroxide. The twin objects, he wrote, were '(*a*) to render such bones, refuse or waste more suited for fertilising purposes, [and] (*b*) to extract the gelatine, glue, or size'. While the process did involve alkaline hydrolysis, it is hard to see any obvious continuity between Hobson's patent – which does not seem to have been particularly revolutionary, and didn't dream of human corpses – and the emergence more than a century later of alkaline hydrolysis in something close to the form Sullivan and Oakes are practising. Another patent, filed in 1994 by two doctors at Albany Medical College, New York, might be a more plausible point of origin.

In biomedical research, chemical compounds will often be 'labelled' with a trace of tritium or another radioisotope to allow scientists to identify where the compound has been metabolised in the body – the body usually being that of a rat, mouse, rabbit or sheep. The process patented by the two doctors, Gordon Kaye and Peter Weber, promised to reduce the expense of disposing of carcasses that had been isotope-labelled, which were classified as low-level radioactive waste under government regulations. Previously, the main means of getting rid of such carcasses in the United States was in one of two special interment facilities. A single sheep could cost hundreds of dollars, as the body first had to be packed in lime and placed in its own special burial flask. In Kaye and Weber's process, which did not differ in principle from what Hobson described a century earlier, the carcass was sunk in a mixture of water and sodium hydroxide. Their innovation was to use a pressurised steel vessel to achieve temperatures above boiling, which had the effect of expediting the process – though it still took about two hours to dissolve three rat carcasses. All that remained, other than bones and teeth, and any surgical clips or sutures, was a solution of amino acids, fatty acids

and peptides whose radioactivity was well within the regulatory limits for disposal in the sewage system.

In 1994 Kaye and Weber formed a company, WR$_2$ ('Waste Reduction by Waste Reduction Inc.'), and gradually refined what they called their Tissue Digester. At this stage, as the name suggests, no thought had been given to applying the process to the human dead. At the time, Sandy Sullivan was living in Watford, on the outskirts of London, and employed as European vice president of Steris, an American firm specialising in sterilising equipment for labs and hospitals. It was at Steris that he met Joe Wilson, who ran the firm's US arm. Wilson had recently become aware of WR$_2$'s work on alkaline hydrolysis, and after failing to convince his bosses to acquire the smaller company, left to become WR$_2$'s president and CEO. He invited Sullivan to run the company's European wing, WRE, which, as it happened, was based in Glasgow. Sullivan, who had grown up ten miles from the city, in Kirkintilloch, and was in the middle of a divorce, was relieved to have a reason to return to Scotland.

Over the next decade, WR$_2$ became increasingly involved in the disposal of human, rather than animal, remains. In 1995 it sold a tissue digestor to Shands Hospital at the University of Florida, though this was more in the order of the original Albany rat-boiler, a clamp-lidded cauldron designed for body parts. It was not until 2005 that the company was commissioned to install its first single-body unit, at Mayo Clinic in Rochester, Minnesota, for the disposal of cadavers that had been used in teaching and research. Hardly had the system begun operating, however, than it malfunctioned. But by then, as the clinic's director of anatomical bequests discovered, WR$_2$ had gone bust. Sullivan offered to help. 'It was a very basic unit, and it couldn't get rid of brain tissue.' This was one of several problems. To solve it – to keep the boat of the skull from yawing and spinning uncontrollably as the liquid recirculated – Sullivan designed what he calls the FACT system, 'focussed agitation cranial targeting'. The device was nothing more than a perforated steel 'sleeve', fixed to the end of the unit, into which the head was slid, keeping the skull in place as the alkaline solution was jetted through the nasal cavity and eye sockets. 'You can tell if there's brain tissue left,' Sullivan said, as we were approaching Harrogate. 'It stinks. *Stinks, stinks, stinks.*'

After WR₂ collapsed, he took what he'd learned and founded Resomation Ltd. Sullivan didn't 'invent' alkaline hydrolysis, then; nor did he come up with the single-body unit; the only element of his current machine he has actually patented is the FACT system. But, as he puts it, 'you couldn't sell the process if you end up with brain tissue at the end'.

Resomation's only significant competition is an Indiana-based firm run by Sullivan's former colleague from WR₂, Joe Wilson. Bio-Response Solutions was founded in 2006, a year before Sullivan's company, as a service for disposing of pets and contaminated livestock. Wilson's machine is quite different in appearance from Sullivan's. The body is placed in a narrow steel cylinder, which is tipped feet uppermost to a 35-degree angle. Like the Resomator S750, the Aquamation HT-500 does not have a viewing window.

When he gives talks, Sullivan sometimes quotes Machiavelli: 'He who innovates will have for his enemies all those who are well off under the existing order of things, and only lukewarm supporters in those who might be better off under the new.' On other occasions Obama must be recruited: 'We are the change we seek.'

England has been slower to come round to alkaline hydrolysis than the United States, the Netherlands, Australia, New Zealand, Ireland or, for that matter, Sullivan's native Scotland, where he expects Resomation to become legal later this year. Even the 150-year-old Cremation Society of Great Britain now accepts the process as a future adjunct to cremation. As was true of cremation long after William Price cremated his son, alkaline hydrolysis is not strictly *against* the law, since no law exists prohibiting it. And yet carrying it out in England and Wales has, hitherto, proven almost impossible.

Sullivan has learned that people's natural reticence when it comes to the rituals surrounding death is most constructively met with self-reflection rather than annoyance. Which isn't by any means to say he hasn't had moments of intense frustration, in fact he's sometimes thought of chucking the whole thing in, over the twenty-plus years he has been trying to launch his product in the UK. More than once, alkaline hydrolysis was about to be formally legalised only for some bureaucrat to intervene. Just as one borough council, Sandwell, was about to buy a unit, the local water authority, Severn Trent, decided it wasn't willing to grant a trade effluent licence – not because the effluent did not meet safety thresholds but because of 'concerns about the public acceptability of liquefied remains of the dead going into the water system' – even while Severn Trent apparently accepted that this was a misconception.

But we are the change we seek. 'If I don't do this, nobody's going to do it.' And consider this: a century ago it was unimaginable that by the end of the millennium the majority of England's dead would be burned in an incinerator and sent up a chimney. The same degree of assimilation, Sullivan is convinced, will happen with alkaline hydrolysis – is already happening, even if the law is slow to catch up – for the simple reason that it is a proven technology (well over 10,000 bodies have been Resomated, most of them in the seven Resomators that have been sold in America) and cheaper than the alternatives – not to mention far less environmentally damaging. Why would you, as your last corporeal act, choose to expel 27 kilograms of CO_2 into the world your daughter must inhabit?

A name that may turn out to be as significant in the history of final disposition as that of Iesu Grist is Catherine Rose. On 2 April 2019 hers was the first of five bodies – and thus the first in the UK and in Europe – to be subjected to alkaline hydrolysis in a trial Resomator specially installed at Sheffield University. 'They kind of learned on her,' her daughter, Barbara Rhodes, told me. In Sheffield, three of the five bodies had been embalmed, and Rose's was the only woman's. The main objective was to prove that the effluent met the water-authority requirements for release into the waste-water system.

In collaboration with the universities of Sheffield and Middlesex, Sullivan had assembled a working party of industry experts to oversee the process, including Yorkshire Water, the Federation of Burial and Cremation Authorities, the Institute of Cemetery and Crematorium Management and Professor Douglas Davies, Director of the Centre for Death and Life Studies at Durham University. Because the Certificate for Burial or Cremation, known as the Green Form, does not include alkaline hydrolysis as an option, 'cremation' was scored out by hand and 'water cremation' written in its place. The tests were a success, as Sullivan knew they would be. Satisfied with the quality of the hydrolysate, Yorkshire Water – and subsequently several other water authorities – agreed to permit its discharge into their sewers. Catherine Rose's daughter, Barbara, was sufficiently at ease with the experience that when her husband died four years later she arranged for him to undergo the process. Philip Anthony Rhodes thus became the first in Europe to be Resomated on a *commercial* basis – in Oakes's machine in Ireland. 'Philip came home from Elizabeth's in a Ryanair bag,' says Barbara.

In 2024, the first British Resomator for public use was finally installed in Houghton-Le-Spring, outside Durham, with Co-op Funeralcare marketing the service as the 'biggest change to funerals in over 120 years' – that is, since the legalisation of cremation.

It was a rare moment of public vindication for Sullivan, seventeen years after he had founded Resomation Ltd, and eight years after Co-op Funeralcare had abandoned its stake in the company. But Sullivan has learned that vindication is not victory. His recollection of what happened next is that the Home Office determined that the hand-amended Green Form would not suffice for future Resomations, and that a new form would therefore have to be drawn up. Perhaps it would be blue. This would require a change in primary legislation. For its part, Co-op Funeralcare says its decision to 'pause [its] plans in this space' was due to a lack of regulatory clarity. 'Whilst we believe Resomation could be a more sustainable method than pre-existing forms of committal,' they told me, 'without a pilot, we were unable

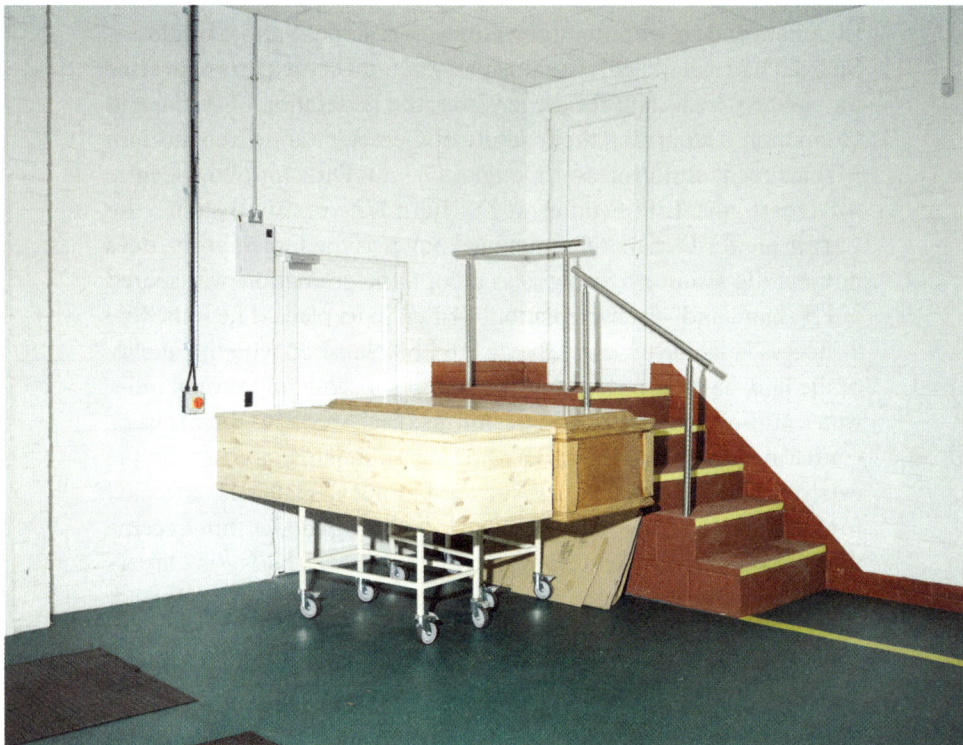

to gather the necessary data to confirm this, and therefore could not proceed with our initial plans.' Meanwhile, the Law Commission is carrying out a project to consider, among other aspects of the funeral industry, the regulatory framework around alkaline hydrolysis, with a view to publishing a draft bill in due course. Sullivan, who as we've seen is an optimist, reckons it'll take about two years for any new legislation to be made law.

After two hours we reached the small industrial estate in Houghton-Le-Spring where England's first Resomator is installed. Between Herrington Tyres and the Hand Car Wash is a disused coffin factory. Sullivan led me down to the basement. The machine, a monument in stainless steel, shone dimly in the cold light. 'It's basically gathering dust,' said Sullivan.

3

Every human person has an innate dignity that calls for the utmost respect of the body both in life and in death. Reverence and respect for the human remains of those who have died has been, and should remain, a guiding principle for the proper disposal of these remains . . . While the process of alkaline hydrolysis may not be intrinsically wrong, we believe it fails to show due reverence and respect for the human remains of the deceased by subjecting the dissolved human remains to being flushed into the sewer system. Apart from a situation of dire need, such as a public health emergency, we oppose the use of this process and call upon the Catholic faithful to reject its use.
– Statement of the Catholic Bishops of Missouri, 2018

While alkaline hydrolysis is legal in twenty-six states, Catholic opposition to the practice in America has sometimes been strident, with the clergy's criticism reserved in particular for what it views, however erroneously, as the treatment of human remains as mere sewage. One eloquent American defender of the procedure, however, Sister Renée Mirkes, has noted that 'the flashpoint of indignity with alkaline hydrolysis – specifically, pouring the liquid remains down a drain – is found in similar form in the seepage after burial and in cremation through rain'. The Vatican has yet to comment, but in Ireland, where even the burning of the body has never been totally normalised, the problem ecclesiastically speaking turns out to be more prosaic.

When Elizabeth Oakes wanted to find a priest to speak before one Resomation, she rang Navan Parish office: Not a hope, they said. The problem wasn't doctrine; the problem was the national priest shortage. But if you're driving to Navan on the R147 you pass Dalgan Park. I had noticed it from the bus: a retirement home for missionary priests.

'I thought surely there's a priest there that has half his wits about him that would say a couple of words. And there was a lovely father, and he agreed. So I went up there, whipped him out, put him into the car and down here.' He only paused once during his address – *What* was the procedure called, again? Otherwise he'd had no qualms whatsoever. With the business done, Elizabeth took him to do his grocery shopping, then ran him back to Dalgan. 'He was delighted and the family were delighted.'

The funeral industry has been less cooperative. In early 2024 Oakes hosted a meeting of the Irish Association of Funeral Directors. 'These are all the big boys, the big boys' funeral homes. They had soup and sandwiches in the pub, and then they got a detailed tour of the facility. They really understood exactly what I was offering.' Afterwards she recruited her husband to ring some of the businesses that had sent representatives. He was, he told them hoarsely, considering Resomation for his dear departed aunt. Speakerphone on.

'You should have *heard* what they were saying! "That's an American thing, it's not available in Ireland yet"; "Wouldn't recommend it, we don't know where she takes the body." Another fellow said, "Oh, *that* thing, it's about *6,000 euros!*" There was fire coming out my eyeballs!' She should have known better. The big boys' main interest, she believes, is in selling coffins, and since a coffin cannot be put in a Resomator, why *would* they be interested? She has since decided to focus her efforts on selling Resomation direct to the public. About €3,700, all in, compared to more than €6,000 for the average Irish funeral.

'They're not going to respect me until it starts hitting them in the pocket; until they say: "Well, feck-it, she's going to take them out from under us if we don't start going with her."'

Oakes's Resomator occupies its room in Navan like a bear occupies its den. It seems to radiate potency. It might, somehow, weigh 100 tonnes, rather than its actual 2.5. It asks to be polished, asks to be stroked. It is evidently an object designed for voyaging – a minisub, a pod for Neptune. You can tell it's in use because of the scatterings of white powder here and there around the place, as if the room has been dusted for prints. All but unavoidable when the stuff is so fine. A horizontal chalky band on the inside of the Resomator door, like a scum mark on a bath, shows the mean water height after the ninety-eight times it has been used since Pure Reflections opened in November 2023. Oakes often lets it run overnight, when electricity is cheaper, but in the case of a child she will stay in the room for however long it takes, an hour, two. There have been several children, more than she expected.

Before I met her I'd assumed that final disposition, whatever the form, aspired not merely to *destroying* the body but to dematerialising it utterly. I had sat in my mother's dining room, remembering that kilo of grey grit in the dresser and wishing it gone. But if what Oakes and Sullivan are offering represents a level of perfection, it is because of what is *preserved*, preserved in all its celestial, imperishable whiteness. Philip Rhodes, Oakes's first Resomation, had filled a carrier bag, but even a baby (there has been one eight-week-old, the first infant to undergo alkaline hydrolysis anywhere in the world) will leave enough white powder for a 125-millilitre vial. The same cannot be said of cremation: a trowelful of coffin ashes if you're lucky. The Bishops of Missouri might take note.

Sometimes – and Oakes's hesitancy is not because she's embarrassed, but because the subject has come up before and she doesn't want to be misunderstood – sometimes, she *will* talk to them, talk to them as she binds their naked bodies in a woollen shroud. Nothing much, just a few words. God, your wife's going to miss you. I met your daughter and she's very sad; won't you look out for her, now? You'll be fine, you'll be fine. I'm going to be looking after you. You don't have to worry about anything. I know you've had a really hard time, and you suffered a lot, and it must have been difficult. But I'm going to look after you now, and everything's going to be okay. ∎

UNRULY LIGHT

Ming Smith

Introduction by Tobi Haslett

What unifies Ming Smith's images? What draws five decades of mostly black-and-white photographs into a single affecting ensemble, transcending surface differences in subject and composition? The answer is not quite style; it's closer, I think, to tone. Each picture seems to express a sensuous riddle and arrives at a tonal mixture of darkness-distance-warmth. These are images *of* strangers or celebrated performers, *of* children, cities, rooms, or skies. But that *of*-ness can feel secondary, at times even incidental. The fierce burst of articulate detail in one photograph and the smeared silhouette in another are linked by a mystic deference to the stirring fact of the phenomena. Documentation is not the point here. Some restless, formless element thrums deep within the portraits and stalks through every streetscape, trailing and sometimes meddling with the transmission of the message.

'I do a lot of night shooting,' Smith once told an interviewer, 'and even in the dark, I look for the light – the way light comes in.' This explains the streaks, beams, hazes, glows and abstracted reflective flashes that claw through the black space in her pictures, serving both as pictorial syntax and ingenious personal signature. Look at any photograph from her *Jazz Series* and you see in an instant: this was taken by Ming Smith.

But it's possible to place Smith's idiosyncrasy within a larger history – including that of jazz itself. Among her best-known work are a series of pictures she took in 1978 of Afrofuturist musician Sun Ra. She would later snap some of her most compelling photographs in her early thirties while touring with her husband, the musician David Murray, and his band, the World Saxophone Quartet. One of those images appears on the cover of their 1980 record *W. S. Q.*: the men of the quartet reduced to subtle blots of grey and black, the glare of their respective saxophones slashing the picture in a visual screech.

By that time, Smith had passed through her own powerful group experience. In 1972 she had become a member of the Kamoinge Workshop, a collective of black photographers established nearly a decade earlier in Harlem. The name had been taken from the glossary at the back of *Facing Mount Kenya* (1938) by Jomo Kenyatta, the anti-colonial leader who later became Kenya's first prime minister; in Kikuyu, *kamoinge* means 'a group of people acting together'. The moniker broadcast not only the 'African consciousness exploding within us' (to quote co-founder Louis Draper), but also the wish for a robust, if intimate, forum, an institution that could cultivate individual talents while also confronting a shared predicament.

What could black photography be? Which forces was it struggling against, and what objective could it coherently strive for? These were old questions, debated grandly in the salons of the Harlem Renaissance and now refreshed with frank vitality in the era of civil rights. Kamoinge would go on to arrange group publications and exhibitions, even securing a makeshift gallery space. Visitors included Henri Cartier-Bresson and Langston Hughes, by then a kind of elder statesman.

The task was to practice fidelity to their people – to hold fast to social truth without lapsing into romance or the bleakness of cliché. Hence the disciplined reflexivity among the participants in the workshop. Critique sessions grew notorious for their bluntness, even brutality. The intensity of the meetings followed from photography's historical link to documentary realism, which for black artists involved the bitter, ambivalent pressures of speaking for a group. Kamoinge sought new ways to capture black existence while asserting its variety and complicated dynamism. By 1972, Draper could write that 'we could no longer stomach the steady diet of run-down tenements and sad-eyed tots' because such shots so often became 'an imposition rather than a commitment'.

It was around this time that Smith, fresh out of Howard University and making ends meet as a model in New York, found herself at the studio of workshop member Anthony Barboza. After overhearing him take part in a spirited debate about the purpose of photography – *was it an art form or was it just nostalgia?* – she struck up a friendship. She shared some of her work and was soon invited to join the collective: Kamoinge's very first woman.

An emblematic episode, and not just for its lamination of Smith's glamorous personal myth. Look at her pictures and it feels fitting that she crossed paths with Kamoinge just *after* the 1960s – overhearing a couple of men while waiting to be photographed herself. In one photograph included here, the portraits of John F. Kennedy and Dr Martin Luther King Jr hang at sloppy angles behind Smith's guileless husband, appearing both heroized and marginalized, displaced by the motion of history, folded into the fabric of time. It is a photograph of photographs. It's also gently ludic, as if to suggest that the booming questions of blackness and representation might now benefit from a more angular approach.

'It was a community,' Smith recalls of Kamoinge, 'but eventually I didn't really hang out with them. I was too much of a loner.' She was also a dancer – she'd trained with Katherine Dunham – and a working fashion model. That's how she became friends with and even photographed Grace Jones, years before the latter got into music. But Smith had taken pictures since childhood in Ohio, thinking of her various other pursuits as secondary or side hustles. She'd joined Kamoinge to learn, and she did: about printing, about paper, about all the decisive technical details that before she had fumbled through alone in the only photography class at Howard (where she'd majored in microbiology). She learned too from Kamoinge's many 'cold-blooded' critiques.

But her life was taking place elsewhere. It was shot through with fragments of a different Manhattan, one somewhat removed from the older, male participants' complex of concerns. 'I didn't live in Harlem,' she says, by way of explanation. 'I lived in the West Village.' The geographical contrast is a classic one – Amiri Baraka's exodus from the Village to Harlem was an extravagant, allegorical episode in the history of black American art, marking his repudiation of downtown bohemia and his embrace of the Black Nation. So it's interesting to imagine a twenty-something Smith, for whom that uptown train trip was no more than a commute. Her 1979 photograph of Baraka, not shown here, is admiring, semi-candid and delicately blurred.

The blur is now seen as Smith's trademark. She achieves the effect by slowing the camera's shutter speed and standing very, very still. This technique flattens tonal ranges, gently erasing the distinction between foreground and background, at once collapsing pictorial space and driving the image further away. There's something glyph-like in the resultant streaks of unruly light. Like writing, these photographs are attempts at particularity and explicitness, that nevertheless swing out into the pure form of the mark. They measure the distance between the writer and the thing she wants to touch. ∎

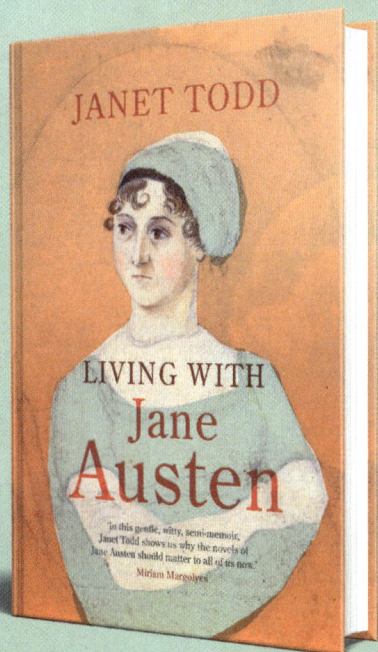

Robert Walser

Note to Self

Note to self: Take a walk
to go see Hermann Hesse
if I can remember his address uh
We need to talk
about whether I too may speak with lyricism
Apparently the public thinks it exclusively is him
able to feel that life
is perpetual trouble and strife
Will he perhaps allow me
to believe that I, like he,
might feel likewise weary
Tomorrow I think I'll trot
to this much admired fellow
I'm positive I can bring
him to laughter
at the crowd of followers running after
him and will not
be begrudged the chance to twitter and sing
now and then, soulful, adagio,
that anyone with a famous name
wishes at times he did not have the same

Gentle Rain

The rain fell, so, so gentle,
on the monumental
fame-bewreathed
genius-bequeathed
Great Man
in a manner impossible to convey,
there's just no way
I can.
He was stand-
ing serious, silent, [...] in hand.
His look at his wife was gruesome –
as together they peered through some
rain at the mountain's eternal snowbank
and she a coffee drank –
beautiful and cold,
enchantingly young and old.
The Great Man stuck his hands in the pockets of his pants
and took a glance
back over the products of his earlier urges.
Around the sanatorium stood birches,
whispering.

Translated from the German by Damion Searls

TRANSLATOR'S NOTE: The German word for 'man' is *Mann*, and with 'the Great Man' Walser was likely referring to Thomas Mann, whose sanatorium novel *The Magic Mountain* had just been published.

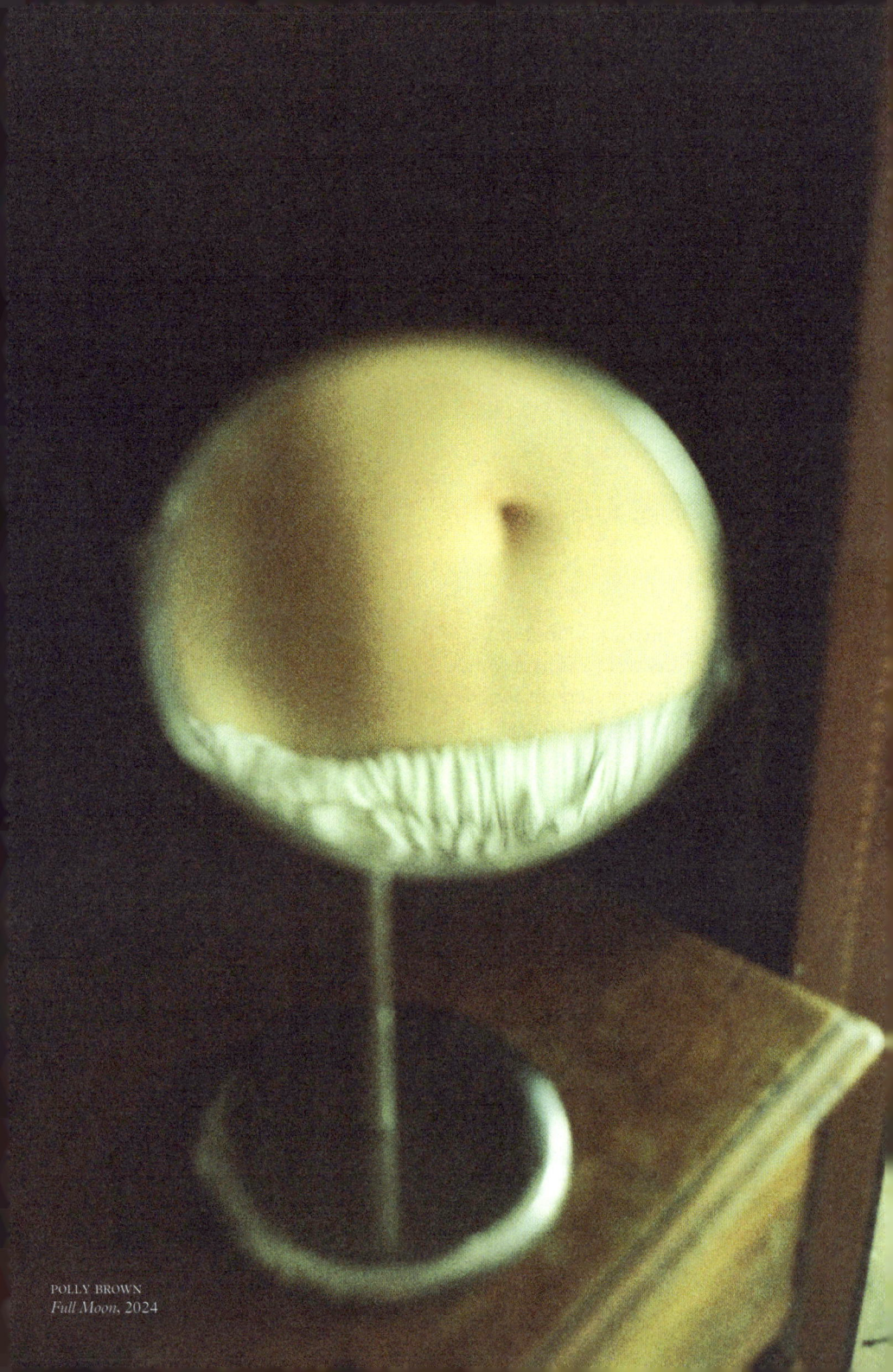

POLLY BROWN
Full Moon, 2024

KILLING STELLA

Marlen Haushofer

TRANSLATED FROM THE GERMAN BY SHAUN WHITESIDE

I have to write about her before I begin to forget her. Because I'll have to forget her if I want to resume my old peaceful life.

Because that's what I'd really like to do: live in peace, without fear or memory. It's enough for me to run my household as I did before, to care for the children and look out of the window into the garden. If one behaves calmly, I thought, one cannot get involved in other people's business. And I thought of Wolfgang. It was so nice having him around me every day. Should I have endangered our peaceful companionship over Stella?

No, things couldn't have ended worse for me if I had. Stella is avenging herself on me, and taking from me the only thing to which my heart still clings. But that's nonsense. Stella can't take her revenge, she was already so helpless when she was alive, how helpless she must be now. I am taking Stella's revenge on myself, that's the truth, and it's as it should be, however much I might try to resist.

Of course I've always known that the day would come, it didn't need Stella for that to happen. Sooner or later Wolfgang would have been lost to me. He's one of those people who has no illusions and accepts the consequences. I don't have any illusions either, but I live as if I did. I used to think I could start over again from the beginning, but it's much too late for that now, in fact it was always too late for that, except I didn't want to acknowledge it.

There could no longer be any point in anything, because Wolfgang moved away from me. And that's good for him.

I read somewhere that you can get used to anything, and habit is the strongest force in our lives. I don't believe it. It's only the excuse that we need to keep from thinking about the suffering of our fellow human beings, or indeed about our own suffering. It's only the excuse that we need to stop thinking about our own suffering. It's true, a human being can endure a lot, not only out of habit, but because a faint spark glimmers within them, which they secretly hope will one day allow them to break the habit. The fact that they usually can't, out of weakness and cowardice, does not speak against it. Or are there perhaps two kinds of people, those who get used to things and those who aren't able to? I can't believe that; it's probably just a matter of constitution. Once we reach a certain age, we are gripped by anxiety and try to fight against it in some way. We sense that we're in a hopeless position, and make desperate little attempts to escape.

If the first of these attempts is unsuccessful, as it generally is, we surrender until the next one, which will already be weaker, and which will leave us feeling still more miserable and defeated.

So Richard regularly drinks his red wine, chases after women and money, my friend Luise pursues men who are young enough to be her son, and I stand at the window and stare into the garden. Stella, that stupid young person, escaped successfully on her first attempt.

I would much prefer it if I could switch places with her, if I didn't have to sit here and write her pitiful story, which is also my pitiful story. I would much prefer to be dead like her, and not have to hear the little bird crying. Why does no one protect me against its cry, against dead Stella and the agonising red of the tulips on the chest of drawers? I don't like red flowers.

My colour is blue. It gives me courage, and detaches everyone and everything from me. Richard thinks I only wear my blue clothes because they suit my face; he doesn't know that I wear them for protection. No one can hurt me when I'm wearing them. The blue keeps everything far away from me. Stella loved red and yellow, and it was in the red dress I gave her that she ran in front of a yellow-painted truck.

That radiantly yellow death that hurtled towards her like a sun, I think it was beautiful and terrible like the death we know from the ancient legends.

I had to identify her. Her face was unharmed, but greenish-white and much smaller than it had seemed to me when she was alive. The disturbed and half-deranged expression of the last few days had fled from it, making way for an icy silence.

Stella had always been a little clumsy and shy, and even when she was cheerful, her regular, wide face was immobile. Then it blossomed from within to her lips. Stella had been very happy for a short time, but she was unable to learn the rules of the game, she couldn't adapt and she had to perish.

A frivolous and greedy mother had stuck her in a boarding school as a child. I remember observing her then, about five years ago, in church. She knelt beside me, her face turned towards the monstrance, her eyes wide open, her lips arched slightly forwards, open and devoted. And with the same expression she later stared at the evening paper behind which Richard's face was hidden. Wolfgang saw it too. He blushed and grew pale, and finally he choked on something to distract my attention from Stella. At fifteen he knew just as well as I did what was happening in front of our eyes, and he was trying desperately to protect me from that knowledge, while my sole concern was keeping him out of the game, and so I did exactly what I shouldn't have done, namely nothing.

While Stella, unable to conceal her single big emotion, slipped inexorably into her disaster and Richard tried to deceive us with his smooth bonhomie, I made an effort to remain oblivious to everything. For Wolfgang's sake and also for mine, because there's nothing I hate more than scenes and arguments, and even a tense atmosphere is enough to leave me disturbed and uneasy for weeks.

The loneliness and peace of my room, the view of the garden, the tenderness that filled me at the sight of Wolfgang, was I supposed to put everything – and for me it is everything – at risk for the sake of a girl who ran dully and inexorably into her fate, condemned from the very beginning to be broken, with her simple, foolish emotion, by our disintegrating, divided world?

Well, it wasn't worth my trouble, but it should have been, because Stella's was the young life that I allowed to run headlong into a murderous, metal machine.

One can perish in very different ways, out of stupidity just as easily as out of an excess of caution; the former seems more worthy to me, but it is not my way.

Luise, Stella's mother, didn't come until after the funeral. She'd been travelling, and nobody from her little provincial town knew where she had gone. By the time we were finally able to contact her it was all over. Richard had sorted it all out, well and appropriately, as he tends to sort everything out. Luise, and incidentally she had been with her boyfriend, a young postgrad student, in Italy, now sat facing us in our sitting room, sobbing.

Richard gave her platitudes, which sound more convincing from his lips than from mine, words of genuine sympathy. His eyes were deep blue and moist, as they are when he is agitated or drunk, and I couldn't help thinking of the wreaths on the bare hill. There weren't many wreaths, by the way, because in this town Stella had only us and a few friends from school. I thought of the hill and of Stella's body, bled dry and crushed, in its wooden prison. For the first time I was filled with pity. It was foolish and absurd, because Stella was dead, and yet pity swelled within me like a physical pain that sat like a lump in my chest and radiated all the way to my fingers. And yet that pain was no longer meant for Stella, but for her dead body, which was now doomed to decay.

I heard Richard talking, but didn't understand any of what he was saying. Gripped with horror, I only saw his eyes, which were so moist and alive. Every hair of him was alive, his skin, his breath, his hands, and the sight of it took my breath away.

Seen from outside, we were a middle-aged couple trying to comfort a mother who was bent with pain. Except Luise is not a mother bent with pain. Stella's death was very timely for her. We knew that, and she knew we knew, but she sobbed and wept as her role demanded.

Now that Stella's legacy, the pharmacy, has come to her, Luise can marry her postgrad, who would never have taken her without the dowry. She can buy this strong young man and persuade herself for a while that she was lucky.

Stella had become a burden to us all, an obstacle that had finally been cleared out of the way. Of course it would have been even better if she'd had a happy marriage, emigrated, or otherwise somehow disappeared from our field of vision. But she had disappeared at any rate, and we were able to forget her for once and for all.

I could tell by looking at Richard just how much he'd forgotten her already, since for him forgetting is a physical thing. His body has already forgotten Stella; tall, broad, and hungry for new women and new sensations, he sat next to me and patted Luise's thin bird fingers with his broad well-tended hand, which is always dry, warm, and pleasant to the touch.

And Luise's whimpering fell silent under that warmth, under the sound of his calming voice.

'I always told her,' she groaned, 'pay attention when you're crossing the road. I would just like to know what she was thinking of.'

'Yes,' Richard said sorrowfully, 'we would like to know that too, wouldn't we, Anna?'

He looked at me and I nodded. There wasn't even a hint of irony in his voice. I apologised and said that I needed to check on the kitchen. I didn't go into the kitchen, however, but into the bathroom and started putting on a bit of rouge. Pallor doesn't suit me.

Stella had been pale in the last few weeks too, but she was nineteen, and suffering refined her face, making it more adult and charming. A woman over thirty needs to be able to stop suffering, it doesn't do anything good to her appearance by then.

When Stella came to us, her skin was slightly tanned. She was beautiful, but lacking in charm and grace. She was a bit too healthy and strong for modern tastes. Indeed, it later took a heavy truck to crush the life out of her body. It was so considerate of Stella to make the whole thing look like an accident. And it showed how little Luise had known her daughter that she believed she had stepped off the curb unintentionally. Because Stella's dreaminess was that of a sleepy, strong, young animal finding its way through the bustle of the city as if in a trance. Not even the driver of the truck, a simple, ignorant young man, believed it was an accident. Stella wanted to die, and with the same unreflective self-abandonment with which she had once dropped into life, she fell out of the same life that had neglected to hold on to her with a bit of love, kindness, and patience. We have cause for gratitude. How embarrassing it would have been had she taken sleeping pills or thrown herself out of a window. Her elegance, which was an elegance of the heart, showed itself in the manner of her death, giving us all the opportunity to believe in a meaningless accident.

But what use is all of this if the only person who should really have believed it does not believe it and never will. Stella will always stand between me and Wolfgang. The time of childish tenderness and trust has passed. Wolfgang abhors his father and despises me for my cowardice. He will only understand me much later, when he goes from one room to the other as I do, alone with my unease and the knowledge that the prison is completely inescapable. But by then I will have ceased to be, just as my father has ceased to be, whose ironic laissez-faire attitude filled me with insecurity as a child. The eye that fell upon me when I played with my dolls is the eye with which I follow Wolfgang when he goes to play tennis with his friend, and with which he already observes his little sister's games.

If Wolfgang were with me now, he would try to save the bird in the linden tree, and I would need to deter him, because if the mother bird doesn't return the little one will be beyond help, it can't eat on its own. Only its mother could save it, and I'm starting to doubt that she's coming back. It has grown smaller than it was, I'm sure of it, even though it was already so tiny in the morning that I couldn't imagine a smaller bird. I can see it clearly now, a little bundle of feathers opening its beak and its eyes wide with fear and hunger. Its mother isn't going to come. I've closed the window again. The sun is shining on the little bird now. Maybe it will go to sleep and I'll have a few hours of peace if I know it's safe. All this crying is draining its strength away far too soon. Perhaps it's thirsty, in fact it must be. But how ridiculous to be bothered by a bird. Richard would laugh at me. I just have to believe that its mother will find it. Sometimes I find myself thinking that it's my inability to believe that attracts calamity. Perhaps Richard would never have become the person he is today if I had blindly believed him, perhaps everything would have been different if my father had not looked at us so strangely the day I brought Richard home. How could he have known, who gave him the right to know what was to come, and who gives me the right to pursue Wolfgang with my eyes just as I pursued Richard and Stella?

We need to get used to looking past people and things, we should never allow our thoughts to deceive us. It would be even better, of course, if we could stop thinking, because even our thoughts kill.

I thought: 'He will destroy Stella.' I thought it for long enough for it to happen in reality. I know that Richard is afraid of my thoughts. Superstitious, like everyone with an energetic constitution, he fears only what he cannot grasp and understand for himself. But he is strong enough to push that fear aside, as he pushes aside everything that would get in the way of his plans.

Why did nothing warn me on that September evening, when Stella came to us? Why didn't I simply turn down Luise's request? It didn't suit me at all to take this strange young woman into our home, and even Richard wasn't exactly thrilled with the idea. He only agreed for my sake and because Stella was only supposed to stay for ten months. Luise is my friend, that is to say she has claimed to be my friend for thirty years. I've never liked her, not even at school, because even as a child she was stingy, duplicitous, and hateful. Luise always wanted to have my things, in those early days she stole my erasers, patent leather belts, and sausage sandwiches, later she wanted the men who wooed me, and now at last, with the help of her daughter, she has destroyed the peace I'd struggled so hard to find. She is a bringer of misfortune, Luise, ugly, dried-up, and boy crazy. But I've never managed to persuade Richard that she's just a burden to me. He simply doesn't understand that there are some people you despise and still cannot escape. Never in his life would Richard have found himself in such a situation. He shrugs off everyone who isn't of use to him in some way or other. Even Stella wasn't much use to him for long; a few weeks, nothing more. She made him far too uncomfortable. What could a seducer like him do with this clumsy, earnest child? No woman has ever bored him as quickly as Stella did.

Richard had never seen her before. Luise always tended to travel without her daughter, and he had formed a quite mistaken impression of Stella. Even today I can't believe that Stella was really Luise's daughter, even though there can be no doubt about it. Stella's father must have been an irresponsible fellow if he managed to spawn a child with Luise. He seems to have immediately regretted this development and tried, by drawing up a will that was as refined as it was shortsighted, to protect his child from his wife by making Luise the beneficiary of his financial assets while Stella would inherit the pharmacy. But he really shouldn't have arranged his will like this, because as a result he created an implacable enemy for his daughter. The best thing that Luise ever did for Stella was to put the child – who was often terrified, crouched in a corner at home, becoming more and more of a hindrance – in a convent. There, Stella found so much love that she was able to store it up and live off it for eight years. Of course she really should have studied pharmacy, but that training was not what Luise had in mind – the less Stella understood of what she was supposed to understand, the better it was for Luise. But since Stella had to do something, in the end, and her mother had no use for her whatsoever alongside her women friends, dogs, and lovers, she hit upon the idea of foisting Stella off on me, at least for a year, or as long as her business studies course lasted. In quiet despair, Luise must've said to herself that the day of Stella's maturity was drawing ever closer. That wouldn't have been her downfall, of course, because she still had a legacy, and she had certainly become rich enough over the past few years, barely hampered by an old and half-demented guardian. But then again there was also the matter of this young man whom she was determined to marry, but whom, as she was probably well aware, she could only buy. It was a hopeless situation for her, I admit.

So Stella came to us, pushed aside once again by her mother, and also not eagerly awaited by us.

Our household, in fact, is set up in such a way that it cannot withstand an intruder, or even a guest. For reasons that are only too obvious. Richard's friends will never be my friends, and Richard finds my friends uncongenial. Apart from this, no one else is familiar with the countless taboos that we must observe in our dealings with one another, and which must be respected even by the children. Consequently, our topics of conversation are somewhat restricted, but of course that's better than ceaseless friction. Then there's also the fact that a stranger would destroy my relationship with Wolfgang: everyone disturbed the two of us in those days, even little Annette, and of course Richard too. For that reason I didn't take on a maid as such, but a cleaner, a morose and sulky person who has no interest in us, we are nothing more to her than the people whose floors she cleans in return for a decent wage. She simply does her work, entirely governed by ideas and worries about people that we don't know or care to meet. People on the moon couldn't be any stranger than we are to her. Even though it's never mentioned, there were two sides in our house: Richard and Annette, Wolfgang and me – and we adhered strictly to the rules of the game. Richard had brief and slightly too cordial conversations with his son, to which Wolfgang responded with perfect politeness, and Annette would sometimes sit on my lap, and of course I put her to bed and she would kiss and hug me. But that isn't entirely true. I think Wolfgang has always loved his father, even though he sees straight through him, and if there is a secret pain in Richard's life, its name is Wolfgang. His son's otherness must cause him suffering, if Richard allows himself to suffer, because in fact Richard is seeking a friend, and Wolfgang will never be his friend. Where little Annette is concerned, I would probably love her instinctively if she weren't so much like her father. It isn't her fault that the very sight of her sometimes fills me with horror. I see her blossoming little face, I feel her warmth and hear her laughter, and know that they mean just as little as Richard's warmth and laughter. Both of them, Annette and her father, are born decoys, traps that God, or whoever, has set for other people, the heavy, loyal, imaginative, and emotional ones. Perhaps Annette is also too healthy and happy to be truly loved. This child will always achieve what she wishes for, and will never wish for anything unattainable. She is just as weak and helpless as a young tiger or a carnivorous plant. Richard is proud of this daughter, but basically he knows exactly who she is: a good-natured companion as long as he indulges all her moods.

But since he has never loved anything as much as himself, he must also love this little image of himself. Sometimes he gives Annette a mighty slap, which she takes with a quiet whimper. He has never struck Wolfgang, who is one of those children that one doesn't strike. Richard is much too clever to show weakness and put himself in the wrong.

During her first weeks with us, Stella was a terrible bother to all of us. Richard, who loved drinking his red wine, smoking and reading in the evening, suddenly felt forced to make conversation with a girl like Stella and found it terribly tiring and utterly pointless. Annette was simply jealous, as she is of anyone who lays claim to the interest of those around her. Wolfgang felt disturbed by the change in atmosphere, and I had a sense of being too quiet and not knowing how to deal with young girls. It seemed impossible to guess Stella's thoughts and respond to them. This tall, pretty, slightly too well-built girl was an alien element in our house, and she must certainly have felt that herself. She was more timid than shy, inhibited by her years of life in the convent, and I thought she must have seemed a little strange there too. She wasn't at all cute, childish, and silly as young girls tend to be. In fact she looked like a woman who is only still a child by chance. And as quiet as she was, it was impossible to ignore her. The dreadful brown clothes that Luise had bought for her were unbecoming enough, but she could not simply be ignored.

I had tried to adapt the spare room in which Stella was expected to live to the needs of its young new resident, arranging a few knickknacks around the place, the kind that young girls like, and covering the dark furniture with lace doilies. Then, when I actually saw Stella, I wished I could have cleared all those odds and ends away, but by then she had already seen them, which meant that it was no longer possible. So the horses, dogs, and ballerinas stayed on the chest of drawers and looked quite strange beside this tall, earnest girl. I imagine that Stella never really studied. She sat in front of her exercise books and her textbooks and was simply bored. She was bad at maths, and probably the slowest of her class at shorthand. In fact I had no idea if she had any real talents or skills. She was good with animals and plants, she liked doing menial work, and knitted jackets and socks from coarse grey wool for some poor people or other. Then she sent those rather shapeless things to her old convent. Richard liked to tease her about her charity work. Then she would open her wide, white eyelids and laugh quietly and clumsily, like someone who has yet to learn how to laugh. She only knitted them to avoid accusations of laziness, and so that she could spend hours alone with her thoughts.

I knew nothing at all about those thoughts. Sometimes I doubted that she was thinking anything at all, her face was so still. She liked engaging with Annette, and the child finally began to return her affection. At first Wolfgang observed her with a mixture of curiosity, shyness, and prejudice. In that too every inch my son; it would never have occurred to him to approach a stranger. When it became clear to me that I would never be able to have a real relationship with Stella, I began to abandon my efforts and went back to living as I had done before, as if there were no young girl in my spare room. She still disturbed me, but I knew that the disturbance would not last for very long. I was always friendly towards Stella, just as friendly as I am with my cleaner, the mailman, or Wolfgang's friends from school.

I started yielding to my own thoughts again, walking from one window to another, smoking or with my hands pushed into my sleeves, gazing into the now bare garden. I bought flowers, which became increasingly expensive as the cold season progressed, I dutifully went for walks with Annette, and I talked to Wolfgang about the books that he was constantly devouring, some of which were perhaps unsuitable for him. Of course I also took care of the housework, got annoyed with Annette, who was lazy and slovenly at school, and, as usual, discussed with Richard all sorts of matters relating to the children and the housekeeping. I did everything according to routine; for me reality meant staring into the garden, wandering restlessly around the house, and feeling warmth in my breast at the sight of Wolfgang.

Something had happened to me years ago that left me in a diminished state, an automaton that just gets on with its work, barely suffers, and is only turned back for seconds at a time into the living young woman that it once was. The touching curve of Wolfgang's neck, the roses in the white vase, a draught billowing the curtains, and all of a sudden I'm aware that I'm still alive. Then there's the other thing, which fills me with fear, with horror, with the feeling that something's going to jump out at me at any moment and break down the invisible wall.

I know that can't happen, but it forces its way into my mind, time after time, staring at me from the faces of strangers in the street, rising in the howl of a dog, filling my nostrils in the butcher's shop with the stench of blood, and touching me like a cold hand at the sight of Richard's full, cheerful face.

Something must have happened to me years ago; since then I don't think I've been able to tolerate the idea that, incomprehensibly to my brain and heart, good and evil are one. To be able to endure that knowledge, one would need the vital force of a giant. But giants do not find themselves in this situation; for them, thinking is replaced by a sturdy cudgel. They prefer to live. Thinking people must always give up living, and living people do not need to think. The act of salvation is never performed, because anyone with the strength to carry it out is unaware that they must do it, and the knowing person is incapable of action

Stella was one of the living. More than a person, she was like a big grey cat or a young deciduous tree. She sat at our table, thoughtless and innocent, waiting for fate. Richard would have needed only to reach out a hand to grip her tanned wrist. He didn't, but he smiled as he cut up the meat on his plate, calmly, relishing each movement.

Richard is a born traitor. Equipped with a body that grants him constant pleasure, he could live contentedly, were he not gifted with a dazzling intelligence. It's this intelligence that turns the pleasures of his sensual body into crimes. Richard is a monster: a considerate paterfamilias, a valued lawyer, a passionate lover, traitor, liar, and murderer.

I have known all this for years, and if I knew who I could hold responsible for this knowledge, I would kill them. I used to see only guilt in Richard, and I began to hate him. But now I have known for a long time that he is not to blame if I react like this to the fact of his presence. There are so many others like him, the whole world plainly knows and accepts it, and no one puts him on trial. Whose fault is it that I can't just accept things as they are? I am slowly giving up hope that someone, I don't know who, will one day take a stand, and even if they did, I wouldn't know how to respond. My rage went up in smoke long ago; all that remains is the horror that dominates me completely, and that I inhabit, in which I am trapped. It has entered me, it has saturated me, and it accompanies me wherever I go. There is no escape. My worst thought is that even death could not be deadly enough to extinguish it at last.

But horror and the knowledge of the truth that one is not supposed to know belong to the order of everyday life. Yes, I cling to this order, to the regular mealtimes, the work that returns every day, the visits and walks. I love that order, which allows me to live. One day I was struck by the touching equanimity with which Stella wore her clothes, those brown, claret, and purple horrors that were either too big or too small for her, and which testified to Luise's wickedness. 'We should buy her decent clothes,' I said to Richard, 'and she would be a beauty.' He glanced up from the newspaper, gave me a surprised look and said, 'Do you think so?'

I know his weakness for delicate, distinctive women. I went on to praise Stella's merits. He laughed and rocked his head regretfully back and forth: buying clothes for her was none of our business. In two years, once she was in possession of the pharmacy, she would start dressing decently. 'Luise,' I said, 'is a disgrace.' Richard raised his shoulders comically, shook himself a little and laughed. Suddenly I had an idea. What if I taught Stella how to dress? I closed my eyes and saw her coming down a flight of stairs in a white dress, smiling with her lips in a Cupid's bow, her reddish-brown hair shiny and loose, young, beautiful and seductive. I saw Richard's white, firm hands holding the newspaper, and was filled with a kind of satisfaction that he couldn't see this beauty, obstructed as it was by his penchant for an artificial, refined prettiness.

Over the following weeks the seamstress came to the house and sewed a few dresses for Stella, out of cheap materials, but in bright colours suitable for a young girl.

The transformation was complete. Stella stood in front of the mirror and saw herself as what she really was for the first time. 'You're beautiful, Stella,' I said, straightening a crease. She didn't look at me, and spoke seriously into the mirror, 'I'm beautiful,' amazed, surprised and finally overwhelmed by the new feeling that my words and her reflection had awoken in her, and then said again, 'I'm beautiful.'

Now I could actually have triumphed. Luise, the dragon, had been outwitted. It was entirely possible that the newly transformed Stella could bring home a fiancé who would ensure that in the future Stella's fortune would not be turned into Luise's clothes, hats, and lovers. But strangely I was unable to rejoice in this idea. Incidentally, I have never been gratified by a triumph, it usually makes me embarrassed, or puts me in a slightly painful state of mourning. Perhaps it's because my triumph means the defeat of someone else; I transform myself into that other person and suffer on their behalf. Luise, however, was so repulsive to me that I couldn't summon that feeling for her. What troubled me in my joy was Stella's face in the mirror, that gleaming face, that young, blossoming flesh, and that gaze devoted entirely to her new brilliance. I felt a creeping unease. Stella was no longer the child that she had been. There was a void in her breast, and it would draw the world towards it. And I didn't like that. It was not within my power to guide the flow that would fill that void. 'Stella,' I said quickly, 'Stella, shouldn't you practise your shorthand today?'

She covered her eyes with her hands in a touchingly childlike gesture and turned towards me. Her arms fell to her sides, the gleam in her eyes was extinguished, and she turned towards the door with a sigh. That evening Richard hadn't noticed that a new Stella was sitting across from him. But Annette noticed it and so did Wolfgang, who gave me a thoughtful, quizzical look.

Stella, in her strawberry-coloured dress, ate hardly anything and stared dreamily into the distance. Fully in command of her healthy young body, she absent-mindedly took little sips of her tea.

The bird is still sitting in the linden tree. It hasn't stirred from the spot all night. It isn't screaming any more, just cheeping faintly. If I close the window, I can't hear it any more. It's so tiny now that it can barely be called a bird. Its mother hasn't come, and I don't think she's going to.

When I'm alone in the house I'm always aware that this isn't my house. Sometimes I feel like a lodger here. All that belongs to me is the view of the garden, nothing else. Once I even imagined that I would at least have something I could call a home, but since Stella's death, the gilded cage has turned into a dungeon. If I'm not mistaken, the garden has even moved further away from the house. It's moving away from me, slowly, almost imperceptibly, one day it will disappear completely, and I will stare out of the window into the void and think, that's where the linden tree used to be, and over there the patch of lawn with the viburnum bushes. Perhaps this has something to do with the windows. They are gradually becoming more opaque until they finally obstruct my view. ∎

*The Destination
for Art and Culture*

Aesthetica

THE ART & CULTURE MAGAZINE
www.aestheticamagazine.com

Issue 123
February / March 2025

PICTURES OF RENEWAL
Images of Brazil's Atlantic Forest
highlight its beauty and fragility

SENSORY EXPERIENCE
Ryoji Ikeda's audiovisual pieces
are a light and sound spectacle

FUTURE CONSTRUCTS
Celebrating the artistic legacy
of pioneer Aleksandra Kasuba

STUDY IN GEOMETRY
Contemporary abstract scenes
inspired by icons of modernity

*In-depth features and visual
narratives with today's most
innovative practitioners.*
Save 70%. £12 for 12 months.

REBEKKA DEUBNER for *Granta*
Oeuf Mayonnaise, 2025

BENOÎT

Michel Houellebecq

TRANSLATED FROM THE FRENCH BY LUKE NEIMA

I'm getting old, and of course my friends are getting old, and there are now quite a few people whose death I'm afraid to wake up to, but Benoît wasn't one of them. I just didn't see it coming. The news of his death plunged me into a state of horrified shock, and deep down I still can't really believe it. I'm often about to call him to ask if he wants to do something together, visit a monument, eat in a restaurant, see a show, before reality catches up with me. This must be what the shrinks call *denial*. It's strange because I don't go in much for denial; I usually take tragic news on the chin, without my mind assembling the slightest escape. In the end, I don't think you ever come to terms with the death of someone you love all at once; you have to come to terms with it over and over again, sometimes many times. The last people I had to mourn died after long illnesses, and you gradually resign yourself to it with each visit to the hospital. But with a sudden death it's afterwards that you have to kill them inside yourself, and even then you can only kill them little by little.

It's probably for the same reason that I didn't manage to write the tribute to Benoît Duteurtre that I'd planned, so I'll have to make do with my memories. I had put my favourite books by Benoît on my desk, and suddenly I realised that I couldn't read them, that I couldn't even physically open them. I was afraid to open them. I felt that reading the words in them would sign his death warrant. Since he won't be writing any more, the words would become definitive, and I don't want there to be anything definitive between us. We'll be seeing each other again soon enough, anyway.

S trangely enough, our first encounter was an argument in print. At the time Jean Ristat was attempting to revive *Lettres françaises*, the magazine run by Aragon after the war. Ristat asked me to write an article on Prévert, who had just been published in the *Pléiade*. I wrote the article, which was frankly negative (and in fact I still don't like Prévert), and sent it to him, though with some trepidation – the magazine was still financed by the Communist Party. Jean laughed out loud at the piece, and published it without the slightest hesitation, without the slightest cut; but in the following issue he published an article by Benoît, in which Benoît defended Prévert. (Jean Ristat was a rather peculiar Communist; he died in 2023.) I didn't meet Benoît until two years later, in 1994, at one of the meetings held by another magazine, *L'atelier du roman*, where I also met Philippe Muray and Sempé. Milan Kundera came more rarely, as he was no longer on top form. There are more and more dead people in this article, I can't help it.

I don't know when I'll be able to read his books again, but in any case it will be brutal. There will be gentler things, like how I'll never be able to order an *œuf mayonnaise* in a restaurant without thinking of him – literature can do that, when the description is perfect. His description of the ideal *œuf mayonnaise* appears at the start of *Le Retour du Général* (2010). The novel belongs to a genre he was very fond of, which could be called 'soft speculative', by which I mean books set in a plausible version of the future, which don't involve sweeping scientific and technological changes. In the novel, we learn in the first few pages that the European Union has just banned mayonnaise, which, after all, is not that far-fetched. They've already come close to banning raw-milk cheeses. There's no telling what those people are capable of. This reminds me that one of my fondest memories of Benoît was being with him at the Cirque d'Hiver, during what was billed as an evening of debates about Europe. It wasn't much of a debate at all, as we agreed about everything, and shared the same hostility to a federal Europe.

Basically, Benoît's books come in two main types; I like both, I really don't have a preference. The first are the 'soft speculative' books, which can get fairly polemical. A perfect example is *La petite fille et la cigarette* (2005). The second type, which aren't fictional at all, are memoirs of childhood and early youth. It's a world that feels distant, almost unreal in its naive optimism. An example of these is *Les pieds dans l'eau* (2008).

I can easily locate myself in these remote memories. We were essentially of the same generation, and our sensibilities were shaped by similar experiences. We discovered the same poets and rock bands at around the same time, and we both went on language exchanges in Germany at the same age. Back then, Benoît would cycle miles to buy the latest Led Zeppelin album. Personally, I'd have only gone out of my way for Pink Floyd. Not a huge difference: I liked Led Zeppelin, he liked Pink Floyd. I never really asked Benoît why he liked 'Alan's Psychedelic Breakfast', that weird Pink Floyd song. It starts with a bit of music, but mostly what you get are the actual sounds of someone making an English breakfast, with dishes clattering, the distinct sound of bacon slices frying in the pan, etc. Little by little, the music develops, expands, until it takes up the entire sonic space. I think the delight he took in this song tells us something about his aesthetic. Music played almost as important a role in Benoît's life as literature. Almost. In any case, it's easy to imagine one of his novels beginning with a simple scene like that: making breakfast.

We weren't on the same level when we talked about music. I can't remember a single time when I mentioned a musician he didn't know, whereas the opposite happened quite often. Our sense of literature was more comparable, and our tastes often very similar. If I had to define what the writers of my generation who met at *L'atelier du roman* meetings shared, I'd say it was the desire to return to realism. In Benoît's novels, as in mine, you know where the characters live, what their jobs are, how much they earn. Neither of us had the ambition to equal Balzac, to take up his overwhelming project of describing the whole of the society of his time, but both of us tried to grow in his great shadow.

Jacques Prévert aside, we were almost in complete agreement about poetry. In retrospect, we'd mostly written our pieces on Prévert for the pleasure of polemic. Perhaps I was drawn to the early nineteenth century, to early romanticism, more than him. He was partial to the *fin de siècle*, to the symbolist movement. But basically we agreed on the essentials. He was someone I was always happy to talk to, and there aren't that many people I'm happy to talk to. All of a sudden my life has gotten poorer.

We still had a lot to live for, a lot of discoveries to make together. I'll never get to show him the masterpiece that is the Limoges train station. He would have loved it so much, it's exactly his favourite period, architecturally speaking. But I have wonderful memories of those few days when he showed me around the New York he loved. As for wild game, we had mixed results; we discovered this shared culinary passion too late. There was one magnificent *hare à la royale*, but we didn't get around to the grouse. Without him, I won't be as interested in game. Hunting season is short; so is life.

When I come across a breed of cow I don't recognise, I'll think about Benoît, because in my opinion, with *À propos des vaches* (2000), he came close to writing the definitive book on this remarkable animal. Were there any breeds of cattle unfamiliar to him? I imagine so, but you'd have to go pretty far afield, outside of France at any rate.

And whenever I take a train with a proper restaurant car, I'll be thinking of him. He so aptly evoked the sensuous little pleasures you find on old-fashioned trains in *La nostalgie des buffets de gare* (2015).

The word 'nostalgia' has to be singled out. It's certainly the one that first comes to mind when you think of his work, and it's one of the sensations I most enjoyed in his writing, especially as I'm incapable of it myself. It's true, though, that in some ways things were better in the 'good old days'. But the nostalgic is not a reactionary, a word that has become a mark of infamy, and it's wrong that he sometimes got called one. The reactionary wants to turn back the clock; the nostalgic knows full well it's impossible. And yet this is where things get so surprising and beautiful. Because there's something not entirely sad about nostalgia. It goes hand in hand with the incongruity that you sometimes feel in life. It comes with a strange smile, half resigned, half ironic. I can't think of anyone other than Benoît who, in that tone of cheerful incredulity, could say to me, some thirty years after our first meeting: 'It's strange, we've become old.' And it's a pity, a real pity that he couldn't say to me, in the same tone: 'It's strange, we've become dead.'

In the end, I'm going to have to talk about what's unbearable about this loss. Benoît intersperses many of his books with autobiographical elements, but he didn't write a real autobiography, even though no writer had more talent for one. He had what I utterly lack, the power of acute sensorial recall, which allowed him to recover an instant of the past, to bring it to life in all its colour, its every luminous flickering, its familiar sounds. Just think of the pages of *Les pieds dans l'eau* where he writes about the afternoons of his childhood on the beach at Étretat. The time would have come, it would certainly have come, in a few years perhaps, when he would have wanted to gather all his memories, to offer us a wonderfully delicate and sensitive history of the second half of the twentieth century. That's what his readers have lost.

I'm a writer too. I take literature seriously. It means a great deal to me. With a little difficulty, I suppose I can see how it's respectable to mourn all the books a dead author wasn't able to write. But there's also something inhuman about doing that, and I'm not ready for that kind of asceticism. And for me, anyway, there's something even worse about Benoît's death. He wasn't meant to die, not now, not at this age. He possessed all the ideal qualities of affectionate generosity, tolerance, mischievous irony and, not least, wisdom that would have made him one of those old codgers who manage to make you like old age, who almost make you want to grow old. Now it's going to be harder. ■

Krystyna Dąbrowska

Cell Phone

Each time I'm in her country, my translator
lends me the phone of her dead husband.
The smooth black slab's like a miniature gravestone.
It doesn't have dates of his birth or death,
but connected by umbilical cord to a power source,
it comes to life with messages for the dead:
Jim, your friend commented. Jim, get updates.
Not only the phone is on a first-name basis with him.
When my translator calls to ask me about some word
in a poem, and I don't pick up, the phone
responds with his voice. 'I didn't say anything,'
she tells me later. 'A year on, it's like he's still here.'
As if he were here and could click on push alerts
from CNN: the price of gas, immigration, the blizzard,
taxes. Instead, I'm the one who clicks. I add my accounts
and contacts to his contacts and accounts,
the pictures I take go into his album.

At first, they huddle at the edge like shy guests,
but over time, they push their way in
and are surprised when a selfie of their host
appears like a ghost behind them.
Jim was a poet. Now his cell phone,
leading me through new terrain where it's my only
map, slowly becomes a poem. There's so much more
of me in it, so I keep delaying the end.
I take it on a transatlantic flight to a country
he never visited – just a couple of lines yet,
now one more, before I hand it over to my translator.

Translated from the Polish by Karen Kovacik

CHANTAL JOFFE
Hannah Arendt, 2014
Courtesy of the artist and Victoria Miro

THIS VERY COMPLICATED CAST OF MIND

Interview with Renata Adler

W hen *Granta* asked Renata Adler about contributing to this issue, she off-handedly mentioned an unpublished piece she had been commissioned to write years before by the *New York Times* on the occasion of the death of her friend, Hannah Arendt. The article was a 6,000-word memorial that included a detailed appreciation of Arendt's oeuvre. Adler, however, shelved the piece after writing it. 'I thought she would have hated it,' Adler told *Granta*. After retrieving the article from her archive this past autumn, Adler looked at it with different eyes. 'If anything,' she said, 'it's too distant.'

The piece is not only a forthwright reckoning with Arendt by a writer from a younger generation with a shared German émigré background, but also marks the points of contact and contrast between the two writers (though Adler refuses to be compared with Arendt). Adler first met Arendt in 1963, shortly after Arendt's two-part report on the trial of the SS commander, and high-level organizer of the mass slaughter of European Jewry, Adolf Eichmann, appeared in the *New Yorker*. The Eichmann articles were not only controversial for coining the phrase 'the banality of evil', but also for calling attention to the leaders of the Jewish councils in Europe who, according to Arendt, had to a certain extent cooperated with Nazi directives. Adler's unpublished piece is concerned in particular with

Arendt's understanding of politics, and her moral understanding of the responsible way to be in the world. For Arendt, neither friendship, nor even the individual self, can exist without making reference to the public realm. In this sense for Arendt, as Adler writes, conversation does not merely sustain the world, 'it *is* the world.'

Readers can view the original, unedited version of Adler's essay online at granta.com. What follows is a supplementary conversation, in which Adler relates some of her memory of Arendt.

Renata Adler was born in 1937 in Milan, the daughter of German Jewish parents who left Nazi Germany in 1933. In 1939 they settled in the United States. Adler grew up in Danbury, Connecticut, and in 1962 became a staff writer at the *New Yorker* under William Shawn. She is the author of the novels *Speedboat* and *Pitch Dark*. Her works of reportage include *Reckless Disregard: Westmoreland v. CBS et al., Sharon v. Time* and *Irreparable Harm: The U.S. Supreme Court and the Decision that Made George W. Bush President*. Her essays have been collected in *Toward a Radical Middle, Canaries in the Mineshaft*, and most recently in *After the Tall Timber*.

1

EDITOR: How did you first come into contact with Hannah Arendt?

RENATA ADLER: I was fairly new at the *New Yorker*. In fact, I was *very* new at the *New Yorker*. The pieces on Eichmann's trial had just come out in the magazine.

EDITOR: This was the two-part report Arendt wrote from the trial in Jerusalem where the SS commander Adolf Eichmann was tried, convicted, and executed by the young Israeli state for his work in facilitating and coordinating the mass slaughter of Jews and others under Hitler.

ADLER: That's right. I ran upstairs to Mr Shawn's office, and I said, look, I think – I know this sounds peculiar, but I think the magazine needs to run another piece, very quickly, whether by Miss Arendt or by somebody else, but preferably by Miss Arendt, which explains what the Eichmann pieces really say.

EDITOR: This is 1963, and you were twenty-five years old. Why did you think the articles required additional clarification?

ADLER: She stressed collaboration between Jewish leaders and the Nazis to the point that I just thought it's going to be highly offensive, and also perhaps misleading in a way.

EDITOR: They did offend a lot of people. Irving Howe wrote that *Eichmann in Jerusalem* 'provoked divisions that would never be entirely healed' in the Jewish New York intellectual world.

ADLER: I thought the pieces might be misunderstood.

EDITOR: Did you disagree about the substance of them?

ADLER: No, I trusted her completely.

EDITOR: Then what was wrong with them?

ADLER: There was perhaps an element of snobbery to them, which I think she never was quite aware of. An edge of contempt. I loved her dearly, I admired her enormously. But I think the 'banality of evil' – although I can understand why she used the phrase – it isn't right. It isn't right. 'Banality' is a strange word to use. It's an intellectually strange word to use, no? It really trivializes something. There could have been another way to express it, I'm sure.

EDITOR: Even if 'banality' is pejorative, it might have had a different inflection in her ears, no? It was a word that she would have learned in a German gymnasium. The 'Banausos' – from which 'banality' derives – were the manual laborers of Ancient Greece. Couldn't it have had a more clinical meaning for her?

ADLER: But it's trivializing and dismissive in English. In the way people used to use the word 'middle class'. But I think I can understand why she used it. Because she was also writing against the glamorization of evil. There's a long history of romanticizing evil. No matter whose devil it is, no matter where evil is depicted: there's something quite elegant about it. You don't get a devil who's a pudgy fat boy. So in another way Hannah's choice of words is exactly right. Exactly what she wanted to do was deglamorize evil. Even now, even again, the devil is not a glamorous character. It's not something with a wonderful tail.

EDITOR: But William Shawn didn't think it was necessary to run a defense of Arendt at the time in the *New Yorker*, so then what happened?

ADLER: Sometime later, when the book *Eichmann in Jerusalem* was published, Mr Shawn appeared in the doorway of my office. He said that Miss Arendt would not mind if I were to write a letter to the *New York Times*. The letter, which he himself would edit, would be a response to the awful review by Michael Musmanno, who had been a judge at Nuremberg. [Ed. Musmanno's review appeared on 19 May 1963, and argued that Arendt's book read like a defense of Eichmann against the Israeli prosecution.] *The Times* did not run my letter. Then Mr Shawn appeared in the doorway of my office again, and he said that Miss Arendt would not mind, if I would agree to it, for him to run my letter as a Notes and Comment in the *New Yorker*. He did run it. Mr Shawn appeared in my office again. He had this way of appearing in the doorway of one's office. He said Miss Arendt would like to invite me to tea.

EDITOR: What were your first meetings with her like?

Hannah Arendt, Passport Photo (sheet of four), 1933
Courtesy of the Hannah Arendt Bluecher Literary Trust / Art Resource, NY

ADLER: I thought of her more as a sort of parental figure in the beginning. There was scolding. When I went to the *New York Times* to become the movie reviewer, she said, 'When are you going to get serious?'

EDITOR: Did she give you a sense of what she thought of your writing?

ADLER: That's the funny thing about this note on this scrap of paper I recently found, which she had sent me. She says she likes a story I've written.

EDITOR: What story?

ADLER: I don't really remember. I'm still so embarrassed by it that I've never looked at it again.

EDITOR: How can you be embarrassed about it, but not know what it is?

ADLER: I just remember the embarrassment!

EDITOR: Didn't Arendt take film seriously as an art form?

ADLER: I think not. She would have thought about my writing about it as selling out. But then so did my brother. So did Hannah's husband Heinrich Blücher. So did Harold Rosenberg.

EDITOR: Your novels *Speedboat* and *Pitch Dark* appeared after Arendt died, but did you ever discuss your fiction?

ADLER: It did come up, but I don't remember how. She had a literary side. There's that wonderful sentence about her friend Randall Jarrell.

EDITOR: The one about 'the precision of his laughter'?

ADLER: 'The precision of his laughter'! I mean, 'the precision of his laughter'. Who else could say that? She was capable of phrases like that. So when it gets reported that Mr Shawn didn't like Hannah's writing because her prose was turgid, I think: You can't even say that. It just isn't true. I mean, 'The precision of his laughter'!

EDITOR: You've pointed to how Arendt achieves a special kind of authority in her prose. And you've also respectfully pointed to how this authority in her writing, alongside a drive toward fundamental concerns, comes with certain costs. The authority, you suggest, can sometimes crowd out precisely the kind of dialogue she aims to build with her readers. What's your own feeling about authority in your own writing?

ADLER: I don't think in terms of authority. When I think about prose I think about Evelyn Waugh and Muriel Spark, that kind of crisp style. Of course I don't write anything like that, except that I sort of try to in fiction. What's a good sentence? That kind of crisp . . . something. Hannah writes in such a different way. So, no, I don't feel the authority thing, and now that you mention it, I wonder if Hannah did.

EDITOR: This crispness you pursue on the page – what is it exactly?

ADLER: One thing it is, much to my astonishment, is monosyllables. I like sentences to end on the monosyllable. Or I really just tremendously like monosyllables. That's not a Hannah Arendt thing. But that's only in fiction. I don't really seem to do that in non-fiction, where the sentences are sometimes longer than I remember. But I do care about the word. Some writers do, and some writers don't. Some writers care about momentum or rhythm, but I think I'm very aware, maybe too aware, of every single word, although I bet an awful lot go by, because of course you can't be aware of every single word. Hannah was also aware of every single word, but in quite a different way. She didn't attach as much importance to cadence or rhythm.

Hannah Arendt and Mary McCarthy under tree in Castine, 1971.
Courtesy of the Hannah Arendt Bluecher Literary Trust / Art Resource, NY

2

EDITOR: You were both émigrés from Germany, albeit from different generations. Was that part of the bond?

ADLER: We must have spoken German in the beginning. Hannah would invite me to New Year's Eve, to a party for refugees. Fellow refugees who were friends of Hannah's. Some of them were quite old or seemed old to me. Of course, I went.

At the time I had a superstition, which was that I needed to be in bed, and perhaps asleep, well before midnight on New Year's Eve. I don't know why I had that. I can't think of another one that I had like that. So I would go to these parties, and there would be these refugees – a generation older than I, at least. Then I would leave, saying I had to be in bed. And I thought, they all don't believe me. They think I have something better to do, right? Some possibly, I don't know, romantic, illicit thing to do. What else would they think? On the other hand, why would you go to a party of refugees at Hannah's apartment on Riverside Drive if you had something better to do? It was very odd.

I remember a conversation on another evening, I guess where there must have been other refugees – one of them turned to me and said, 'Renata, I didn't know you understood German.' And Hannah said, 'Yes, the pity of it is that she used to speak it.' Now, what was peculiar to me about that conversation is we'd been speaking German at all of the parties. They weren't predominantly in English at all. So it just meant my German was declining.

EDITOR: What were the parties like?

ADLER: Intellectuals, necessarily. I can't remember who they all were, but certainly Helen Wolff, who was Kafka's publisher. They were pretty reproachful with me, because I hadn't finished my PhD. They kept saying I should at least finish it. I thought so too. I kept asking for extensions because I had another job.

EDITOR: Do you remember what the apartment was like?

ADLER: Only to the degree that it was very like my parents house. I think there were Oriental carpets, but I may be making that up completely. I wasn't really paying attention. Maybe my parents' milieu and Hannah's were more alike than I imagine. I remember telling her that I really did not understand my parents' account of their life in Germany before the war. I just didn't get it. It made no sense to me. Then she started telling me a story. It was part of a story my father had already told me.

EDITOR: What was the story?

ADLER: There was a Jewish family in Germany, and they were very rich. Their last name was Moses, which they changed to Merton. It became a joke in the Jewish community: 'Have you been to Italy to see the Merton by Michaelangelo?' So already this is not such an attractive thing. Anyway, it was apparently quite common for wealthy Jews to marry less wealthy Czechs with titles. A girl from the Merton family married a Czech aristocrat named Czernin. So the woman became Trix Czernin. Trix was short for Beatrix. Then during the war, nobody saw anybody. When Trix turned up in America, she was married to my mother's cousin Bill, who, as unlikely as it seems, was a dairy farmer and war hero. He lived in Amenia, New York. My parents and I went to visit cousin Bill. (In the meantime she had been a secretary to Simenon, so you can see how this gets confusing.) We were all relaxing there together. Suddenly my father said to Trix, 'What's happened to the money?' And she said, 'Oh, I don't know.' And he said, 'Is it with your brothers or what?' It's not a question my father would have normally asked. It's certainly not a question you would ask of somebody you had a formal relationship with. She said, 'I don't know.' But they hit it off. Right away they knew each other. He said, 'No, no: what really happened to it? Where did it go?' She said, 'I really don't know.' He said, 'You really don't know?' She said, 'No.'

He said, 'Undenkbar.' ('Unthinkable.') After the war, after everything everybody has gone through, the thing they find unthinkable is that Trix Czernin doesn't have any money. On the way back in the car I was sort of puzzled by it all. My father said, 'You don't understand. It would be as if I.G. Farben or General Motors went bankrupt.' I thought: No American would be so astounded if somebody failed. I thought, isn't it strange that of all the things he would react to with real astonishment, as if it were the most amazing thing he ever heard, was that Trix Czernin had no more money.

EDITOR: How does Hannah Arendt come into this?

ADLER: Years later I'm having lunch with Hannah. I said, 'You know something very strange? I don't understand a thing about my parents' life before they came from Europe. Nothing makes sense to me. I don't understand it.' Hannah said, 'Listen, I have a story that will explain it all to you. There was this family in Germany called Moses; they changed their name to Merton. That became a local joke: "Have you been to Italy to see the Merton by Michelangelo?"' Now this is so terrible, I so regret it: I interrupted. I should have let the story go on. But I started to say, 'Oh, you know' – I was going to say that Trix Merton married Cousin Bill, right? But I didn't get very far with the interruption, because Hannah was going on. 'Trix Merton became . . .' I kept interrupting, if only because Hannah said she had chosen this story to explain what my parents' life was like before they came. I kept interrupting. I even started to recount the conversation Trix had with my father. Hannah said: 'She has no money?' She wasn't interested in any other part of what I was saying. She said, 'No money?' Hannah said: 'Undenkbar.'

EDITOR: What? The exact same reaction?

ADLER: She had written *The Origins of Totalitarianism*. She knew as much about all of that as anybody. And she was ready to criticize the people who collaborated in any way. I'm sure she would have stood up. When one asks now, who would have stood up? – she would have stood up. But to find it unthinkable that somebody lost all her money. It so easily becomes, even in my mind, an antisemitic story. And to think that I interrupted her in telling a story she said would explain everything about my parents' life before the war.

EDITOR: She didn't finish the story?

ADLER: No! But if I hadn't interrupted . . .

EDITOR: So your father and Hannah were, in some sense, coming from a similar place.

ADLER: They were coming from a similar place. But the difference between Hannah's family milieu and my parents' is that my parents were never politically active. I have pictures of both my father and my grandfather (my mother's side) in uniform in the First World War on the other side. They didn't really go into battle or anything. I didn't really quite understand what they did. They said that they were never really soldiers. But my father used to talk about learning to ride in the cavalry.

EDITOR: How did you as a German Jew Americanize so thoroughly?

ADLER: Because of my parents. People that my parents knew in Germany, people who came here early enough to survive – they all seemed to my father to be, first of all, Democrats, second of all, on the liberal side, thirdly, to have a sense of superiority over Americans culturally, and in other ways. Americans would ask my father what he thought of this or that. And he would always say, 'Oh, it's wonderful. It's the best, you know, ever, ever anywhere.' The only exception that he made was for wild strawberries – what a funny thing to say – he said in Germany they might have been slightly better. And the

CHANTAL JOFFE
Hannah Arendt, 2015
Courtesy of the artist and Victoria Miro

response was, 'But the wild strawberries here are exactly what we're most proud of!' So after that he no longer claimed that German strawberries were slightly better. His friends were all critical of how uneducated Americans were. He said, 'This country welcomed us. What do we know? Everything's superior.' In order to be American, he thought he had to be Republican. And not only him. The whole family had to be Republican.

EDITOR: What about the Second World War?

ADLER: All I knew about the war, really, was that we collected milkweed pods for parachutes. There are no milkweed pods in parachutes. We also sold war bonds. We were supposed to sell war bonds. We were reading a lot of comic books. In the comic books, the villains of the war were the Japanese. They were always committing hara-kiri or saying some word like 'Banzai'. They were always torturing people. Once I mentioned it to my father, and he said, 'But the Germans were much worse.' I didn't know what he was talking about. But then I started reading a different kind of comic book. And there they were all saying, 'Achtung!' and 'Jawohl!', but it came as news to me that the Germans were the enemy. I found that out pretty late, considering.

EDITOR: When did you learn about the camps?

ADLER: It came very late. It came, I think, through movies. I wasn't allowed to go to the movies much at all. The first movie I ever saw must have been a war movie, because it was called *Winged Victory*.

EDITOR: Why were you not allowed to go to the movies?

ADLER: I don't know. I just wasn't allowed to go to film. I was too young to go to film.

3

EDITOR: What about your connection to Arendt via Mary McCarthy?

ADLER: Mary McCarthy was very nearly my mother-in-law, when I was together with Reuel Wilson. Mary and Hannah were great friends.

EDITOR: McCarthy was perhaps her closest friend, no?

ADLER: Yes: she made Mary McCarthy her executor. And it was at times a funny friendship. I remember reading somewhere that when Mary had breakfast with Hannah in New York, Hannah was always having anchovy paste, which I remember, strangely enough, from my own parents. There was quite often anchovy paste. So when Hannah came to stay with Mary, she, Mary, as a friend, put out anchovy paste with breakfast, but Hannah ignored it as though she had never seen such a thing in her life.

EDITOR: Why?

ADLER: She didn't want to have been observed that closely.

EDITOR: You have written about Arendt's attitude toward the public, how she was a public person who didn't want her privacy entered into.

ADLER: But then why did she leave the correspondence with Heidegger? I would have thought she would have destroyed that.

EDITOR: It's curious.

ADLER: Yet I can imagine her girlhood, and I can imagine that. There she is, she's waiting outside at night on a bench, even outside his

CHANTAL JOFFE
Hannah Arendt, 2014
Courtesy of the artist and Victoria Miro

office. If there's a light in the window, she can come. When there's no light . . . or it's the other way around. I don't know where I read that. But she was eighteen.

EDITOR: Another aspect of your relationship with Arendt is the generational divide. You were brought up in the Cold War, in Truman and Eisenhower's resolutely anti-communist America, whereas she would have had a different introduction to the left. She was not a Marxist by any means, but she would have been familiar with Marxism as an intellectual tradition. She was friends with people like Walter Benjamin. Did you think of her more as a Cold War liberal or as someone with these more left-wing tendencies coursing through her?

ADLER: I didn't even think of it that way. At the time I knew her there was the New Left. The New Left – she thought she understood them. I really didn't. She knew the Cohn-Bendit family from Paris, and even offered to fund figures in the New Left like Daniel Cohn-Bendit if they got into trouble. I wrote disparagingly about the New Left, because there was this wonderful movement – I thought at the time – being brought down by these New Leftists.

EDITOR: The civil rights movement?

ADLER: Yes, the civil rights movement. For instance, the New Left was mocking Martin Luther King. I kept thinking, 'Why are they focusing everything towards the Vietnam War, when we have this amazing movement going on?'

EDITOR: But Martin Luther King was dead against the war.

ADLER: Yes. But I thought, 'They're distracting attention from the only thing that we are winning.'

4

EDITOR: You're usually quite critical in your writing, even of what you admire, but when you write about Arendt there's a kind of fealty. It's as if you're suddenly thrust into the position of trying to size up her historical stature.

ADLER: I knew I loved her as a friend. I knew I admired her as a writer and as an intellectual and as a human being, but I didn't have what I presumptuously call 'understanding'. I didn't really understand her at all. Well, 'at all' is going too far, but I didn't really understand this very complicated cast of mind. I remember her saying that it was just as well that people died before they became too old, because they get too dogmatic, or they get too boring. She was really saying something much more complicated, which I've already forgotten.

EDITOR: Do you have other memories of Arendt?

ADLER: Strange things. She has a line where she says: 'Events, by definition, are occurrences that interrupt routine, processes, and procedures.' Doesn't that strike you as brilliant? I have a memory so distinct, but I don't see how it could have happened. I was living on 49th Street, three floors up. Hannah is coming up the stairs with a German Shepherd. She knew I wanted a dog. I can't remember where she got it. How could I do anything but say how grateful I was? Then she said, 'Of course you have to medicate his ears.' The phrase is so strange that I couldn't be making it up: 'Medicate his ears'! Now I have very strong feelings about dogs. But somehow I didn't want that one. Nor did I take it in the end. So that's it. ■

In the latest NLR

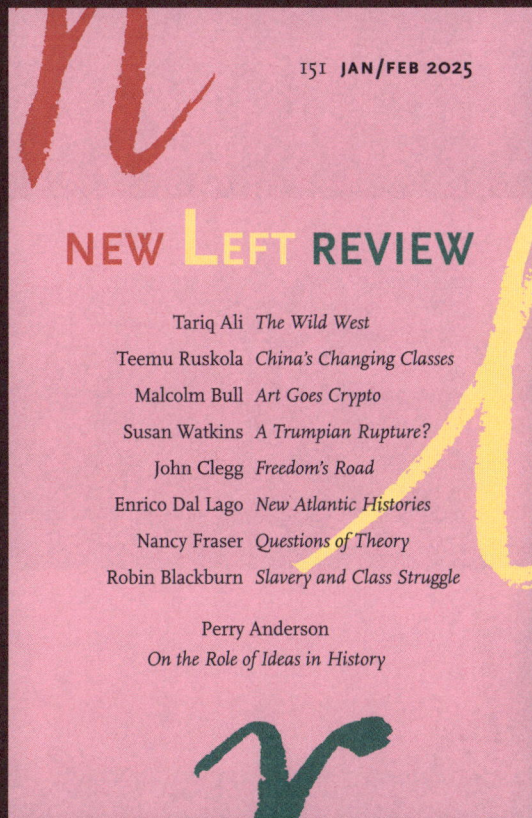

151 JAN/FEB 2025

NEW LEFT REVIEW

Tariq Ali *The Wild West*

Teemu Ruskola *China's Changing Classes*

Malcolm Bull *Art Goes Crypto*

Susan Watkins *A Trumpian Rupture?*

John Clegg *Freedom's Road*

Enrico Dal Lago *New Atlantic Histories*

Nancy Fraser *Questions of Theory*

Robin Blackburn *Slavery and Class Struggle*

Perry Anderson
On the Role of Ideas in History

Subscribe to *New Left Review*

Six issues per year

Print or digital formats

Full online archive since 1960

Courtesy of the author

V.S. NAIPAUL:
THE GRIEF AND THE GLORY

Aatish Taseer

'I'll read it with great interest,' V.S. Naipaul said, as he took the bound proof of my first novel in his hands and peered up at me with a mixture of alarm and fatigue.

Then Naipaul's wife, Nadira, ushered me out the door of their Wiltshire cottage, suggesting that we take a walk. I was acutely aware that I was moving through the landscape of one of my favourite Naipaul books, *The Enigma of Arrival* – hills and downs, and 'flat wet fields, with the ditches as water meadows'. Beyond lay a narrow river, the Avon (not Shakespeare's Avon), on whose swirling glassy surface, a black swan would occasionally glide by.

Naipaul's life there was hard won. He had grown up in colonial Trinidad, where his north Indian family had been sent as indentured labourers by the British, a practice that continued long after the abolition of slavery in 1834. He had come from that 'dot on the map' to Oxford on a scholarship in 1950. The twenty years that lay between what he described as 'the blackness' of his time at Oxford, which included the death of his father, and when he came to feel at home in Wiltshire were years of tremendous intellectual growth, travel and the creation of a dazzling body of work; but they were marred, in his mind, by feelings of homelessness, financial precarity (his income through the 1970s averaged £7,600 a year) and what he described as a 'fear of extinction'. Having tried and failed to emigrate to Canada, it was not until the early 1980s, when he was fifty, that his life in England acquired the stability I witnessed then.

When Nadira and I returned an hour or so later, soaked to the bone from an October shower, I glanced into Naipaul's drawing room, with its two rose-coloured armchairs and facing shelves, full of Penguin classics in black and orange – and saw that my novel, which I had called *The Temple-goers* (a Naipaulian formulation for Hindu India), was gone.

'I've read thirty pages,' Naipaul said when we reconvened for drinks (Bushmills and soda). 'We'll talk about it later.' But then we began to talk about it. He asked me what I thought about 'it', his fingers working rhythmically against the suede arm of his chair. 'It feels slow and laboured,' he said, sounding agitated. 'You are doing the details and jazzing it up with the sex, I presume, but there is no sense of the narrative. You need to give a line, *a line.*' He rose very quickly and went around the room. He was looking for Somerset Maugham's *Cakes and Ale.* 'I don't want you to write like Maugham,' he said, 'but read him for narrative.'

The 'narrative line', he explained, is something that 'cuts through the fiction, small things attach themselves to it, but don't worry about the small things'. He gave the example of *Wuthering Heights*: 'I have just returned from a visit to my landlord – the solitary neighbour that I shall be troubled with.' *Great Expectations* was another example. 'There's the Pip, Pirrip business,' he said, referring to how Pip gets his name. 'Then there's the scene with the convict. It is an arresting beginning,' he said, with yet greater urgency.

I was twenty-eight. I had published one book, a memoir called *Stranger to History*, in which I had gone in search of my Pakistani father from whom I had been estranged for most of my life, and who was, at the time, serving as the Governor of Punjab. Naipaul, at seventy-seven, was in the twilight of a glittering career spanning half a century, in which he had received practically every accolade the republic of English letters had to offer, including what he only ever called 'the

Swedish Prize'. I should have felt grateful that one of my literary heroes was reading my work, but all I could think of was my poor novel, which six months away from publication, already typeset and in print, was receiving its first savaging – from a Nobel laureate, no less.

'I suppose you can't do any significant rewriting at this stage,' he said, seeming to come back to himself. I admitted that I couldn't. 'Well, leave it as it is. Take this as advice for the future. I hope you know that this is not about your talent. You know I have a great feeling for your work, for your mind. This is why I want you to learn about the importance of direct narrative.'

He spoke then about what would be his last book – *The Masque of Africa* (2010). 'I spent eight to nine months in East Africa in 1966 . . .' he said, reciting the opening from memory. 'Then a quick round-up of the other times I came. That gives rhythm,' he explained. 'But let's not speak more about it. I think you will be able to detect what I mean. I'll read some more.'

But he could not let it go. Moments later, he asked me again what the novel was about and where it was headed. The tension in his voice seemed to come from a place other than my novel, as if he were reliving his own fear of falling, his own missteps getting started as a writer in 1950s Britain. 'There's the trainer,' he said. 'You were quite obsessed with that trainer,' he added pointedly, alluding to something we had never openly discussed. I was not out yet, but in the words of my mother, 'This book could only have been written by someone who was gay.'

At dinner that evening, in a long room with a Japanese screen of a red-breasted bird picking its way through the snow, Naipaul consoled me. 'I don't want you to be cast down,' he said. 'We all need people to guide us. My father would have been a better writer than me,' he said, 'if someone had been there to guide him. He was writing in the 1930s and thought it was his duty to write about Hindu ritual because it was this strange, odd thing in our lives. But really, he should have been writing about his own life – his childhood, the people he grew up with.'

The table was lit with candles. Nadira came in and out of the room as we talked, serving the delicious scallop risotto she had made. 'This is not about your talent,' Naipaul continued. 'You have a feeling for the natural world, for language, but I want to tell you something about narrative. All writing is about narrative.'

He wanted to know if I had understood. I was not sure I had. I was so full of grief at having let him down. 'It's terrible to disappoint Vidia,' a woman at a book launch in London had once told me, and now I knew what she meant. I mumbled something about wanting the narrative to mirror the protagonist's own confusions. He seized on this. 'Blur the narrative to correspond with the narrator's blurred state?' he asked. 'Yes,' I replied, hoping not to damn the novel completely. He searched my face. 'It is possible,' he said, 'to create the feeling of a character adrift without needing to have the narrative be adrift.'

After dinner, he was suddenly tired. When he had gone upstairs, Nadira tried to comfort me. He had read with great interest, she said, with her uncanny ability to ventriloquise him. 'He got us out of the house so he could read. He is tired because he has been reading. He reads with great concentration.'

–

I first met Naipaul on a late-summer evening in London in 1999. I was eighteen, and about to set off for college in America. My mother asked me to join her for dinner with Nadira and Naipaul at the writer's flat on Cranley Gardens. Through slanted windows, the lights of Harrods were visible. 'You know what Vidia calls it?' Nadira asked, as she brought salmon and wild rice to the table. 'Harrabs!' she said, and everyone laughed. It was my first taste of Naipaul's humour, with its slight courting of danger. Over dinner, conversation turned to my going to college. Naipaul told me not to go. 'Except in the case of the "exact sciences",' Nadira filled in, 'Vidia is against it.' When my mother looked to him for further explanation. 'Indians, Tavleen,' he said, turning to her, 'they go to these places, they get dazzled by the institution and they come away having learnt nothing but the babble.' My mother looked somewhat taken aback. 'What should he do instead?' she asked. 'He should go boldly into the world,' Naipaul said, looking at me, his eyes brimming with mischief.

Nadira and my mother were friends and colleagues, who had known each other since covering the Afghan jihad in the 1980s. At the time, she was dating a newspaper owner called Rehmat Shah Afridi, who had been a close personal friend of Osama bin Laden during the jihad. She wrote a regular column in a Pakistani daily called 'Letter from Bahawalpur'. Having drifted apart, they reconnected in 1998, when Nadira Khannum Alvi turned up in Mumbai, reborn as the new Lady Naipaul.

I met Naipaul a couple more times in my early twenties. Once, in 2002, in New Delhi. I was at Amherst College writing a thesis on Gandhi, and while teaching a bartender at the Maurya Sheraton Hotel how to make a martini, he blew a hole through the core of my thesis statement. When I mentioned how Gandhi, through a programme of celibacy and dietetics had overcome the body and therefore the British, Naipaul pointed out that the British could still have simply killed him, 'And what kind of victory would that have been?' He was fascinated by Gandhi's flaws, but would always say, 'It is of a great man that we speak.' We crossed paths again in 2006, at Antonia Fraser's book party in London, when I was preparing to sell my first book on proposal. But it wasn't until 2007, during his trip to New Delhi to participate in a BBC film about his life called *The Strange Luck of V.S. Naipaul,* that our relationship ceased to be an adjunct of my mother's friendship with Nadira.

It began with Nadira asking that I accompany Naipaul the next day as the BBC crew filmed him riding the newly built Delhi metro. Over the next ten days, now at the National Museum, now drinking Jack Daniel's at his suite in the Maurya Sheraton, we became friends in our own right. I had by then read all his work and it was a joy for me to be able to talk to him about the more technical aspects of writing. In its intensity, and because the air always crackled a little when he was around, those early days of my friendship with Naipaul resembled the friendships one forms in eighth grade, when all you want to do is spend every waking moment with your new friend.

One evening, after the crew had left, Nadira and Naipaul came to my flat for dinner. I had never had him over on my own before and was a little daunted. She said he wished to tell me something. Filing away small spoonfuls of the yellow dal he specifically requested, he looked gravely up at me and told me not to obsess about my father, who I had been estranged from for most of my life. He was in part the subject of my first book. 'You've done it now,' Naipaul said. 'You've looked at it from every angle. You have to move on.' That need to keep moving both as a writer and a human being and, above all, to never allow yourself to be bogged down by corrosive people or situations, was the paramount Naipaulian lesson.

He ran like a thread through the defining moments of my life. He was there after I made the journey to Lahore to rediscover my father; and he was there again, in 2011, when my father was assassinated by his own bodyguard. His killing was on the front page of every major newspaper in the world, lamented by the likes of the Pope and Hillary Clinton. He had died a hero, fighting for a poor Christian woman, accused of blasphemy. To me, though, he had been a distant, and later domineering figure, with violent prejudices against Jews, Hindus and homosexuals. A man I once heard tell my younger brother, 'I don't care if you're a rapist, or a murderer, but if you're a fag, I'll fucking kill you.'

Nadira, who knew my father from Lahore, was among the first to message me when he was assassinated: 'Your father has been shot. He was killed by his gunman. We are here. Nadira.' Shortly after, I was with Naipaul in Wiltshire. He asked me how I was doing. I must have begun to speak of my father in a way that struck Naipaul as false, channelling what others were saying about him, because he stopped me short. 'But your father,' he said, 'was your great enemy, so you must also be relieved that he's dead.' It was the kind of absolution only Naipaul, who loved the human heart, with all its capacity for malice and generosity, could offer. And it freed me from the guilt I felt at being released from the heaviness of my father's presence.

Naipaul brought a heaviness of his own. When I married a man from Tennessee at a small ceremony on Manhattan's Upper East Side, Naipaul didn't come. He was in New York at the time, but his aversion to homosexuality prevented him from attending the wedding ('Vidia is busy,' came the terse email from Nadira). It did not prevent me from attending his funeral a few years later. I watched his body disappear on a conveyor belt into the maw of an electric oven. I took notes, 'kept the record', as he often liked to say.

He wanted to be judged solely by 'the work', and in a sense he was. 'Nasty man, great writer,' they said at his funeral. Even when I fell out with Naipaul, I never fell out with the work. And even when he was monstrous, he was far more interesting than most. He taught me about Japanese painting and Chola bronzes, about the plants and trees in the garden in Wiltshire, which he had planted himself, and how to read history laterally, always making sure to judge a period or event in one part of the world against what was happening elsewhere. From reading the annotations in his books – the single note in blue ink at the back of Troyat's biography of Pushkin: 'Pushkin had read so much that he couldn't see with his own eyes' – I learnt to read with a pen in hand. Following his example, I began to use Garamond size sixteen when I worked, which only the house style of this magazine prevents you from seeing.

Our relationship contained the same admixture of cruelty and tenderness that defined all his close relationships. It was as if he could only rest after reconciling himself, and those around him, to the severest version of the truth. There was something clarifying in surviving Vidia, just as it was clarifying to see 'the work' survive the man. 'The trouble with Vidia,' Nadira wrote, when the business about my novel got ugly, is that 'he does not give anything of himself, but when he does, then it is 100 per cent, and it can be unnerving.' He had a Brahminical adherence to the idea of vocation, and it gave our relationship its edge.

Why – you might ask – would I actively seek out the opinion of someone I knew could be so unkind? I was young and full of hubris. A part of me wanted to subject myself to the severest critic I knew and see where I came out. A part of me felt that what Naipaul had to teach me was more important than the passing damage he could do me. I have never met anyone as exacting as him, so much the real thing. He redefined the meaning of what it is to be a writer for me as one who cannot lie, even as I wondered what inadvertent violence he did the truth by only ever looking at it in so harsh a light.

–

I thought he had said all that he wanted to say to me that day in Wiltshire, and so I remember feeling distinctly unnerved by the email I received a few days later, after I had returned to New Delhi, where I was living at the time: 'Darling, Vidia wants to talk to you. We tried ringing your Indian number. Please call Wiltshire. Love you and MISS YOU, your aunt.'

I called and Nadira answered. 'Vidia has finished the book and is very agitated,' she said.

There was some shuffling about on the other end, a picking up and putting down of receivers – Naipaul wanted to take the call in his office. 'What I'm going to say now,' he began, after enquiring briefly about my journey home, 'is in the context of your great talent. I say it not to cast you down but to draw out that talent. I've finished the book now. You began writing non-fiction and made a transition to fiction. But fiction is very different, I want you to learn about narrative, about changing the pace of the narrative, about tone. The subject you've tackled is immensely ambitious, which is nice, but I wish you'd tried something simpler.'

The narrative didn't change, he explained, even after the murder in the novel. There was something still about it. The main character didn't change. There was no development. 'I don't want you to be subtle,' he said. 'I want you to be direct. Don't be so subtle.'

He asked if Andrew Kidd – his former publisher at Picador and now my agent at Aitken Alexander – had helped me with any of this. Naipaul was distressed that he had not. He wanted me to go back to Pushkin's stories for narrative and economy. 'With Pushkin, there's a coat hanging in the room, and the scene is there,' Naipaul said. 'See what he does. He's very clear, isn't he?'

And what was this business about Spain? 'Was it necessary, or did you just put that in . . . ?'

I tried to explain that it reflected the narrator and his girlfriend's failed attempt at life in the West.

'But you must state it simply and directly,' Naipaul said, and writing the line for me, began, 'Despite my great love of India, I found myself in Spain, then this happened, then that happened . . .' You must make things easier for the reader. And don't feel that by doing this you are being in any way less subtle.'

As I listened to him, I marvelled that this man, known to be so ungenerous – who had implored a young girl who brought him a piece of writing 'to promise never to write again'; who, when asked to judge a literary competition in Uganda, only awarded a third prize – was so natural a teacher.

Our conversation now turned, in an oblique way, to the homosexual element in the novel. Naipaul had made clear his distaste for homosexuality: 'I was myself subjected to some sexual abuse by an older cousin,' he told his biographer, 'I was corrupted, I was assaulted. I was about six or seven. It was done in a sly, terrible way and it gave me a hatred, a detestation of this homosexual thing.' I feared his scorn. I had seen it directed at the writer Vikram Seth. When asked by a friend why Seth was spending so much time in Brazil, Naipaul's eyes gleamed with suppressed amusement. 'Boys?' he said with a mock gravity. 'Yes, yes, yes . . . A lot of boys in Brazil.' When he asked me what my mother thought of my novel, I sensed he was anticipating her disapproval as a conduit to express his own. I said that she had found the characters unsympathetic and the story dark. 'But that wouldn't matter,' said the author of *A Bend in the River*, 'if the narrative line was clear, it wouldn't matter that it was dark, you see. These new pieces you're doing . . . is the narrative in them clearer?'

'I hope so.'

'Good, good. I want to see them when they're done, *before* publication. Have they sold this anywhere else?'

'No. Only in the UK.'

'I think they would find it hard.'

He stressed again that I was making a transition from non-fiction to fiction; most people do the opposite, which is easier.

'Do you think I'll be able to make the transition?' I asked.

'I think it's a transition you'll make very well,' he said. 'I wouldn't be saying all this to you if I didn't think that.' But he had also made it clear that it was *not* a transition I had made yet with this, my first novel.

–

I was worried about Naipaul reading *The Temple-goers* for reasons other than those he had outlined. There were characters in the novel based on him and Nadira, whom we had not discussed. Moreover, the man who believed fiction could not lie ('An autobiography can distort; facts can be realigned. But fiction never lies: it reveals the writer totally') was circling around a difficulty that had a deeper origin. The emotional mechanism of the novel – a triangle in which the protagonist, Aatish Taseer, develops a passion for his trainer, Aakash, which weakens and destroys his relationship with his girlfriend, Sanyogita – had been imported wholesale from my life in England.

The character of the trainer came to me when I moved back to India in 2006. It was a time when I read seriously – as Naipaul would say, 'in a gobbling way' – worked on my book, and went to the neighbourhood gym in Sundar Nagar. There I met Ashish, the man who would become the model for my trainer. I was intrigued by his restlessness, by an unevenness that made him in one context an adherent Brahmin to his family, full of caste prejudices, and, in another, a man of hookah bars and nightclubs, conducting a secret affair with a rich girl. I was intrigued by how the different characters within him remained distinct, never speaking to one another. To me, it represented how we lived in India then – how I lived too – on multiple moral planes, never seeking a unified self, never seeking to be, as Naipaul was, the same man everywhere and to everyone. 'Your main character, this gym trainer,' Naipaul said, his voice trembling with anger, in a second phone call, a week on from the first. 'You make him do so many things. He's a bisexual, he's a religious man, he's a trainer, but the problem is that he's uninteresting. He comes across as someone who eats a lot and talks a lot. Is he really like this in real life?'

I think he was. Ashish must have caught me looking at him one day, when we were both changing in the gym, his chest hair thick between his pecs, the outline of his cock visible through the cheap cotton of the bronze-coloured VIP underwear he wore. He asked me if I knew a trainer at the gym called Sunil. 'I think he comes after you leave,' Ashish said. 'Anyway, *he* was called for a personal training to the house of a gay. They took him there blindfolded and brought him into the gay's office. The gay puts sixty thousand down on the table and says, "Sucking." Sunil ran out from there, but they had bodyguards and Alsatians and Dobermanns, and they say, "If you don't sucking, we'll let them out and they'll make *keema* out of you."'

'What did he do?' I said, thinking to myself that he was trying out a new persona for my benefit. 'He's sucking, man,' Ashish said matter-of-factly. 'He's sucking, sucking, for one hour, sucking . . .' He screwed up his dark lips so that their pink interior was more visible.

It was this country, with new kinds of people in new environments, feeling its way to a new way of being, old unintegrated selves existing alongside adopted selves, that I felt was my natural material. I never fully knew if Naipaul's objection was against that material itself, or whether truly it was technical. Had my novel revealed something about me that made Naipaul recoil on some deeper level? I couldn't say. What I do know is that I had had about as much direct contact with the man, not the writer, as I wanted. Any more, I felt, would harm my own development, my voice, the distinct way of looking that comes to every writer from his distinct set of circumstances.

–

Once I got off the phone with Naipaul, I tried to distil something optimistic from his reaction. 'So this is what I'll do for the next few months,' I wrote in a note to myself. 'Read huge amounts and work on narrative. On smaller, simpler pieces and subjects. I will treat what he said as my first review and console myself in the knowledge that not everyone has V.S. Naipaul as their first reviewer.'

But Naipaul was not content to leave things there. Ten days after we spoke, another email from Nadira arrived.

18 October 2009

Dearest Aatish,

Vidia has been brooding a lot ever since he finished your book. He is at a crossroad himself on what should he do that would not offend you in any way. First of all I must tell you that he has never read a book through, but for you he did. He saw many narrative flaws and a lot of little hiccups that Shruti or Andrew should have spotted and made you go over them, but he says again that you do have the talent to be a very good writer and to be that you have to be ready to learn.

I told him that you would not hold this against him, but that you will in time remember him with kindness. Aatish,

Vidia is willing to teach you narrative structure personally if you are willing to work with him.

He learned the hard way by himself and your book reminded him of his very early work when he was twenty and trying to write. So what do you say?

Are you willing to come and be taught?

He has never done this and if you say no you must never tell anyone.

He will teach you in complete secrecy because you are an upcoming writer and he feels that he will teach you to walk and then run.

I am nervous sending you this, but you may find it hard to understand but we do love you like a son.

Nadira Khala

Reading it on my Blackberry, I felt a chill. The enclosed world of Wiltshire, with its strange intensities heightened by solitude, was so distant from the complexities of Delhi, where Indian writing in English was itself a rarefied sphere, soon to be the locus of class wars, cultural revival and Hindu nationalism. To be taught by Naipaul would be an honour, but it also seemed to contain the risk of annihilation. And I did not like the hush in Nadira's tone, the whispered secrecy of 'if you say no you must never tell anyone.' It was meant to be generous, but it felt vaguely threatening.

For the sake of perspective, and to open a window on the close air of Wiltshire, I decided to confide in a friend who was translating my first book from English into Hindi. Amitosh had grown up in a small town near Delhi, full of Hindi and Punjabi literature and theatre, before moving to Bombay to pursue a career as a Bollywood actor. We had been friends for only a couple of years, but he struck me as someone who understood the practice of apprenticeship, both in its historical context, and in the way it worked within the Hindi film industry.

'This *guru-shishya* (preceptor-student) idea is a bad one,' he said. 'If you were fifteen, it would be one thing, but you're not at the age where you can go and sit at his feet. And, besides,' he added, 'there's no mantra, no *ucharana* (recitation) that he can teach you. You have to make your own way, Aatish.' Moreover, he said, confirming my worst fears, Naipaul will look for what you have learnt from him in your next work. If you defy him, you're the ungrateful student; if you follow him, he takes the credit. 'Either way,' Amitosh said, 'Naipaul plants his flag. And who knows,' he added, speaking from his experience of the malice Bollywood reserves for newcomers, 'he might even be wanting to stifle you.'

I laughed, and said that surely Naipaul, with his life's work behind him, would have no desire to do that.

'This particular desire,' Amitosh said, 'never leaves you, no matter how old or successful, you get.'

Listening to him, I was reminded of a story Naipaul liked to tell. An older writer goes to see his longtime editor and asks him if he's publishing any promising new writers. 'Oh, yes,' the editor says, and rattles off some names he's excited about. 'Oh good,' the writer says, after listening a while, 'I want you to stamp on them very hard.'

–

I answered Nadira as tactfully as I could. I said that I loved those moments in Naipaul's writing, where he evaluates his own missteps and mistakes. 'I want very much to make my own mistakes,' I wrote. 'Those moments of slipping and falling, understanding why, and working through to a better model are among the most powerful moments in writing. A writer is made by those moments.' I also said that I was forced to ask myself a question that had become part of my reckoning. *What would Naipaul do?* Would he go and learn at the feet of another writer? 'And my feeling – though, of course, I could be wrong – was that even if there had been someone to learn from, he would not have gone.'

I was about to hit send, but then, out of what must have been my growing fear of Naipaul, and the fear that perhaps I was throwing away a remarkable opportunity, I drafted a new email, one that was at once more equivocating and, inadvertently, more offensive: 'I am overwhelmed by the generosity of his offer. But tell me, what do you have in mind when you say come here and learn? Do you mean Wiltshire? And for a few days or weeks? Or would he prefer I sent him writing? I ask both for practical reasons but also because there is a kind of influence I don't want to expose myself to . . .'

The reply came in the form of a phone call. Nadira cooing on the phone about how I should not take it badly. Vidia, she explained, was just worried about how brutal publishing culture was these days and how people wouldn't give me a second chance. I realised that the latter formulation was a reworking of one of Naipaul's own sacred rules when it came to people: 'No second chances.'

Then he came on the phone. I could tell from the thickness of his voice that he was enraged. The same mixture of insight and humour that I had heard him use against any number of subjects, from Arabs ('they're very wicked people; a little war won't hurt them'), Africans ('the African story is a very short one'), and Indians ('they live for the pleasure of lying'), to the welfare state, was now turned on me.

'I've been brooding about your book,' he began. 'I feel it's a kind of journal that could have gone on and on. You had this ambition to write a novel, but you just loaded it with experiences that happened to you. You haven't understood the fictional form. You haven't understood that it must present a complete experience to the reader. The comprehension of that experience cannot be going on through the book. You have no natural talent for fiction,' he added, 'but you felt you must do this thing anyway.'

It hurt to hear this, but some part of me stepped back and felt a kind of appreciation for how, in a world where everyone wanted to be liked, here was a man who seemed almost incapable of lying, especially when it came to writing.

'I was thinking of how I would talk to you about this book,' he said. 'I was thinking I might put it to you as a series of questions, but you have all these answers,' he said, cutting off my attempts to respond. 'And they're not enough. You drag us off to Spain. You have reason, you say, but it's not enough.' He returned to his original line of attack. He was angry at Andrew and Shruti Debi, my Indian publisher, for letting me down, for not telling me to go back to the work. 'They're setting you up for a great disappointment.' He was convinced, despite the UK proof sitting in his house in Wiltshire, that the book had not sold anywhere but India. When I reminded him that Viking had bought the book in the UK, he returned to his central theme. 'That's very good, but they're setting you up for a great fall. Have Andrew and Shruti not talked to you about the book's shapelessness?'

I said they hadn't and that they had liked it very much.

'No,' he said. 'It's confused.'

Then he began to use a strategy I had seen him use in his work: targeting the lies we tell ourselves. It was one of his great lines – 'The only lies for which we are truly punished are those we tell ourselves.'

'But perhaps you know all this,' he said, 'perhaps you know what I am talking about.'

I didn't reply.

'That is enough for today,' he said. 'You must send me some new work, and when you come to see me, we'll talk about it.'

'Thank you, Sir Vidia.'

'You *should* thank me,' he snarled. 'Because I have written books too, you know. And, in 1951, I wrote a book like this one, which I loaded up with experience and, though I knew it wasn't headed anywhere, I carried on, feeling that I could get by on good writing and style. So I did and hoped for the best. But probably you know what I mean. I could have done an Andrew on you, but I didn't want to do that. I, out of my concern and love for you, wanted to help.'

I thought we were done, but it continued. He now minded the character of the writer and his wife. What was the point of them? The book was too long. 'You felt you had to write a long book,' he said, 'so it's nearly 120,000 words . . .'

'It's not even ninety . . .'

'Oh,' he said, 'I must have counted the lines wrong. Leave this book. We'll speak after you've thought a little about why you want to write fiction. There are many other kinds of writing, travel, history, *journal writing*,' he added with sarcasm. 'All very impressive. The novel was a form that became popular very late in the nineteenth century. And I think it's at its end . . .' he said, as if I had just dealt it a final fatal blow. He was no longer drawn to the book's ambition, nor did he believe I could make the transition to fiction. 'I think you'll find it very hard,' he said.

When I got off the phone, I remember feeling my very existence as a writer depended on my ability to weather this dressing-down.

Even then, I valued my time with Naipaul. He had shown me a darkness I always knew was there. Though I don't know to what extent he himself was aware of it. Once, when we were in Delhi, and a man asked him what his work was about, Naipaul said, 'It does not have a single unifying theme, but I have tried and not been able to find a philosophical explanation for the problem of cruelty.' I don't think he would have thought of himself as capable of cruelty. In the 2008 BBC film that marked the beginning of our friendship, *The Strange Luck of V.S. Naipaul*, he says, when asked about his reputation, 'I'm a very gentle person, and, I feel, it's not in my power to damage other people, or things, whereas other people can, as it were, damage me.'

—

Nadira wrote me a letter shortly after, trying to soften the blows, saying that the only other time he had tried to help someone was his brother Shiva, who had sent him 'a very lazy draft' of *North of South* (1978).

'Vidia literally rewrote the book,' she said, 'which ironically is the only book that everyone praises Shiva for doing. It was such an unpleasant exercise that he promised himself that he would never help anyone again.'

Shiva died of alcoholism in 1985 – and now after having had a taste of Vidia's 'help' I confess that a part of me wondered if Vidia, whether inadvertently or deliberately, had crushed him. He had seemed in a kind of nervous fog as we spoke, half blinded by rage. And, later, when we made amends, Nadira said he had no memory of our conversation at all.

The distant past was growing closer as Naipaul got older. The conversation about my novel had always been tinged by the resurgent memory of his own beginnings. When I once asked him how it felt now, towards the end, he said, he would not do it again. 'It was too hard . . . *too hard*,' he repeated bitterly. ∎

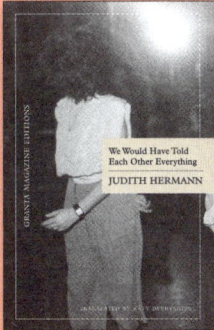

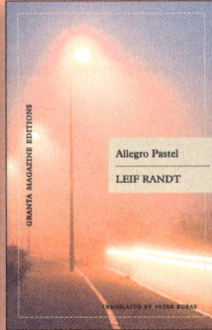

The Granta Writers' Workshop

NATURE WRITING, SHORT FICTION, THE NOVEL, LONG-FORM JOURNALISM, MEMOIR

'One purpose of art is to get us to wake up, recalibrate our emotional life, get ourselves into proper relation to reality.'
– GEORGE SAUNDERS

Image © Julie Cockburn

newyorktyrant

newyorktyrant Me irl
View all comments
3 October 2014

GIAN

Tao Lin

You were born in West Virginia in 1974. I was born in Virginia in 1983. I grew up in suburban Central Florida. You went to college in New Orleans, earning a degree in philosophy. We both moved to New York City in 2001.

In 2005, around when I graduated from New York University with a journalism degree, I saw an advertisement in the *Paris Review* for a new literary magazine. The ad said 'submit' in large lowercase font; in place of the letter i was a drawing of the backside of a naked, obese man wielding a sword.

I sent a short story with a very long title to submissions @nytyrant.com and asked where I could get more information on your magazine. Someone, probably you, replied, 'The *New York Tyrant* is a brand spanking new strictly short-fiction publication that will publish issues quarterly which will be beautiful books on the inside and out.'

Seven months later, I got an email that said, 'The Tyrant thanks you for the opportunity to consider 'Cull the Steel Heart . . .' After due consideration, however, we have come to the unfortunate conclusion that your story is not a good fit for our publication. Rejection is never a happy occasion, but rest assured that the anger and disappointment now stirring deep within your heart will only lead to greater things. Again, many thanks.' Signed, 'The Editors'.

'I hate you,' I replied. 'No, just kidding. Thanks for the note.' I submitted another story, then withdrew it when it was accepted elsewhere. 'Damn,' someone replied. 'This is a good fucking story. Have anything else?' I submitted another and withdrew it a month later and got this response: 'Damn it, man. Give us a fucking chance.'

'Dear Tao,' you emailed me two weeks later. 'Was at KGB the other night but had to leave before you read. Sorry I missed it. Look, we are already collecting for the second issue. If you have anything, send it our way. I promise I will read it as soon as it arrives. Your first two submissions got yanked so fast, we couldn't do anything for you. But we love your shit, so please resubmit. Yours, GianCarlo.'

I submitted a story and withdrew it a week later. Three months later, I sent a fifth story, which elicited no response, and six months after that I emailed you a sixth story, which you rejected eight months later, in June 2007: 'Hello. We're gonna pass on this one, though. Thanks though.' You signed the email 'Giancarlo' and didn't ask me to submit again.

In 2009, you founded Tyrant Books to publish a novella by Brian Evenson, who'd sent you his book after getting two emails in a row from people surnamed Brown – one from your editorial assistant, soliciting Evenson's work for your magazine – while working at Brown University. Brown, Brown, Brown – 'I act on things like that,' said Evenson in an interview.

Like Evenson, you paid attention to what you called 'things that appear in strange ways'. The name *New York Tyrant* had come to you in a dream, and you later noticed, and explained in an interview, that 'the letters TRN found in the word TyRaNt, can also be found in that order in my last name diTRapaNo'.

Evenson's novella was published in November. In December, you emailed me to say you'd started writing for *Vice*. You asked for a review copy of my first (and to this day only) novella, which had come out in September. The email was signed 'Gian'.

The next July, on my birthday, you emailed me, 'Happy Birthday,

Tao. I won't say to have a great day, because that's so hard sometimes. So have a good day.'

I thanked you, and you asked if I knew a doctor who'd prescribe Adderall, which you'd noticed me mentioning online. I gave you my phone number. We began texting.

We met in person four weeks later, briefly, outside New York University's Bobst Library, where I worked on my writing every day. I traded you Adderall for Percocet.

'How many of these should I take?' you texted me after.

'I'm good with half of one but I weigh 125 so maybe just one whole one,' I replied, back in the library, seated at a computer. 'Open it and pour the little balls into your mouth.'

'Ooh fun. Thanks, Tao.'

The next night, we met at an in-progress reading in a dark room above a bar. I sat in the back, at a low table, across from you. You slid your phone across the table.

'hi tao,' you'd typed. I typed a reply, then slid the phone back. 'sip' you saw. I'd mistyped 'sup', or it had been autocorrected.

I don't remember what we did that night, but the next day you texted me, 'It was great hanging out with you last night. Still can't believe I lost those fucking pills.'

'I had fun. We should do it again some time. Thanks again for the oxy,' I texted about the semi-synthetic opioid you'd given me.

'sip,' you texted.

'Heh,' I texted.

A week later, you emailed me instructions on how to get painkillers from a Dr Zhao in Chinatown: 'Go in and be like, "I got in a car crash when I was thirteen and I have back pains. I need a prescription of oxys (if you ask for oxys). It's what I take and I've just moved to town."'

There were nine more sentences, then: 'Anyway, good luck. This is like Lord of the Rings. I'm like a troll leading you to the gold. (Oh yeah, this troll charges a finders fee of five pills from your first prescription.)'

When I went, I was told that Dr Zhao wasn't accepting new patients. I bought three coconuts, drank their water, and returned to the library.

In mid-August, we met at Bar 2A in the East Village. You gave me five oxycodone tablets you'd bought from your dealer for me, and I gave you a hundred dollars.

Walking back to the library, I felt a pang of disappointment when I looked at the drugs. I texted you, 'Hey. 4 of these are blue with cursive Vs on them.' You replied, 'I know. They look different but they are all oxy 30s. Trust.' And I trusted you again.

Late in August, I texted you asking how you were doing.

'Good, I guess,' you replied. 'I'm always bored. Even with drugs.'

'Damn. Do you have an LSD contact? That might help (also if you do I'm "in the market" for some, hehe).'

'No, but I can ask around. I love it if it's pure LSD-25. Might know someone with mushrooms.'

In September, *Vice* published your review of my second novel. The review, titled 'I Like Tao Lin Now', began:

> I never fucking liked Tao Lin. I'd probably have liked his books more, given them their fighting chance, if he and his books hadn't been constantly shoved down my throat every day of the week for the past few years. Shit gets old, quick.

The anti-me rant continued for nineteen sentences, then: 'But something must have happened to me, or to Tao Lin, or to the both of us, because I've been swayed. I kind of fucking love this guy now.'

We were texting regularly by then, mostly about drugs. It was 2010. I'd started using recreational pharmaceutical drugs the year before, mostly out of curiosity and boredom. They fascinated, excited and comforted me, allowing me to become a dramatically different person – cheerful, calm, uninhibited, unworried, social – for hours at a time.

I don't know why or when your drug use began. Your cluster headaches, which started when you were sixteen, were probably a large factor. 'In efforts to deal with this pain, I've orally ingested, injected, snorted and/or smoked oxycodone, hydrocodone, fentanyl, Demerol, Dilaudid, cocaine, heroin, codeine, morphine and more, all to no avail,' you would write in a 2016 article on the excruciating condition, which annually 'shut down' your life for periods of one to six months.

You introduced me to MDMA and your drug dealer. We helped each other relieve boredom. In text messages and emails, I asked you questions like, 'Any parties or want to sell oxys to me?' and 'Any chance of me getting more MDMA tonight?' and 'Want to trade me mushroom for addy?' You asked me questions like, 'Where can I charge my iPhone in Soho?' and 'I have some oxies. Wanna buy?' and 'Know of any parties tonight?' We discussed masturbation:

Me: In a hotel in rural Georgia. About to chug an energy drink and 'jack off'.

You: lol. Does the energy drink increase the pleasure of the jack sesh? I never tried. Adderall makes me beat off like a madman.

Me: It does, I feel. More blood flow. Addy actually makes me hornier but harder to get/remain hard.

You: Yeah, same with coke. But that doesn't stop me. I'll pull on it either way. Like a madman.

Me: Me too. Me too . . .

We saw each other irregularly, at literary events, parties and small gatherings. You always looked deeply stoned, with heavy eyelids and a placid, dispassionate gaze. Sometimes you smiled and grinned a lot; other times you seemed somewhat depressed. Like me, you were shyer in person than online. We were both early, prolific, gleeful, brash tweeters.

In February 2011, you texted me, 'I love you. Happy Valentine's Day to you and Megan!' Then, 'Don't know why I said I love you. I do, but like I'm kind of fucked up.' Two weeks later, I texted you, 'Felt an urge to txt you "I love you" & on only little Xanax and Vyvanse,' and you replied, 'I love you same.'

We had many ideas – some materialized, others were jokes. Drug corporations, we mused, should sponsor the literary world – PEN/ Oxy Award, National Xanax Book Prize. You said *Vice* TV should send us to South America to drink ayahuasca. I published a selection of your tweets in my online magazine. On 24 June, you emailed me, 'I was scrolling through the last year of our drug-addled text messages. Some funny stuff in there. Could be an "epic" Vice post someday.'

I said our texts were positive and considerate. You said we were 'really polite and nice'. I said someone could 'build a sitcom' out of our messages. You said, 'The dialogue is perfect because it's actually real.' You typed our text messages into a document, and I created a photo collage of us looking at our phones.

On 1 July, *Vice* published our text messages from July 2010 to June 2011, which you titled 'Andrew: a Dialogue of Texts in the Year of Drugs and Kindness' after (1) our dealer and (2) the main topic and tone, you felt, of our messages. (After you died in 2021, I learned that some-to-many of your friendships had featured taunting and insults; we never had that; we only ever praised and defended each other.)

I felt compelled to publish our potentially worrying, arguably unseemly texts, in which we discussed buying, selling, trading and using a broad assortment of illegal drugs, because I had no family in the US besides my brother, with whom I wasn't close; because I also wasn't close to my parents, who lived in Taiwan; and because I delighted and specialized, as an openly autobiographical writer, in creating art from life.

As an independent publisher, freelance journalist, and occasional, intimate memoirist, you also didn't feel the need to censor yourself, and for whatever reason, or reasons, you seemed unconcerned with your family learning about your drug-heavy lifestyle. 'I like my life to be an open book,' you would say in a 2016 interview. Asked in a different interview if you'd ever write a novel, you said, 'I feel like my life is my book.'

In January 2012, you texted me saying your new dealer had asked you about books. I joked that he wanted to be in our next 'year of texts', and you said, 'Lol totally. He wants the fame. He's tired of living a life of drug world anonymity.'

'We should start our own drug dealing thing next year,' I said.

'Publish books from profits, like lit gangsters, would be fucking chill.'

'Get writing residencies at Yaddo and use the time to figure out how to make our own MDMA.'

'Show up to Yaddo with a truckload of chemicals and hazmat suits.'

'We'll need our food delivered once a day, and no interruptions please.'

In March, you texted me: 'We need to hang more. I feel like you're like my best friend but I never see you URL / irl / I never see you URL lol.'

'Lol'd and tasted metal in my mouth,' I replied. I'd been spending most of my time alone, working on my third novel.

In June, you emailed me:

> Supposed to fly to Italy tomorrow to see my dad because he's sick but am in the middle of a cluster headache season so I could get into trouble over there without my neurologist. I 'loaded up' on $1,500 of Imitrex shots and Stadol (nasal spray morphine, will save some to 'party' with you) yesterday to try and deal with them myself over there. I feel like my affection for painkillers is like my subconscious making up for all the pain of 20 years of these damned headaches.

TAO LIN

Two weeks later, back in New York City, you said in an email, 'Went and got more nerve blockers injected into my head yesterday so I have been headache-free for like 20 hours now. Seems like a long time.' I said time had started 'moving way faster' for me. I asked if you'd experienced something similar, and you said:

Yes, in my late twenties is when it really started flying. A year is like nothing now. It used to seem like a lifetime. Also, there was like a four-year period where I did nothing but party and I don't remember anything from that time. Maybe a couple of monumental moments, but mostly a blur of watching the sunrise every morning. I don't mind time flying though. I feel like I've done everything I want to do in life. Now I'm just like waiting for disease or tragedy. I don't know. Life is nice sometimes, but it mostly seems annoying/ridiculous.

You hadn't had alcohol in two months because it triggered headaches. You'd been taking Suboxone, a drug used for treating opiate addiction. 'I can like get work done, feel good, sleep good, and I haven't been depressed or anything,' you said, adding, later in the email, 'Oh yeah, I smoke weed all day, every day, but I have done that my entire life it seems,' which I hadn't known. We'd never discussed cannabis, which in 2012 I didn't yet particularly enjoy.

In July, on my twenty-ninth birthday, you sent me a song you'd composed on your piano. 'I taught myself like three years ago,' you said. 'I have hundreds of songs. Can't read music, don't even know the names of keys.' In another email, you said, 'I have to record them to remember them. Otherwise they disappear.'

You sent me another song, and I said it sounded like the soundtrack to *Gattaca*, one of my favorite movies – in which a sickly, determined man overcomes expectations to achieve his dreams – and you said, 'I fucking love that movie.'

At a bar later that month – soon after *Vice* published a second year

254

of our texts, including the text where you said you felt like I was your best friend – you introduced me to a man I'd never met or heard of before. I remember him and/or you seeming kind of sheepish as one of you said he was your best friend.

Discussing the *Vice* post by email, you said, 'Would be sweet if one of us died and then the one remaining (hopefully you) would just do one of lonely unreplied-to texts to no one,' regarding a potential future post of a third year of texts.

I said the last text would be 'are you there?' and that if we both died the post could have an epilogue of texts by two other people, saying 'did u hear gian and tao both died?' and 'yeah lol'.

'yeah lol,' you said. 'laughing.'

One reason we got along so well, you would explain in a 2013 interview, was because we shared 'a humorous and enjoyable nonchalance regarding "overdoing it" and our possible deaths'. Other reasons: We strove to be 'open books', valued novelty and eccentricity, felt a kinship with emotionally troubled outsiders, and were captivated by drugs and literature, braiding them and centering them in our lives.

B esides texting each other around a thousand times in 2011, 2012, and 2013, we also emailed each other that many times during those three years (when our communications plateaued), usually about writing-related matters (we wrote for the same magazines, both ran small presses, and published some of the same writers), but also about other things.

I sent you a mattress recommendation. You sent me a link to a fully head-enclosing pillow. I sent you comically bleak drug-related excerpts from a John Cheever biography. You sent me a video of a person smoking *Salvia divinorum*. I sent you a song titled 'Kids of the K-Hole'. You sent me an audio file – 'ketamine concerto' – of you playing your piano in your apartment on ketamine.

You again invited me to submit work to your magazine, which you were considering ending – it was a 'moneysuck' that no longer

TAO LIN

'excited' you – to focus on publishing books. You'd published four
by then – a novella, a book of drawings, two novels. I submitted
an excerpt of my third novel – my seventh submission – and you
published it in the tenth and last issue of *New York Tyrant*.

You told me about your skin. 'I suffered from horrible, grotesque,
not-ever-wanting-to-leave-the-house-and-see-anyone acne all
through high school and some of college and afterward.' I said your
skin looked 'great' now, and you thanked me. 'I could have turned out a
lot worse, like deep ass scars and shit,' you said. 'I took Accutane twice.
It's like this hardcore acne medicine that apparently causes suicides.
But I think all of the suicides were caused from the acne. Whenever
I see someone young with terrible acne, I kind of pray for them.'

In October, I said I was worried because I kept extending an
in-progress drug-binge, and you said, 'I get in that postponing the
end of binges too. Man, I think I'm really fucked up maybe. Whenever
I like don't do painkillers for more than a week I have these vomiting
attacks. And only eating painkillers helps me feel better. It's like not
even my mind but my body that keeps "forcing" me to do drugs. I
think I've ruined my stomach with drugs. Oh well. I'm sure it'll be fine.'

Hurricane Sandy – the largest Atlantic hurricane ever measured
and second to hit the city in as many years – arrived a week later,
resulting in widespread blackouts, thousands of downed trees,
scattered looting and other chaos. Combined with a global doomsday
meme that claimed the world would transform or end in December,
the natural disaster encouraged me and you and our friends to
use even more drugs, including one night at your Hell's Kitchen
apartment on the West Side of Manhattan. This was the only time I
went into your home. It was low-lit and cramped.

Two weeks later, in mid-November, you came to my place in
Kips Bay on the East Side to interview me in anticipation of my third
novel. We talked from 1 a.m. to 4 a.m., seated on my bed with 'a
small party going on in the other corner of the room', you wrote in
your introduction to our conversation, which *Vice* published after we
edited it down to half the length.

In a deleted section, you said the characters in my second novel seemed to make fun of 'obese people'. You asked if I thought the obese people who'd read my book would be hurt by this. I said I hoped not. I tried to explain that the characters actually empathized with overweight – and other marginalized – people, identifying with their suffering and underdog status, and you seemed to express something similar, saying:

> I don't know, I feel like a lot of my attraction towards like fat guys or whatever comes from some kind of sympathy. Like I feel bad how they've been treated all their lives and like it's, to be honest, sometimes I feel like that's something . . . and then I think that there are other people that have been treated bad for other reasons and I'm not attracted to them at all so . . . I feel like there's some kind of endearing quality in the fact that they've put up with a lot of shit for their entire lives and for some reason that makes me love them or something. I don't know. It's really weird that it manifests itself through sex.

In a 2010 essay about *A Confederacy of Dunces*, which your dad gave you when you were twenty-one, you'd written that you 'fell hard' for the novel's protagonist, Ignatius, a 'waddling, unkempt mammoth toddler'. You wrote, 'Until then, I'd always thought of myself as straight. I walked straight and I talked straight. I dated girls, I slept with girls, when I jacked off, I jacked off to girls.'

You quoted a scene in which Ignatius masturbates in his room, climaxing after his childhood dog appears unbidden in his mind, jumping over a fence, chasing a stick. 'This is the page where I went fag,' you wrote. 'The solitude and isolation, the very sadness of it all, didn't turn me off – on the contrary, it was the hook. Sex scenes had always been filled with gorgeous people. Ignatius wasn't gorgeous. But he was sexual.'

Your mom hadn't believed you when you told her you were

gay. She 'came around', but at first 'it blew her mind, and she was kind of not into it', you said on a podcast. Your dad, who was 'more worldly', a fan of Oscar Wilde and Gore Vidal, was supportive from the start. In multiple interviews, you praised your parents; like mine, they gave you the freedom to pursue what you wanted to do with your life.

You gifted me an action figure of a masked, big-bellied man in a yellow jumpsuit, who probably represented you, I realized two years after you died, when I saw a drawing of it on your Instagram with the caption 'Me irl'. I sent you a link to my favorite song by Swearin', titled 'Fat Chance', and said it made me feel 'deep empathy', and you said, 'what a great song. there should be like a fat music genre.'

In December, I reached a low point with my pharmaceutical drug addiction, which continued for another half-year, until the summer of 2013, when I finally began, with the help of psilocybin mushrooms and the persuasively optimistic ideas of psychedelics-promoter Terence McKenna, to effectively wean myself off pills and powders, replacing them with cannabis and psychedelics.

You got my new interests. You smoked weed as assiduously as McKenna had, and you dearly prized psychedelics, specifically 5-MeO-DALT and psilocybin, for ending your cluster headaches, which are also called 'suicide headaches', that year – 'nothing has provided me with even a 100th of the relief that psychedelics have', you'd write in your 2016 article, which ended, 'I've now been pain-free for three years. Unless you suffer yourself, you have no idea just how beautiful that actually is.'

In early August 2013, seated on my bed peaking on psilocybin at around 3 a.m., I sobbed from joy and gratitude that I finally felt empowered enough to begin to end my pill addiction. I'd wanted to do this for more than two years by then, but had lacked the determination.

A little later in the trip, I texted you, saying that an alien was 'in me', using my body to learn about 'this thing we've got set up: family'.

You replied, 'You don't think they have families?' I laughed and called you; this was probably the only time we talked on the phone.

Years later, while writing about this in my non-fiction book on psychedelics, I asked you about the call, and you said:

> I can remember saying, 'Don't forget that you're on drugs so whatever is happening will wear off once the drugs do. Just don't forget that you're fucked up at the moment.' I think we were laughing? You also said you thought I was controlling you but I convinced you that I was, in fact, not controlling you. You might have said something about my voice being soothing. I was a little worried at first but after talking to you for a bit, I knew you'd be fine. I was doing shrooms like every day for my clusters during that period so felt like I could kind of understand the trip you were having.

In late August, I emailed you praising your profile of Junot Díaz in *Playboy*. You said your dad had read it and emailed you, 'I am so proud of you I am about to burst. I'm telling all of my friends about my brilliant son.' You said, 'He's never really complimented me before, or said he was proud. The email made me instantly cry. But like a joy cry.'

That fall, isolating myself in my apartment, I used large amounts of cannabis to buffer the dysphoria and other withdrawal symptoms – which would continue for many more months – from ending four years of amphetamines, benzodiazepines and opiates. I distanced myself from most of my friends, who remained mired in pills and bleak worldviews, but we continued talking, in part because of our new shared interests in Terence McKenna and psychedelics.

In March 2014, you encouraged me to pitch a column on McKenna to our editor at *Vice*. After I emailed our editor, outlining a potential weekly column, I emailed you, thanking you for your encouragement, and you said, 'It was an encouragement of a selfish nature because I want to read that shit.'

One day, I emailed you, 'i can hear so much shit going on in apartments around mine when i'm very stoned. i hear someone talking to his dog and i've never heard anyone talking to their dog and i like never hear a dog. i hear like 5 dogs right now.' I lived in a six-story building, two and a half blocks west of the East River, a 45-minute cross-town walk from your place, two and a half blocks east of the Hudson River. You replied:

> lol. It's weird that in my building i sometimes feel like I can hear nothing from my neighbors and then other times, I can hear all kinds of shit. Like the guy upstairs with the piano who I started hearing play the songs I write and play on my piano. Like he heard me and then learned them and played them and I could hear it. Sometimes we would play at the same time and kind of play to each other I felt. Like I would play some, then he would as a kind of response.

In April, we discussed our ethnic and sexual identities. 'I wish Asians did more for me, they don't do shit for me,' I said wryly. 'Totally,' you said:

> I wish gays did more for me. I feel like I don't reap enough minority benefits from being gay. Maybe if I added it to my twitter bio. But I guess if anyone ever attacks me (in writing or irl) I can always say that they are a homophobe or scream 'I'm being hatecrimed!!' Really need to exploit this minority position in society. Gays just don't like me, I think. I only have one gay friend (Mark Doten) and the

gay community has always treated me weirdly. Like just because I have none of the stereotypes, they don't feel like I am truly 'one of them' but I guess they are right. I don't feel like one of them.

(On a podcast, you said people never thought you were gay and that you couldn't 'act stereotypically gay' even if you tried.)

I replied, 'Felt strong connection with you on this, replacing gay with Asian.' Other East Asian Americans seemed to readily gather into friend groups, but not me. I tended to drift away from groups, toward other alienated individuals.

'i'm extremely stoned,' I emailed you in May. 'i just started daydreaming and thinking of how productive we're being during these past few years and how it'll be interesting to look back on things in like 10 years, in terms of literature. made it feel fun to keep going and see what happens,' and you replied, 'Totally totally totally, all counts.'

'dude,' you emailed me in June. 'I did some h last night and I fell asleep standing up in my bathroom for 4 hours.' You seem to have snorted or ingested heroin irregularly, not addictively; once, in 2012, when I said I was buying some heroin, you said you hadn't done it in years. 'I slept, standing straight up, for four fucking hours. I woke up mid fall face first into shower curtain and bathtub. Wish I could have that on video somehow.'

Eleven months later, in May 2015, you said you'd been eating 'a large nibble' of psilocybin mushroom every four days:

I felt my headaches coming on twice this year and so ate like half a dose you would take to trip and it clears my head up and the headaches don't start. It's so amazing. It's like the only thing in life that I feel like being political or an activist for. Gonna freakin' march on Washington or some shit lol.

You sent me a link to our second year of text messages, from June 2011 to July 2012, and said, 'rereading this, dying laughing. feel like it didn't get the accolades it deserved.' I liked that you revisited our projects, folding time over itself, stretching it, slowing it. Once, you sent me our *Vice* conversation and said, 'Just did some coke and am drinking beers to sleep and looking at old shit that makes me smile.'

That December, while visiting my parents in Taipei, I updated you on my evolving drug use – 'Been alternating days of weed capsules and days of LSD while in Taiwan.'

'Nice weed and LSD cocktail,' you said. 'Should be good. Seems I am inundated with powders here in the city. There is always some kind of powder around to sniff.'

You were going to Italy in two weeks. 'When I was just there, I think I fell in love,' you said. 'I mean, I did fall in love, but I can't tell if it was just for four days or if it is still happening to me. I'm totally sabotaging every aspect of my entire life lol.'

Your Italian grandfather emigrated to the US in the early 1900s. My Taiwanese parents arrived in the 1970s. You were the youngest of five kids. I was the youngest of two. Growing up, we spent summers in our ancestral homelands.

'Falling in love, that seems good,' I said. 'There are pros and cons. I would say more pros. Who is the person?'

'This guy I met in a train station in Campoleone, IT. Soon as we met he took me to have dinner at his mom's lol. Going back on the 30th. We'll see. I could just be being retarded. I feel like I'm halfway creating all this in my head. Oh well.'

A month later, in January 2016, you said, 'Went back to Italy and I am in love. Breaking up with Chris and moving to Italy in April to live with this guy. Crazy.' In an interview that year, you said you felt healthier, happier and 'more at home' in Italy. In the same interview, you said, 'I used to do a ton of drugs and I've never been ashamed of it or tried to hide it or anything. I love getting high.'

I also wanted to leave New York City, where I increasingly felt beleaguered and nature-deprived, but I stayed to write the first draft of my psychedelics book – an expansion of my McKenna column – and because in fall 2017 I also fell in love.

In March 2018, you emailed me, 'remember the doctor i went to and tried to get him to see you?' about Dr Zhao with a link to an article titled 'Doctor made $1M selling Xanax before bust: cops'.

You invited me to Italy, where you and your new husband lived in an apartment in the center of Rome. You'd started a writers' workshop called Mors Tua Vita Mea ('Your Death, My Life') at a family villa in Sezze – your husband was its chef and tour guide – while continuing to publish books, increasing from two a year in recent years to three that year.

That August, you moved to the countryside in Naples and I finally left New York City, living in rural New Jersey and then upstate New York. My girlfriend visited from Manhattan on weekends. In November 2019, I visited my parents in Taiwan for six weeks, after which I went to Honolulu, Hawaii, to house-sit for my mom's friend.

Three months later, in March 2020, when lockdowns began in the US, Italy and elsewhere, I was still in Hawaii, on the island of Oʻahu. I'd decided by then to stay in Hawaii. One night, alone in an Airbnb, I messaged you on Twitter (I'd replaced my smartphone with a flip phone and stopped texting) a link to a book titled *SIP* and said, 'It's our book.'

'lmao NICE,' you replied. It was 29 March in Hawaii, but in New York the date was 30 March, exactly one year before your death. 'Chapter One', you wrote:

> The event was crowded, but at least he had drugs. 'I'll never find a place to sit to listen to this boring shit,' Tao thought just as he saw someone stand from their seat and walk towards the bar. He scurried over to the bench and sat down, filled with the small joy of not having to stand for an hour. Tao was blankly staring at the glass table at his knees when a cell phone appeared, seemingly

out of nowhere, on the table before him. The screen was illuminated and open to the Notes app. One word, three letters: sip. What could it mean?

In my memory of that night ten years earlier, in 2010, it was me who had typed 'sip', but now, after reading your message, I wasn't sure. I replied:

Gian made his way to the back of the reading, choosing a seat at a table where he couldn't see the readers and wasn't facing the stage. He noticed a small Asian person sit down across from him. It was that annoying Chinese-looking kid who was always promoting his books online.

You replied:

Tao looked up from the phone and across the table. Smiling, and obviously on opiates by the look of his eyelids, sat this guy named Gian who had just written a Vice piece about me. It was called 'I like Tao Lin Now'. This confuses Tao. Why didn't Gian like him before? What has he done to him? But Gian had confessed his new feelings in the article and the love in the article dominated anything between them in the past.

By April, you'd 'gotten used to' the lockdown:

it's kinda how i lived before anyway. i've always worked from home. sucks though because we can't even go for walks or leave the house for anything except grocer and pharmacy. and been running for past few months but can't now. it was so hard to get into i'm afraid i won't be able to pick it up again.

On 1 July, you said, 'man it was 3 months here in the country, only leaving for the grocery store. now it's all back to normal.' You'd been swimming fifty laps a day in a pool. 'i love it,' you said. 'i feel like i'm never gonna see people from america again,' you said. 'kind of scary. what a whack-ass year.'

I said I'd been swimming too, in the ocean, and that my girlfriend, free now to work remotely, was joining me in Hawaii soon. Many people had left New York City, which was ghost-town-like after months of protests, riots, fires, looting and closed businesses.

In January 2021, my girlfriend and I moved from the North Shore of O'ahu to the east side of the Big Island. While listening to a new interview with you one day, I messaged you, 'Liking your talk with Sean a lot. Making me miss you and also want to write.'

A week later, we discussed an idea you had for an anthology featuring the same short story edited by many different editors. We worked on a list of editors to include. We brainstormed which story to use. You said I should publish it. I said you should.

We discussed other things, then you said:

> dude / i tripped my balls off last night / such a long story / but i thought i was god's angel here to do his work / and had all the power in the world / so wild / i called my brother and sister and freaked them out / i was just medicating for my clusters and went too far lol / but so beautiful / the most beautiful experience i've had in my life / i was convinced i would be king of Italy lmao / feel so happy today.

Two days later, seemingly out of nowhere, you said, 'wild to think where we were 8 years ago.'

'yes,' I said. '2013. damn.' The year we were closest to each other. The year psychedelics helped to end my pill addiction and your cluster headaches.

'lmao,' you said, 'i was a freakin mess / "gian r u there" "the aliens" "they're interested in this thing we have" "family" / i owe you for getting me to this place where i finally feel happy and enjoy life.'

'lol, forgot the aliens texts, and calling you,' I replied. 'your voice was coming out of my head, or from in my head, it seemed. was so sweet / nice, glad you feel that way. i owe you for getting me into and out of whatever happened i think.'

'lmaooooo / we owe each other. nice.' We seem to have followed each other deeper into and then gradually out of our unsustainable lives in New York City.

You asked if I had WhatsApp or Signal. 'wanna tell you about something like just in texts or whatever but i don't think i have your number or even if you use a phone anymore.'

I didn't have either app. I gave you my Google Voice number, which accepted texts. I don't know what you wanted to tell me – you never texted – but maybe it was about your new press.

Ten days later, on 1 February, you tweeted, 'I'm launching another press soon. Please stand by . . .' with two images of the logo for the press, which was called DiTrapano.

'sweet logo and name,' I messaged you. The logo was a drawing of your Twitter profile pic – a car whose entire top half was on fire.

'thanks man. it's gonna be huge launch. honor sean molly brodak gabriel.'

'excited.'

'me too like tons. dreamt you said it wasn't good.'

'damn.' That was our last communication.

O n 31 March, while visiting the west side of the Big Island, I learned from a mutual writer friend that you'd been found dead in a hotel in Manhattan, which you were visiting to have meetings for your new press.

A bad batch of heroin was going around New York City and multiple people had died, according to the writer friend. A different mutual friend, who seemed to have some knowledge of the toxicology report, blamed the combination of ketamine and cocaine.

One of the last people you talked to was a mutual friend who was a chemist. On his podcast, this friend said you'd visited his apartment, and that while there you'd briefly left to buy heroin – not for 'some kind of dark, destructive use' but as 'a pure celebration of life', the friend said. You'd told this friend that your dealer had said the heroin had been triple-tested for fentanyl. He'd told you not to believe your dealer.

But then later, in an email, the chemist friend told me he'd analyzed the heroin and had found no synthetic opioids other than heroin, and that he'd heard that only ketamine and cocaine had been detected in the autopsy. 'A combination of cocaine and ketamine could cause a dramatic increase in blood pressure, but still I think that would be an odd way for him to have died,' he said.

Your family didn't release the cause of your death. However you died, it seems to have been an accident. You didn't seem to have anything deathwish-like by then. You were forty-seven and had seemed to be firmly in the start of a happier phase of your life in Italy.

After your death was announced online, there was an outpouring of praise for you and your work. You'd published twenty-four books, many pieces of your own writing, and more than 16,000 tweets. The *Believer* and the *Paris Review* published collections of remembrances by your friends and colleagues. More memorials followed in other venues. The *New York Times* called you 'a defiantly independent publisher'.

'Feel heartened by all the praise of Gian and the sharing of memories of him. I feel like he's out there, seeing all this,' I tweeted. I imagined you passing through the internet on your way elsewhere. As you left, people thought and talked and wrote about you, collectively slowing time by immersing ourselves in the now-completed book of your life.

I posted a screenshot of our messages from six weeks earlier, when you'd said you 'finally feel happy and enjoy life'. I reread our correspondence and collaborations, read all your interviews and writing, and organized a collection of memories from me and thirty-three of your other friends, publishing it in my online magazine six weeks after you died.

Eleven months later, I dreamed I was behind you in a crowd, looking at your backside as we walked in the same direction.

Seventeen months after that, I dreamed we were walking toward each other. You were smiling widely. We greeted each other briefly – as if we knew we'd meet again soon – and continued in opposite directions.

A week after that dream, our writer friend invited me to read at an event in Manhattan for a foundation that had been created in your name.

Two weeks later, I was back in New York City for the first time in four years. It was November 2023.

The bar holding the event was near Hell's Kitchen, I realized while walking there with our friend on the night of the reading.

'We're near where Gian lived,' I said.

'Really?' said our friend.

'Yeah,' I said, waving my arm across the dimly familiar buildings to the west. 'He lived somewhere over there.' ■

GRANTA TRUST

Granta would be unable to fulfil its mission
without the generosity of its donors.

We gratefully acknowledge the following
individuals and foundations:

Ford Foundation
British Council
Jerwood Foundation
Pulitzer Center
Amazon Literary Partnership
Sigrid Rausing
The Hans and Marit Rausing Charitable Trust
Anonymous
Bloomsbury Publishing Plc
SALT
Open Society
The Common Humanity Arts Trust
Jonathan and Ronnie Newhouse Fund

If you would like to contribute, please make
a donation at granta.com/donate.

CONTRIBUTORS

Renata Adler is the author of the novels *Speedboat* and *Pitch Dark*. Her non-fiction has most recently been collected in *After the Tall Timber.*

William Atkins's latest book is *Exiles: Three Island Journeys*. He is working on a book about Sizewell and its nuclear power stations.

Susie Boyt is the author of seven novels and the memoir *My Judy Garland Life*. Her latest novel, *Loved and Missed*, will be published in Germany, Italy, Sweden and Norway in 2026.

Anne Carson was born in Canada and now works mostly in Iceland.

Mark Cawson aka Smiler was a photographer who documented London squats from the late 1970s, 1980s and early 1990s. His work was exhibited at the ICA in 2015.

Joshua Cohen is the author of numerous novels, one collection of stories and one collection of essays. His most recent novel is *The Netanyahus*. He lives in New York.

Krystyna Dąbrowska is the author of five poetry books, most recently *Miasto z indu* (2022). Her poetry collection in English translation, *Tideline*, was published in 2022.

Fernanda Eberstadt's most recent book is *Bite Your Friends* (2024), published by Europa Editions in the UK and US.

Tobi Haslett's writing has appeared in *n+1*, *Harper's* and elsewhere. He lives in Berlin.

Marlen Haushofer was an Austrian author of short stories, novels, radio plays and children's books. Her books include *The Wall*, *The Loft* and *Nowhere Ending Sky*.

Michel Houellebecq has published collections of poems since 1991 and novels since 1994.

Gary Indiana was an artist and writer living in New York and Los Angeles.

Karen Kovacik's book of poems, *Portable City*, is forthcoming in 2025. She has just completed the translation of Krystyna Dąbrowska's collection *Sorrowbalm.*

Tao Lin is the author of ten books, including *Leave Society* and *Taipei*. 'Gian' is part of his in-progress essay collection *Reasons to Live*. He lives in Hawaii.

Audun Mortensen is a Korean adopted Norwegian author of twelve books of fiction and poetry. He is currently a PhD candidate at the University of Oslo.

Yasmina Reza is a playwright and novelist whose work has been translated into more than thirty-five languages. *Récits de certains faits* was published in 2024 and *Serge* is forthcoming in English translation with Restless Books.

Damion Searls is the author of *The Philosophy of Translation* and *The Mariner's Mirror*. His translation of Robert Walser's late poems and a lost novella is forthcoming in 2027.

Iain Sinclair has lived and worked in Hackney for sixty years. His books include *Lud Heat*, *Downriver*, *London Orbital* and, most recently, *Pariah Genius*, a psychobiography of the photographer John Deakin.

Ming Smith is a Harlem-based photographer. Her work has been exhibited at the Museum of Modern Art, Tate Modern, Whitney Museum of Art and Columbus Museum of Art.

Alison L. Strayer is a Canadian writer and translator. Her translations include works by Annie Ernaux, Abdellah Taïa, Yasmina Reza, Mavis Gallant and Virginia Woolf. Forthcoming translations in 2025 include *The Places of Marguerite Duras*, *Dreaming Out Loud* and *The Other Girl*.

Aatish Taseer is the author of several works of fiction and non-fiction. His new book, *A Return to Self: Excursions in Exile*, is forthcoming in 2025 by Catapult.

Robert Walser was a Swiss writer, most notably of the novels *The Assistant*, *Jakob von Gunten* and *The Walk*, as well as numerous short prose works.

Shaun Whiteside is a translator from the German, French, Italian and Dutch. His most recent translations include *Aftermath* and *Vertigo* by Harald Jähner, and *Annihilation* by Michel Houellebecq.

IDLER FESTIVAL 2025

11–13 July   Fenton House & Garden, Hampstead

MICHAEL PALIN
STEWART LEE · ROWAN WILLIAMS
GEORGIA MANN · MIRANDA SAWYER · ARTHUR SMITH
AMY MATTHEWS · BEN MOOR · SAM AND SAM CLARK

**PILGRIMAGE WITH GUY HAYWARD · SUZI FEAY · TOM HODGKINSON
DAISY DUNN · JOE BOYD · ROWAN PELLING · DAVID BRAMWELL
MARK VERNON · ROBERT ROWLAND SMITH · DAISY BUCHANAN
MADDY HARLAND · JOHN MULLAN · HENRY ELIOT · FERDINAND
MOUNT · HARRY MOUNT · SALENA WISNOM · ROBERT WRINGHAM
TIM RICHARDSON · CLARE POLLARD · JOHN-PAUL FLINTOFF
RACHEL DE THAMPLE · LAURA GONZALEZ · DAVID BRAMWELL**

PLUS   Jane Austen vibes, Regency dancing, harpsichords,
beekeeping, literary walks, ukulele, Food by Moro
and more

Tickets on sale now   idler.co.uk/events

"Britain's best literary and arts festival," *Spectator*